LUNAR CYCLE BOOK 2

SHATTERED SKY

破碎天空

DAVID COLBY

THINKING INK PRESS
CAMPBELL, CALIFORNIA

Published by Thinking Ink Press
P.O. Box 1411, Campbell, California, 95009
First printing, 2018

Print edition ISBN 978-1-942480-22-8

Ebook edition ISBN 978-1-942480-23-5

Printed in the United States of America.

Project Credits

Cover layout: Streetlight Graphics

Editor: Anthony Francis

Copy Editor: Gayle Schultz

Chinese Language Editor: Roger Que

Interior layout: Betsy Miller

DEDICATION

To the random musers.

For small creatures such as we, the vastness of the universe is
bearable only through love.

Carl Sagan (1934-1996)

CHAPTER 1
HAPPY ENDING

4/2/2068

California, North American Economic Zone

T-Minus L-Day: 141

Happy endings were supposed to be a hell of a lot easier than this *kōngtóu zhīpiào*. I had been on Earth for a whole twenty-four hours and in all those seconds of all those minutes of all those hours, I had gotten to kiss the love my life a grand total of once.

"This sucks."

Jillian stood next to me, her back leaning against the wall as she looked out at the vast sweep of Edwards Air Force Base. When I looked out at it, it just made me feel queasy and impatient and claustrophobic in a way that I had never felt before. I didn't even need to move my eyes to splash the images all over the wallpaper of my brain: the three or so buildings the size of entire habitation blocks, the kilometer and then some of blackened tarmac that sucked up heat like a sink, and spread through it all the real reason why I was here and not with Sarah.

The troops. Specifically, the ten thousand or so troops that used Edwards Air Force Base as a way of getting to the next leg of their various deployments. Huge cargo hauling VTOLs landed and lifted off, while suborbital streakers burned hard to slow down and let off troops. Their uniforms spanned a spectrum of military minutia I'd never seen before, like looking through the world's *shittiest* spectrometer. In space, the officer pool had been decidedly shallow, with maybe three lieutenants before General Lau. Down here, I saw every single rank that I had been forced to memorize during Basic: Gunnery Sergeants, Staff Sergeants, Second Lieutenants, First Lieutenants, Colonels, Majors, and Captains. It was a relief from the endless stream of PFCs and Corporals and Areos, like sunspots breaking up the eye scorching brightness of the sun.

Most of the Earthers were kitted out differently from Spacer soldiers, too. No laser weaponry, no bounce in their steps, no breathers and enclosed helmets. The enlisted pukes had slugthrowers on their backs, while the officers tended to be unarmed and glittery with medals, but they all trudged along, looking ...

Actually, most of them didn't look that unhappy. For *most* of them, this was a life they had chosen. A comfortable life with good pay, free medical coverage, honor and prestige. A life that I could have—something that fascinated and repelled me at the same time.

I wished they were unhappy. It'd be easier. It'd make more sense, if I could share that misery. Instead of being...

"So, Corp," Jillian said, deorbiting my thoughts.

"Jillian, we're out of the Marines now," I said, rubbing my face with my hands.

"So, Dru," Jillian started again. "What are you going to do once we get out of this?"

"Buy a farm." I stood. The gravity down here was *intense.* I had to actually use my hand and the wall to get my knees to unbend, rather than just kipping up. I had never thought that one-G would be so … so much more than the gravity on the Hub. It wasn't even that I hadn't been exposed to one-G before— it was more that it was *all* the time, everywhere. Standing didn't feel worth it, but I felt too confined by sitting, too passive. I started to pace back and forth, my body wanting to bounce, but gravity glued me to the ground. "I told Sarah I'd be in Quebec Arcology as soon as I could get there. At this rate—"

Jillian shuffled to the left. I shuffled into the space she had vacated. The Space Marine—one of the survivors of the Battle of the Forge, as they were calling the last big battle of the war— behind me shuffled over to take up the spot that I had held. And so, the line continued to process, and so I got closer and closer to getting out of this endless waiting.

But I still felt trapped, stuck in adhesive, forced to do nothing but endure. Endure the sounds—the babbling conversations that overlapped and drowned each other out—endure the smells— the thick, cloying stench of the tarmac, the scent of the scrubland that surrounded the base, the smell of jets and jet fuel—and endure the heat. The pounding, unstoppable heat, pouring through my skinclothes and broiling me in my own juices. I had never imagined that an uncontrolled environment could be so horrifyingly unpleasant.

"I miss air conditioners," Jillian muttered.

"I miss Sarah."

"I miss air conditioners *and* I miss Sarah. She was cute. You never said she was that cute." Jillian chuckled.

"I didn't?" I asked, rubbing my eyes. I tried to ignore the aching feeling that started to suffuse my head, starting right behind my nose and working its way down my jaws. A stress headache. That was what I needed. That was just the *perfect* addition to this day, thank you, body.

The line shuffled forward again. My heart skipped a beat. Did it just start to go just a bit faster? The line, that is, not my heart. I knew that was going faster: The idea of getting out of this heat and into Sarah was just about the only reason why I hadn't started wishing that I wasn't in space again.

"What are you planning to do?" I asked, looking at Jillian.

"That's hard. I don't have any desire to waste my life poking at the ground with a sharp stick—"

"You have no idea what farming actually involves, do you?"

Jillian didn't stop, speaking over my interruption with a grin. "—but I also don't have any friends or family down here. I'm technically old enough to vote and smoke. Not drink, mind you. But I can still take my back pay, rent an apartment ..." She trailed off, shaking her head.

"Why not come with me?" I asked. "I mean, you ... you probably can't stay with the Cayers, but if there's not an apartment somewhere in the Republic of Quebec, I'll speak nothing but English there. We can hang out, you can help farm, maybe I can set you up with a fair-haired farm boy. Mostly to get them off Sarah's back ..."

Jillian snorted. "Earther farm boys, Earther farm boys. That means I'll want to do a *Mkundu ng'ombe msichana* and they'll run away screaming to their moms."

"Think of it as an educational process."

Jillian stroked her chin as we shuffled forward again.

After what felt like five eternities (and I knew something about eternity, having ridden a fully packed ROVer from the Sun-Earth L1 point to GEO) Jillian got sucked into the front doors that the whole line was riding through. She was the first person I'd actually physically seen go in, thanks to the curvature of the line and the building blocking the view. Now that I was closer, though, I saw that a second line was heading into the same place, a far longer line of Earther soldiers going in for their processing. I had to wait for four Earthers to cycle in before I got to head in—hoping that Jillian would be waiting nearby after I got out, or else I'd never find her again.

After losing Liam, Chuck, Jason, David ... after losing all of them, the idea of losing Jillian—even if only for a second—made me want to hyperventilate.

The office that I stepped into was exotic enough that it gave me pause. Normally, stepping into an office was like stepping into private quarters. In space, offices were virtual, with all the paperwork handled by computers, the information thrown up by wallpaper and contained within handheld tablets. On the ground ... well, on the ground, it felt a bit like getting smacked in the face by excess. Everything in the office—the books, the paper in the books, the ink on the paper, the shelves holding the books, the computer, the heavy metal desk, the clock, the ornamental piece of printed artwork depicting an old USA Marine Corps logo in three dimensions—all of it wasn't measured in fuel and credits and effort to get it out of a stubborn gravity well. It took me a few seconds to jerk my point of view around, to reorient myself with a mental burst from my imagination.

The furniture wasn't the wasteful bulk of a wealthy showoff. No, the metal framework of the desk had the blunt functionality of a mass produced, tough, reusable military surplus product. The bookshelves were crammed with books because, down here, netwar attacks weren't regulated and tightly controlled. Down here, a single worm downloaded from the blacknet could wipe any file that wasn't printed out on paper ... so they printed everything out in paper. But what struck me as the most out of place thing in the office was the bureaucrat himself.

He was Latino—an ethnicity I'd only seen on vids till now—and he was a bit portly. The implications clicked home as I saluted and he saluted back.

Dietary restrictions weren't enforced down here. Gym wasn't state mandated.

"Please, Sergeant Zhao, have a seat."

I sat down.

"Sorry about the delays. It's a mad house down here." He smiled thinly at me. He looked at a small laptop set on the desk, his other hand writing quick notes in short hand, a pen scraping against paper. I tried to not stare, but ... but the whole office was so damn old-looking. Pens? Laptops? What was this, the dark ages?

"First things first ..." He paused. "I'm required to inform you that you are no longer of the rank Star Sergeant. The space-borne forces, now that we can integrate them with the official Alliance military, will be folded into the standard military organizational system. Due to your age and lack of battlefield experience and the abundance of qualified NCOs, you will be made a Corporal again without any negative repercussions on your record," he tapped a few buttons on the laptop. "This won't change your back pay, but when you are recycled back into the service after—"

"Excuse me, sir, but ..." I coughed. "What was that?"

He looked at me. "When your leave is over, Corporal Zhao."

I blinked. I blinked again. A ringing filled my ears. "I-I ..." I put my hands over my face, breathed in, then breathed out. Losing a pay grade? Didn't even register as an issue. Hell, after what happened on the Forge, I wasn't sure I *deserved* anything above Private. But ...

I slid my hands off my face and asked the man. "Sir, respectfully, how would I go about, uh, mustering out? Retiring? I've served my term, I thought—"

He held up his hand, silencing me. I shut up, clenching my jaw—hard enough to make my teeth ache. It was what I needed to keep myself from sobbing in his office. Or beating the guy to death with a chair as he explained it.

It.

It being the thing that I would hate more than anything save Omar Kaufman.

It being ... the Emergency Acts of 2022.

"The Emergency Acts of 2022 state that, in a time of emergency—civil insurrection, global unrest, catastrophic climate change, or impending extinction events—the Chinese American Alliance is within its right to conscript anyone deemed of acceptable age, mental health, and physical health. While the state of emergency lasts, the state of conscription persists and the citizens conscripted under said act are compelled by law to perform their state mandated service." He tapped his fingers on the desk. "Or, to put it in English, you're lucky to be getting leave at all, Corporal."

I sank into my chair and listened numbly as he started to move onto the rest of the checking out process. He asked me my name, parents, date of birth—"just checking our records"—serial number, rank—"procedure, have to follow procedure"—and then moved onto a question that actually required a bit of thought.

"Do you have a legal guardian that you will be remanded to for the duration of your leave?" he asked. "Or would you prefer to be put in the custody of one of the CAA's state orphanages?"

Sarah and I had discussed me going to her mother's place after I finished checking out. As a *guest*. It hadn't occurred to me that I'd need to visit there as a legal ward ... after all, I had killed people for the state. You'd *think* that would mean you count as an adult. Legally. Right? Nope. Apparently, when the Emergency Acts gave the senate and the President powers to decide who was 'of age' to be thrown into a uniform, it didn't give them the power to decide that those people were adults. Or ...

Or to think more like Jillian, it totally *did* give them that power and they just preferred their teenage soldiers to be defanged completely while in civilian life.

The bureaucrat kept looking at me, waiting for an answer.

"Mary Cayer," I said, feeling a weird, sinking feeling. That kind of feeling that comes when you take a leap and you're not sure if you are going to reach what you've pushed towards or be left flailing in the middle of the corridor to the sound of your friends mocking you.

"Mary Cayer ..." he said, frowning.

I gave the extra details that Sarah had told me over the years and during our conversation yesterday.

"Ah, she applied to be your legal guardian last night," he said, nodding. "Very well, you are logged as being a ward of Mary and George Cayer. Your back pay, all rated at an E-5, not E-4, will be forwarded to a private account for your own use. Report to the Quebec International Airport for recall on the first of next month." He stood up, holding his hand out to me. I stood as well, taking the hand by reflex. He shook.

"Enjoy your leave."

He let me go and gestured me to the door that led out of the room. I opened it and found myself in the main building of the base, a huge chamber that had even more troopers, most of them waiting for their chance to board a VTOL. They were sitting in a few dozen rows, lined up along the floor and snaking around terminals for VTOL loading, their packages by their feet and their uniforms creating a sea of conformity. I didn't see Jillian.

I walked towards the exit, which was large and obvious, and walked outside. An autobus terminal sat next to the highway that ran along the base. Huge buses—the same kind that had been pioneered in China before the Slump, big enough that smaller cars could drive underneath their rectangular bodies, picked up troops and drove off to who knows where. The autobus terminal also had what looked like half a dozen charging stations for mobile electronics. I had turned in my kit—my armor, my honest to god raygun, even the mining pick I'd used in a pinch—in orbit, so all I had on down here was my skinclothes. That still included a phone built into the sleeve, but I didn't dial for Sarah just yet.

I just stood there.

My emotions felt as if they had done hundred and eighty degree turns once too many times. Jealousy at the other soldiers and their *belonging.* Their happiness at being part of something larger. That...that moment when I had felt like I had been a part of that too.

Fear. The intense, clinging, stinking fear that comes when you know you are not immortal.

Pain. Separation.

Elation at being welcomed back in.

Horror at being dragged, screaming, back in.

"Dru!"

I spun around and saw Jillian stepping out of the exit. Her eyes were streaked with red, her cheeks glimmering and wet. That was almost as shocking as being told I was still drafted, seeing hardass Jillian crying. She stepped closer and in the moments between a blink, she managed to completely wipe her face off with her hands and looked like she had never sniffled in her whole life.

"Hey, you walked right past me," she said, putting her hand on my shoulder, practically shoving me towards the autobus terminal. "So, I've radically altered my whole life course in a few seconds. Got a bit of temporal whiplash."

"Yeah. That ... whiplash ... a bitch ... " I said, vaguely, rubbing my neck, as if the joke had become real.

Jillian bit her lip, then forced a grin. "How about instead of spending that back pay on apartments or jobs—"

"Can't get either ..." I mumbled.

"We blow it on thirty days in Neo-Vegas? Thirty days of binge drinking, gambling, whores—"

"Can't do any of that ..."

Jillian stepped around and looked me in the eyes. "Dru. Come on. Focus here."

I looked into her eyes, shaking my head. "I need to call Sarah."

Jillian closed her eyes. "Dru, you're going to kill her."

I stepped past her, ignoring her as I tapped my wrist. The cloth of my skinclothes shimmered—quantum dot projectors flicking on and showing the holographic display and interface for the phone service. I started to tap in area codes, mentally cursing the fact I'd never programmed in Sarah's speed dial. Never thought I'd be on the ground in these clothes until about five minutes before the ST3A showed up and pulled my ass out of the fire. Jillian grabbed my wrist—the hologram fuzzing around her fingers like ghosts.

"Dru," she said. "Dru, if you go to Sarah, you're going to spend thirty days with her, then go back into the meat grinder. Surviving it once was a miracle. Surviving it twice, with a definite one hundred percent chance of going into space again, is going to take the intervention of pretty much every single deity we both do and do not worship. Thirty days with that hanging over your head ..." She trailed off.

I looked at Jillian, frowning. "It's worth it," I said, my voice holding that steel that put me through the hell of Basic. Squash the feelings, all of them, and find the one you want. Use it. Use that steel. "Besides, it isn't going to be thirty days of moping. It is going to be thirty days of you and Sarah and I working to find a way out of this."

Jillian laughed—her fingers releasing my wrist.

I sighed—quietly—and finished tapping out Sarah's number. "We've broken regs before. We'll find a way out of this. We will survive. We will spend our money responsibly—"

"Damn!" Jillian snapped her fingers.

"—and we will make this." I tapped the last number and my collars buzzed with a ringtone. A few short seconds later, Sarah picked up and I tapped the mic on so that Jillian could listen in.

"Hey, Sarah," I said, feeling a strange mixture of confident and terrified. Like I was going into combat again. "Are you still in San Jose? Because ... my friend and I need a ride." I grinned. "And we have some sneakiness to get up to."

"Ooh, sneakiness. That's my third favorite kind of ness," Sarah said. "Can you take an autobus to the city? Mom doesn't want to risk the highway again."

"Sure," I said, nodding. "See you soon, Sarah-Bear."

"See you soon, Snoogums."

I tapped the phone off.

Jillian mimed vomiting.

Chapter 2: Symptoms

By the time Jillian and I got off the autobus in San Jose it was a little bit past midnight and something was terribly wrong. It started when I stepped up to the doors of the bus itself and felt a moment of panic. It was the weirdest and most disturbing sense of panic I had ever felt, a stabbing feeling right at the base of my brain. I stood there and tried to remember where my *breather* was.

It was so nonsensical that it took a shove from Jillian to get my brain working again. But the anxiety persisted as I sat next to her and waited for the bus to fill.

Jillian and I didn't say much. I pursed my lips so tight they felt like they might fuse. If I didn't, I was worried I'd start screaming and I'd never stop. So, instead of doing that, I focused on the world outside the window and ignore all the little things that were twigging in the back of my brain: the window wasn't properly sealed, the bus jerked and twitched all wrong, like a shuttle wasting fuel. Every jounce and shudder bumped my shoulder against Jillian's, reminding me that the shuttle was wasting fuel. Except every bump wasn't a jet of acceleration or motion of cold gas thrusters. It was just a bus, bumping over a poorly paved highway.

At least the world outside the window distracted me from that worry pretty quick.

First, we drove past an old highway sign that was entirely non-computerized, so it still called the highway "I-5 N" and some of the signs even still claimed that there was a route to Los Angeles. A few of those had been painted over with graffiti that had stuck around long enough to become official, after a fashion: THE FLESH OF FALLEN ANGELS.

Then, there were the gallows.

They weren't very common at first, as we drove through the desert, but then we got into the part of California that had a lot of hills. They were there: tall, silvery structures built on the top of highest hills. Only a few of them actually had bodies hanging from them, each one with a sign hanging around their neck, their heads covered in a cloth bag. They had words like MUR-DERER and RAPIST on them. You hear that California was the only state that hadn't repealed the old Emergency Acts and you don't think exactly what that means until you drive past a few …

And yet, I couldn't look away.

We drove past a fenced-off hill compound that had a few armed guards patrolling the walls. We drove past a large farm, fully automated and looking a few centuries ahead of the rest of the countryside, with its sleek robotics and glittering fields of genetically engineered crops—obvious due to their odd col-oration. Either a way to make them more obvious so that cross-breeding didn't happen or it made them grow better, I didn't know.

Then we came around a bend and I elbowed Jillian, trying to repress the feelings of anxiety that jabbed pins in the back of my head.

"Look at *that*."

Jillian opened her eyes and whispered. "*Mtakatifu kuzimu*, that thing is HUGE!"

San Jose wasn't actually San Jose.

San Jose, the historical city, was the huge boneyards surrounding the new San Jose. But it hadn't just been abandoned to rot. No, the ruins had the look of a place that had been rendered down. Broken buildings, ground up roads, cratered holes where digging had gotten at fiber optic and copper cables. But when the urban and suburban sprawl had been rendered down to chunks that couldn't be recycled or reused, people let nature creep back in. Even with the climate out of whack and the ecosystem gone absolutely buggy, that meant lots of green vines winding through and around ancient foundations and rusted hulks of machinery and autos, with the last road needed cutting through it like a slash of anti-apocalypse, slapping down civilization on ruins.

Sitting in the middle of all of this, at the end of that last road was the arcology herself. An arcology was, in short, a space station at the bottom of a gravity well: a single building that contained the food, the people, the machine halls, the game rooms, the *everything* that a million people needed. But that was where it and my home diverged. Everything in orbit had been dragged, inch by painful inch, out of Earth's crushing embrace.

San Jose just needed a *crane*.

It was a pillar of steel and concrete slabs and smooth plastic that thrust almost three, four hundred meters into the air. Flowering from each of its four sides were large spars that were set in a spiral 'staircase' pattern, so that each spar could be exposed to the air. Those spars were dotted with homes and gardens and solar collectors. At night, the whole thing seemed to glow like a spec-fic torchship: shining windows, glowing decorations, gleaming metal.

It kind of pissed me off how San Jose looked more like the future than anything I had ever seen in my freaking life, and I was from *space*.

Pissed or not, economic and ecological reasons for building arcologies—cities contained in singular, massive buildings—were obvious to me, especially when you could contrast it to the boneyard decay surrounding one. They were a great way to have a city without having the sprawling construction projects that required clearing out land that should be processing carbon and making food. Having a rapid transit system built into the superstructure made massive numbers of cars redundant, the enclosed ecosystem made recycling ridiculously easy, the sturdy construction meant it was hard to destroy or even damage due to natural disaster. All the reasons tumbled through my brain and all I could think was ...

Was ...

"We're not in Kansas anymore, are we?" Jillian said.

I looked at her.

She looked back at me. "*Wizard of Oz*, Dru. I thought you'd get that one fast."

"Sarah just shoves retro-1980s stuff at me."

Jillian rubbed her face with her hands as the autobus drove into the shadow of San Jose. The bus hissed and clicked as the door opened and the other troopers started getting off. My heart pounded as I watched them walk out the door. *Where's your mask, Dru?* my brain whispered. I found my hand sliding to my hip, where a breather—or a P3—would be strapped. I wasn't sure what it'd be good for, but I wanted to grab onto something familiar like that. I kept expecting air to rush out and—

"Come on." Jillian either didn't notice or didn't mention the way that I was hyperventilating. She slapped my shoulder, her voice dropping to a playful *purr*. "We've got your meals on wheels to meet."

"Meals on ..." I snorted, shaking my head slightly. "Jillian, maybe tone down the sex jokes? On Earth everyone's like me. But worse."

"Oh, you mean prudish and monogamous? I'm actually looking forward to that," Jillian said as we stepped off the bus just as the sun started to set. "Speaking of wheels, why is Sarah *in* wheels?"

I blinked. "I never told you?"

"Dru, I don't know how to break this to you, but you're kind of an introverted brooding weirdo who never talks to anyone about your feelings," Jillian said, casually. "You have a really sexy ass, though!"

I scowled at her, turning back to look at her. She grinned impishly down from where she stood in the doorway of the bus, mercilessly tormenting the poor bus' artificial intelligence as it tried to close the doors and get back on its rounds.

"Sarah got hit by a war-pox during the tail end of the Slump, when she was very young," I said, shrugging one shoulder. "By the time they got to a med-tech, it was too late to reverse the nerve damage without a few million spare bucks, and they barely had a farm."

Jillian clicked her tongue and stepped down and off the bus. Night gathered quickly around us as the door closed behind her. I put my hands in my pockets and turned away from Jillian, looking up at the arcology that filled the sky as that sky darkened. I'd seen the sun set in a thousand vids and dozens of sims, but it had never seemed quite so grim there. I wasn't sure what it made it worse: tThe gravity just made it worse,or remembering the Slump. It felt like I could feel like the whole pile of steel and concrete teetering on its foundation was, ready to fall down on me – a cripplingly literal metaphor for the pre-Slump Earth, just driving faster and faster towards a crash. I looked back down at Jillian, who whistled as she kept looking up and up and up.

"Do these things really hold a million people each?" she asked, glancing at me. The attempt to change the subject was so painfully obvious that I kind of loved it.

"Not sure." I tapped out Sarah's number. "Hey, Sarah, we're here at the base ."

"Which part of the base?" she asked. "Military base or arcology base?"

I mentally applied palm to face. "The arcology base!"

"Ah, yes." Sarah paused. "Which part of the arcology base?"

"Your planet is too big and complicated," I said, grinning ever so slightly. It was weird how talking to Sarah for about five seconds could cheer me up so much. I looked around. The area around the arcology was broad and flat, the ground paved and lined with autobus tracks. There were a few non-recycled buildings nearby, most of them looking more like pillboxes than tourist information stations like their signs claimed. Beyond them, there was Old San Jose, where the urban sprawl that had once filled the entire area was being slowly taken apart and recycled and turned back into forest or scrub or whatever the local terrain was around here. It looked a bit like a graveyard from a cheesy VR adventure, especially without anything beyond the most rudimentary illumination at night.

I looked back at the arcology and then tilted my head up slightly, so that I could see that we were by CORNER A, according to the words written out in letters larger than a ROVer.

"Corner A."

"Oh, sweet, I'll be there in a jiffy!"

I hung up with a finger tap and looked at Jillian.

We waited in companionable silence and I tried to not flinch every time the breeze blew against my face. I spotted the dozen or so doors that led into the arcology from Corner A, though none of them seemed that active at this time of night. Of course, if the building was a self-contained city, why the hell would anyone leave? The doorways were all a good ten meters higher than we were—there were long ramps leading from them to the sidewalk of the street. Not sure why. Maybe big buildings needed equally big foundations?

One of the entrances opened and out came Sarah. My heart skipped enough beats to have me declared legally dead as she made her way down the ramps that led up to the doorways, using her hands and her arms—her wonderfully muscular arms—to slow her way down. I'd seen pictures. I'd seen live feeds. I'd seen holosim recreations and I had seen her in my literal dreams. But right now, I was seeing her in the real and I simply *drank* her in. With my eyes. Screw you, I can mix whatever metaphors I want. Sarah had shoulder-length blond hair, framing a rounded face with skin that wandered between pale and bronzed, depending on how her fashion tastes went that week. Today, she was sun-bronzed and warm, like a Greek goddess.

I didn't so much *step* forward as half collapse onto her primitive wheelchair and kiss her. She grabbed me, hands on my shoulders. I picked her up, staggering up as I tried to hold her tightly enough that the moment would never ever have to end. She squeezed, kissed back—ooooh gods that was good, delirium good—and then pushed me away, gently. "Dear, down."

I set her down and she laughed, a bit nervously.

"S-sorry," she said, hands on the wheels. "I ... uh ... don't like getting picked up."

I turned a shade of red normally associated with fusion containment breeches. Jillian did a very bad job of hiding her snicker. I kicked her in the shin. She glared at me and Sarah—ignoring our little scuffle—grinned and turned her chair around by pushing both wheels in opposing ways. "Come on! The City-Soul only lets the door unlock on special order and it relocks pretty darn fast, if you ask me."

"Why?" I asked, walking behind her, pushing the wheelchair.

"Uh, I can push myself." Sarah smiled at me over her shoulder. I felt oddly quashed by that and slid my hands off her wheelchair's prongs. She started to use her arms, keeping perfect pace with us. "As for the why? Well, see, there are looter gangs running around here. More than there used to be, if you believe the local feeds."

I frowned. "I saw the gallows."

She nodded. "It's the war, I think. Rationing isn't still enforced here, not like up north."

"Really?" Jillian asked.

Sarah nodded. We hit the front doors—thankfully, they unlocked as we stepped up to them—and went into the city proper. I tensed as the doors closed behind me, my brain expecting a second airlock and some desuiting procedure. Just walking through made me feel ...

Nervous. Scared. A bit like I should start hyperventilating. Which made even less sense, even if we were in space, because if we were in space, we'd be running out of air if I hyperventilated. But that didn't make me stop getting nervous. Oh, no, that just made me *more* nervous. What if there weren't proper seals here?

It wasn't like I could tell if the place had proper seals. In space, you didn't put wallpaper over every surface; you need quick and easy access to get at the guts of certain parts of the station for emergency repair, modification, or maintenance. The only rooms that *did* have total coverage were the holodecks (which involved no holograms nor took up entire decks, so the name never made sense to me) and the Storm Cellar, which had almost no complex electronics in it.

So, walking down a corridor that was entirely coated in wallpaper felt both comforting and jarring; it felt like being in a place I knew was safe, but reminded me of being bombarded by high energy particles. Joy. The walls were set to verdant grassland while the ceiling was set to blue skies and the floor was set to look like a paved street. The air was full of the sound of buzzing insects and the scent of life—like the hydroponic bay.

I realized that, between my hyperventilating, my tensing, and my heart pounding … I had almost missed everything Sarah had been talking about.

What. The. Hell.

"And if you think that's crazy, you should visit the farm." Sarah gestured to the walls. "This stuff is pretty good, good enough for arcos, but arcos wouldn't know a real forest if it started growing inside their living rooms." She snorted.

We got to the end of the corridor and another door— another flash of panic—opened for us.

"Oooooh."

That was Jillian. I was too busy clenching my jaw.

We were in a courtyard. The middle was dominated by a large, open-air garden, with trees stretching up towards the night sky. Looking up took a few seconds of silent awe: the roof was miles overhead, and the only thing between me and it was … nothing.

"That is *not* safe." I looked back at Sarah, then around at the rest of the courtyard. There were shops and restaurants and doorways that probably led into other corridors, other courtyards. The other thing I noticed was the crowds: even at midnight, there were people walking around. They wore thicker, heavier clothes. They wore straps and belts. They wore jackets. They wore necklaces. They had long hair and spiked hair and dreadlocks with rings and every single other thing you'd never ever want to see in space. I snapped my gaze from them to Sarah, listening to her.

"Oh, there's actual mesh thingies. One every ... uh ... four levels, I think. So, the worst thing that can happen is you fall and hit and bounce a few times ..." She shook her head. "Anywho ... come on!"

She started to wheel away. Jillian and I moved to flank, and I felt a surge of sympathy and relief to see that Jillian looked as tense and nervous as I did. I put one hand on Sarah's shoulder, pitching my voice to be heard over the murmur of the crowd—which wasn't as overpowering as I would have expected. "So, where is your mom?"

"Floor 531," she said. "We rented a hotel room from one of the outside buildings. Figured you'd want to be able to see the stars." She grinned at me.

I smiled back. "Figured right."

We got to one of the many doorways that led into the other parts of the arcology. Rather than continuing through into another set of courtyards, which I was sure had different shops and different kinds of attractions in them but at the moment I couldn't care less, we slewed into a side corridor. This one was positively narrow for this place, being nothing but a rectangle with loads of doors on the sides.

"Into zee elevators," Sarah said, affecting an odd accent. This was not a shock. She liked weird accents. I think it came from imbibing an unhealthy amount of early twenty-first century entertainment. Sarah, being Sarah, managed to make any kind of weird accent sound absolutely adorable.

The elevator doors closed behind us and we started heading up, the elevator zipping along at a smooth and steady clip.

"This place is too freaking big for me," Jillian said, rubbing her face. "Remind me, is Neo-Vegas an arcology again?"

"Yup."

"Damn." She grinned. "I had been thinking about visiting there. Dru, did you relay my plan?"

I leaned over, whispering—very loudly—in Sarah's ear. "Jillian wants to go to Neo-Vegas and do the whole whores slash drugs slash gambling things."

Sarah looked a bit nervous. "Don't, uh, don't mention that, even as a joke, near my mom. She's Neo-Catholic of the Quebec Church. Are you guys up to snuff on Catholic history?"

"They're the kid diddlers, right?" Jillian asked.

Sarah rubbed her face. "Okay, Jillian, get out some paper and a pencil."

"A what and what?"

"Jillian." I frowned at her, warning. She held up her hands.

"I can remember a list."

Sarah nodded. "Good. In this case, label the list: Shit to not say around my mom. One, anything ... ANYTHING about sex."

I winced.

"Two, never talk about the Roman Catholic Church. Ever. Not unless you want her to rant at you for six hours. In French."

Jillian nodded. "Noted. So, um ..."

The elevator chimed and the door opened.

" ... how are you going to handle the fact that Dru undresses you with her eyes every second you two are together?"

Sarah looked thoughtful for a bit.

"Sunglasses?" I suggested.

Sarah snickered and shook her head. "Why don't you roll me over to her? That way, Mom can see you're a caring, loving individual and not just a freaky Spacer ..." She trailed off, but there was a word hanging at the end of the sentence. Slut. I knew that Sarah would never say that, but it felt like ... talking about what to not say around her mother roused up every single issue that had ever sprung up about me being a Spacer and Sarah being an Earther.

It didn't matter over text, even with the minute delays between responses that snuck in thanks to the fact light had to slowly crawl from the gravity well to my home to back again.

It wouldn't matter here. I kept telling myself that.

We got out of the elevator and into a corridor—a looping, curving corridor that had a door every ten or so feet—that made up this part of the arcology. We came to a large archway that led out onto one of those huge platforms. Sarah looked a bit nervous, remarking: "So long as we don't get near the edges, I can pretend I'm still on the ground ..."

"Meh, this is nothing." Jillian shrugged.

"Yeah," I said. "We've been in orbit with just spacesuits."

Sarah nodded. "Is it really that scary?"

"Well, we're ... what? Half a kilometer off the ground right now?" I asked, glancing to the side. The buildings we walked past were set around with gardens, each one looking like, well, I'd seen the like before in videos and on the holodeck: houses. Three stories each, with windows and everything. The gardens all looked like they produced a certain amount of produce, but they were also festooned with flowers and bioluminescent vines that provided most of the illumination up here, all gentle blues and golds. Beyond the buildings, I saw the edge of the platform: walls, then large, sleek looking wind baffles or turbines or something.

"You know ... this place is getting more and more comforting every second," I admitted as we pulled up to one of the more commercial areas of the outer platform. Here, the houses became hotels and shops, most of them only tended by a night watch to cater to the sleepless people walking around.

Sarah rolled her head back to look up at me.

I explained: "It's like a space station. On the ground."

She nodded. "Makes sense."

We walked into the hotel—a flare of tension as the door opened, closed—and went into yet another set of elevators. These, thankfully, didn't take nearly so godsforsaken long to get to the floor they were heading to.

Unfortunately, they also didn't take nearly so godsforsaken long to get to the floor of the building we were heading to. This meant that in a few short seconds that passed in a blur of terror that I swore was almost as nasty as when I had first gone into combat, all three of us were at the door to Sarah's hotel suite. Or, should I say, Mrs. Cayer's hotel suite. Sarah knocked.

The door opened.

Mrs. Cayer wasn't as scary as a drill instructor.

Mrs. Cayer wasn't as scary as a Loonie with a mining pick and a desire to dig my heart out of my ribcage.

Mrs. Cayer was actually not scary at all. She looked like Sarah: add in a functioning spinal column and a decade or two of experience. Then I reevaluated that opinion after a few moments of looking into her eyes. Those eyes reminded me of Portia Brown, the director of the Forge and one of the oldest women I had ever met. I could see, in those eyes, someone who had seen the Slump. She narrowed her eyes fractionally, then nodded, smiling at me.

"It's a pleasure to finally meet you, Drusilla."

She held out her hand. I took my hand off Sarah's wheelchair, taking it. My throat seized up for a second and I struggled to find words. Finally, I pushed some out: "P-Pleased to meet you too."

She stepped back and let us walk in, watching me and Jillian curiously. I gestured to Jillian, hurriedly. "This is Jillian Zhang."

"Heyo!" Jillian waved at Mrs. Cayer.

"She's one of Dru's buddies from the army," Sarah said.

"Marines," Jillian and I said at the same time.

Sarah snickered.

"Well, uh, it's a pleasure to have you both here." Mrs. Cayer took Jillian's presence in stride. She walked us into the hotel room—it had two beds and a connected bathroom, so it felt pretty crowded with four people in it. Sarah patted one of the beds, murmuring to me. "You sit here."

I sat there. The bed was really soft. I tried to not look around the room and spot all the things wrong with it, instead focusing on Mrs. Cayer as she stifled a yawn and asked Jillian: "Do you need help finding a place to stay?"

"Oh, no, I think I can figure it out."

"Are you sure?" Mrs. Cayer asked, sounding quite serious.

"Yeah." Jillian nodded, awkwardly. "Hey, Dru, see you tomorrow?"

I nodded back to her, squeezing Sarah's hand nervously. Jillian stepped out of the room and my back tensed as the door opened and closed. Mrs. Cayer turned to Sarah and me, gesturing to the beds. "So, uh, these are our beds, but I rented an attached room for you, Drusilla. Come on."

She walked to the wall that didn't connect to the bathroom, tapping the wallpaper a few times, bringing up an interface and manipulating a few simple icons until the wall clicked and a black rectangle appeared on the floral graphics that covered the wall. The rectangle slid up, revealing the next room over, which looked exactly like the room Sarah and Mrs. Cayer shared ... but flipped.

I stood, hand sliding out of Sarah's as I stepped over to the door.

"Thanks ..." I looked from Mrs. Cayer to Sarah. Sarah mouthed an apology and I shook my head, not wanting her to feel bad. I figured this kind of thing would be what I'd have to be used to, at least at first. The door closed and I leaned against the wall on my side of the room, listening to ...

Nothing. The soundproofing here was good, good enough that I couldn't even hear a murmur from the next room over.

I walked over to the bed, then lay down. A gesture dimmed the lights.

I had slept alone so many nights.

I could do it again.

I lay there for a time, eyes closed, unable to get to sleep. I had had the same problem last night: Gravity was too intense down here, pressing against me, pushing me into the bed and making me feel like my whole body had turned to lead. I told myself it was that. I told myself and told myself and told myself that the only reason why I curled up on the bed was because ...

I sat up. My eyes were already adjusted, so I saw that the door was open. A dark shape glided in and then the door closed. Sarah pushed up to the bed, grinning at me.

"So ..."

"Hey." I tried to sound nonchalant. That broke down as I felt tears sting my eyes. "Won't your mom get upset?"

"Nah. I'll wake up early and scoot back to the other room before she gets up." Sarah grabbed the armrests of her chair, pushing herself into the bed and onto my lap.

I lay back and Sarah's legs pressed against mine, her arms on either side of my head, looking down.

Her arms quivered and she laughed. "Roll over."

I rolled and pushed her onto her back, shifting so that I took the position she had. I grinned down at her ... paused ...

"Mmm?" She smiled at me. "Not gonna kiss me?"

"Sorry." I leaned forward, whispering. "I was waiting for the light lag."

Sarah laughed.

Chapter 3: A Day in the Life

4/4/2068

Republic of Quebec, Northern Reforestation Zone

T-Minus L-Day: 138

"This ..." Mrs. Cayer turned around and dropped a cloth-wrapped hunk of machinery on the table. "Is a chainsaw."

She threw the cloth aside, revealing matte-black carbon composite and high tolerance plastic, shaped into an ergonomic handle supporting a long razor blade.

"Dispatcher of zombies and deadites," Sarah spoke up from her place at the table, wheeling back and forth on her chair—her way of rolling onto her ankles, so to speak.

"What the ... what is a deadite!?" Jillian looked at Sarah. "Are those the *jiang shi?*"

"Whazzat?" Sarah looked at Jillian. Jillian held her hands up and out, then started jumping with her feet pressed together while hopping in the air.

"Chinese hopping vampires," Jillian explained.

"Chinese ... hopping ... vampires ... "

Sarah's head made a remarkably wooden noise when it hit the table.

"Children." Mrs. Cayer gave each of us the evil eye—the same evil eye she cast at us when Sarah admitted that she had been sleeping in my bed at the San Jose hotel—and we all shut up. "As I was saying, this is a chainsaw. You activate it with this toggle—it has a safety sensor, so if it detects a hand coming near the blade, it shuts down." She flipped the toggle on. The blade whirred to almost silent life, but lights flicked on, illuminating the blade so it looked like one of those stupid energy swords from *Star Wars*. Mrs. Cayer demonstrated the safety sensor by pressing her hand close to the blade, which immediately shut off, the lights blinking in a warning pattern.

"See?" She smiled at me. "We use these to trim the branches on the trees. Then we feed the branches into the recycler and use the biological runoff to feed our algae-stocks and run the carni-culture vat."

I wrinkled my nose. "Cloned meat. *Ugh*."

"Oh? I'd have thought that you'd be used to that in space." Mrs. Cayer had the astounding ability to inject just enough disapproval in her voice to make me feel like I was sixteen again, being lectured by my mom about proper use of station resources. Which was a neat trick, seeing as how I was ...

Sixteen.

In my defense, kill a few dozen people, get your fingers frozen off and all your friends killed, and you stop feeling like sixteen in a hurry. And ... after what happened on Tuesday ...

"Dibs on the chainsaw!" Jillian cut in, derailing my thoughts.

"Awww," Sarah pouted.

I tried to not meet her eyes, but Sarah caught them anyway and smiled. I glanced aside, tapping my fingers on the table. "So, what do I do if I'm not chainsawing?" I asked, taking advantage of English's easy way of verbaging things. I tried to not look or sound guilty.

I didn't know if it was because I was her daughter's girl-friend or Mrs. Cayer could just sniff out guilt, but I had a feeling that she knew that I was fidgeting under her gaze. So, she did the only thing a parent could do: She toggled from a class one gaze to a class two and made me feel like a bug.

Or I was imagining things.

Either one.

"Well, you need to carry the branches. Here." She stepped over to the cabinet, yanked out a burlap sack and tossed it at me. I caught it, trying to rein in my temporal whiplash. The chainsaw had been a bit of a lurch—it looked nice and modern, so it stuck out in a room made of wood and seemingly insulated by nothing more than a few hanging carpets. "Use this."

"Can I get one too?" Sarah asked.

"No, I need you to feed the chickens and do some gene-tests," Mrs. Cayer said.

"Awww ..."

"Just because your friends are staying here for a bit doesn't mean you can skimp on your chores, young lady." Mrs. Cayer pointed at the front door. Sarah wheeled herself out and Jillian and I followed. I gave Sarah a wave, not really feeling up to say-ing anything. She pushed herself over to me, grabbed me by the shirt, dragging me forward and kissing my cheek.

"It's okay," she whispered.

I felt even worse as she rolled away, heading to the chicken coop, which was a small metal building past the fields and the carni-culture vats where the cloned meat grew and the solar power plant and the other buildings that made up the farm. The balmy sun and the scent of the trees filled the air, snapping me out of my funk if only because I felt entirely, one hundred percent at ease.

After all, there was nothing *subtly* wrong about this. This was *all* wrong, so my instinct to twig out and panic wasn't triggered at all. Jillian seemed to feel the same way, as she headed towards the trees with a spring in her step. The trees were huge—bigger than anything I'd seen out of a holodeck—and they had loads of low hanging branches.

Jillian flicked on the chainsaw and sheared through a branch without so much as a tug of resistance. I tried to not think about how nasty that could be when used on a living being—I'd have almost preferred the thing was as noisy as the chainsaws from Sarah's old gore-films. At least those were obvious about their danger. Flashing lights just didn't have quite the same impact ...

"Jillian," I spoke softly, picking the branch off the ground, moving to catch the next one she sheared off. "I ... I gotta talk."

"Sure. What's up, Corp?" she asked, keeping her eyes on the chainsaw as she slipped it through another branch. Hey, give a job to a Spacer, we wouldn't take stupid risks.

I tried to find a good, elegant way to put what I had to say out there, so I didn't just blurt it out and sound like a complete and total psychopath.

"I almost killed Sarah yesterday."

"What?" Jillian looked at me, automatically flicking off the chainsaw and lowering it. "No, wait, seriously?"

I rubbed my hands over my face and managed to smear tree-sap into my bangs by accident. I jerked my hand down and made a face.

Jillian was still looking at me. "Corp, finish this story before I die."

I shook my head. "Well, basically, I was trying to get to sleep when Sarah showed up in my quarters. She crawled into bed with me."

Jillian nodded.

"And things were great. But when I went to sleep, I ... I woke up and I *swore* that I was back in the fight again and that someone was trying to strangle me. I pivoted Sarah around and was about five seconds away from breaking her face."

Jillian frowned at me—breaking me out of my chain of thoughts with her reason and her logic, the *biǎo zi*. "That's not *quite* trying to kill your girlfriend."

"I wrenched her shoulder hard enough that it hurt all through yesterday!" I said. "A-And if I hadn't ... stopped myself ..."

Jillian stepped over to me and put her hand on my shoulder, squeezing as she met my eyes. "Corp, it was just a bad dream. I have had a few since falling down this well, and I figure I'll be having them for the rest of my life. You just need to get your brain to figure out ..." Her finger tapped my forehead. "That all the things we were trained to be ready for don't happen down here. No blowouts, no ..."

She frowned, then jerked her head back. I reacted without thinking. I darted forward into a gnarly collection of bushes—while Jillian crouched behind a tree. She nodded into the forest and, glancing around, I saw a group of people moving through the woods—I peeked around my concealment and swept my gaze around, judging the terrain and the placement of the targets. Concealment wasn't better than cover—so I stepped back and put a tree between myself and the tangos. It felt sturdier than a lot of the cover I had had in space, where cover was usually nothing and more nothing backed up by even more nothing.

There was that about the Earth, at least. It had cover.

My hand drifted to my hip. No P3, no pistol, no pick. Just the sticks, which felt painfully inadequate considering how much hardware floated around on the Earth. The Slump had been the starter of wars and the crasher of economies. The only thing that had sold well through the entire thing was guns. Still, a branch upside the head might get me a weapon ...

Jillian tugged on my sleeve. I looked at her and she mouthed the words: 'Calm down.'

I shook my head, as if to get rid of the spirits clouding my brain. What was I *doing*? I looked around the tree and saw that the people were wearing coveralls and had backpacks and were chatting among themselves with a cheery, unconcerned air. They didn't have guns. They didn't slink around like bandits.

I really needed to start thinking like a civilian, didn't I?

And once I completed that impossible task, I would fly into space without a heavy lifter. Right.

I stepped out from behind my tree as Jillian stood from her hiding place, holding the chainsaw with one hand. I waved at the group and they waved back: There were two boys and a girl. The boys had long, braided hair, while the girl was bald and her eyes were covered by large, thick-looking goggles. She wore a frilly skirt and had leather bracers on her forearms, with huge, thick, rubberized gloves that seemed both entirely impractical and uncomfortable for a forest in the middle of April after a century of climate change.

"Hail and well met, fair maiden!" the woman said, bowing low, her bald head glittering in the sunlight.

"Come on, Regina, we need to keep going if we're going to reach the commune before dark." The boy to her left looked frowny. Something about him made my hackles lift. He looked at me, flicking his eyes over me—checking for guns, weapons. He saw my left hand and smirked.

I clenched my fist, feeling my metal fingers press against my palm.

The boy on the right said something in French. I only caught one in four words, but the gist seemed to be that he wasn't in such a godsdamned hurry.

"Commune?" Jillian asked, her hands still on the chainsaw.

"The WTF Commune. It's about two days that-a-way, as the zeppelin flies." The woman reached up to adjust her goggles. "Ah! I know you! You're Drusilla Zhao!"

"Whoa. You're a vet? From space?" the one who had eyed me asked, perking up.

"Yes. From space." I frowned, my voice as approachable as a vacuum.

"Slash!" *Slash?* "I'm Darren, this is—"

The woman with the goggles took my hand without so much a by-your-leave and curtsied at the same time. "Lady Regina Archibald."

"And this is Pierre." Darren jerked his thumb to the French guy.

"Bonjour."

"Nin hao," Jillian responded.

"Nísī diàn jù," Pierre responded, then switched to English. "I spent three years in Beijing during the Garcia Administration."

"Garcia, I found his stance on welfare repugnant. Feh," Regina said, putting a hand on her forehead. I was starting to seriously wonder if she was an escaped mental patient.

"Listen, this is fun and all, but we need to just head on if we're going to get to the commune. Can we head through your land?" Darren asked.

I looked at Jillian. Jillian looked at me and shrugged. I looked back at Darren, about to answer.

BANG!

A bullet blew through the tree branch that thrust over the three weirdos' heads. I hit the deck, Jillian threw herself down and all three of the weirdies threw their hands up. I looked up from my hiding place, spitting leaves out of my mouth, and saw Mrs. Cayer. She walked, steadily, towards us with a sleek, two-handed rifle cradled in her arms like she had been born shooting it. She worked a lever and a spray of powder blew out of the side of the gun—what was left of the caseless round— and the holographic interface around the gun ticked its ammo count down from 100 to 99 bullets. Jesus, Buddha, and all the ten thousand gods of the Hindu, that was a big hunk of ammo packed into a very small gun.

"Keep your hands very high," Mrs. Cayer said, her voice steady and steely as any DI I'd listened to. "And explain, in English or French, just what the *ce que faites-vous ici?*"

"*Pardonnez-nous. Nous allons vers la commune WTF!*" Pierre spoke up.

"Comm ... Commune? You're heading to a commune on foot?" Mrs. Cayer looked at them, lowering her gun barrel ever so slightly. I pushed myself away from the three of them, then got to my feet, kicking one of the dropped branches up and grabbing it from the air. Club was better than nothing.

"We're experiencing the forest delights, fair—"

"Can it, punk." Mrs. Cayer's voice was brusque and cold in a way I'd never heard before. I saw, behind her, Sarah sitting on her wheelchair with her own gun. Sarah hadn't mentioned a gun in any of her emails. Ever. I felt a cold drip down my spine that had nothing to do with the situation at hand. "What's the real ... reason ..." Her eyes shifted from Regina to Darren. "Push your hair up."

"What? Hey, I—"

"Hair. Up." Mrs. Cayer lifted her gun up to her shoulder and aimed it right at his head. He kept spluttering. Screw this. I reached out with my branch and shoved his hair up. I almost dropped the stick when I saw what waited under there: A metal surface, smooth and bonded to his skin. I could see tiny wires and fibrous cables that wormed their way into his scalp then sunk under the skull into the brain. A headcomputer.

Darren was a transie.

"Get the ... off my land," Mrs. Cayer snarled.

"Racist!" Darren shouted.

Mrs. Cayer fired into the air. "GET OFF!"

Darren, with his hands raised, backed away. His friends walked with him. Once they were a good distance off, they turned and sprinted away as quickly as their legs could burn. Mrs. Cayer lowered her rifle and worked the bolt again. She walked over to me, her eyes flashing. "You call yourself a Marine?" she hissed. "Drusilla, didn't you learn to NEVER let strangers onto your land? Ever?"

I gaped. "This is my fault?"

"You're a soldier!" Mrs. Cayer shouted at me.

Somehow, Jillian and I managed to not shout 'Marine!' right back at her. But it was close. "You should be better than this!" Mrs. Cayer added, stepping closer to me, getting right in my face.

"Mom!" Sarah pushed herself off the porch. Jillian opened her mouth to speak. But for the moment, it felt like I was on the battlefield with a CO shouting in my ear. I slapped the barrel of Mrs. Cayer's rifle to the side, slammed my head into her head—she turned aside at the last second and didn't take it to the nose—and I got the gun in my hand. I stepped back and Mrs. Cayer looked back at me.

I threw the gun to the ground. "T-This is a ... I thought ... we were in a civilian zone. Not a war zone." My breath came jagged, hard, like I had hot shrapnel in my lungs.

Mrs. Cayer stood stock still and slowly let her body untense. She had a pretty good CQC stance. She knelt down, keeping her eyes on me, and picked up the gun.

"Mom! Dru!" Sarah pushed herself over. "What the flying—"

"Sarah, clean this gun." Mrs. Cayer's voice was soft, gentle. Sarah took the gun, automatically. She opened her mouth—

and without even looking at her—Mrs. Cayer cut her off. "Now, Dear."

Sarah closed her mouth, shot me a look—I wasn't sure if it was a look of commiseration or a look of irritation or what—and wheeled her way around, calling out. "Jillian, with me."

Jillian looked at me. "Corp?"

I nodded to her.

Mrs. Cayer and I were alone. I felt like I was looking at General Lau again, the same kind of opposing force, sizing each other up kind of feeling.

Mrs. Cayer rubbed her cheek. "So, Drusilla ... where the hell did you get it in your head that the Earth was safe?"

I shrugged. "I don't know. Growing up in an environment where pushing the wrong button gets you and everyone else killed kind of makes places like this—" I gestured around the forest, my left eyebrow twitching like crazy "—look pretty f ... pretty idyllic."

"Twenty years ago, I served in the Regional Quebec Militia. Thirty years before that, I was in a refugee camp when radiation from Vicksburg blew up along the coast. My uncle starved to death, my mother was raped and murdered by gangers, and I've killed at least three bandits since I had Sarah and run dozens more off. My husband ... ." She put her hands on her hips and I really became aware of just how athletic Mrs. Cayer was. She took a moment, controlling herself. "I can tell you right now, this place isn't *safe*. Not unless we make it safe. Strangers are questioned, not conversed with. Weapons are kept on hand. I thought you knew this."

I closed my eyes. "Sarah didn't ... mention any of this."

Mrs. Cayer didn't respond to that. "All right, let's get you one of the sidearms. Are you any good with slugthrowers? I read on my feed that you guys used directed energy weapons."

"I can hack a slugthrower," I said, bristling.

Mrs. Cayer nodded, curtly. "I wouldn't have let you and Jillian here if I didn't think you would help protect this place. With ... with my husband gone, I need ... mobile people."

I nodded, looking down. "Got it."

I wanted to say something along the lines of: Wait, you just wanted us here because we could shoot straight and not panic when things got real? What about the undying love of my life? What about the whole godsdamn reason I wanted to come to Earth, the only thing that had kept me sane for three years? What about that?

I kept that inside. I didn't want to hear the answer. At all.

"Good." She sighed. "Come on."

>+<

Being armed made me feel more at home.

That made me sad.

Sarah pointedly kept silent, her shoulders set as if she was making herself a wall against her mother as she cleaned the caseless rifle. Mrs. Cayer ignored her daughter ignoring her and instead handed Jillian and me two guns: "Diamond guns. Not actually made of diamond, it's just carbon composite with RFID trackers. Lightweight, not much kickback. They've got a smart magazine, I usually keep it loaded with stun rounds with an alternate loading of caseless bricks."

Sarah punctuated her mother's sentence with the click-clack of her rifle going back together, her face set in a serious 'I'm pissed off but don't want to show it' face.

With those guns on our hips, Jillian and I went back to shearing off branches—more out of fear of Mrs. Cayer's wrath than any desire to actually gather biomass. Jillian cut two down before turning to me. "*Yánzhòng de shì, zài dìyù dàoguà fèiténg de tóngshí hái huózhe huí shì?*"

I snorted. "Hell of upside down while being boiled alive?"

"We have many hells. I only saw fit to make use of them," Jillian said.

"I don't think that *is* one of our hells."

Jillian frowned at me. "Seriously, though ... maybe I was too focused on the trying to not die part of my job description, but what the *hell* was that about?"

I frowned. The disquieting thoughts orbiting my head didn't need any extra remass to fly in and smack me in the face with extinction level anxiety. Still, I forced myself to respond.

"I think Sarah slightly oversold the safety of rural life."

"Wonder why ..."

"Maybe ..."

We both turned. Sarah's voice sounded thick as she pushed herself towards us, her wheels deforming and shifting to handle the rough terrain. Her eyes glinted with tears she was barely holding back. "Maybe b-because in the version of the farm I told you about, I wasn't a pathetic cripple who couldn't be counted on when shit got real. Maybe because I didn't want my girlfriend, who has enough damn problems, to worry about me. Maybe ... maybe because ..." She closed her eyes. "Maybe because I d-didn't want t—"

My hug oomphed her words to a halt and Sarah sniffled into my chest as I squeezed her tight. "It's okay," I whispered.

Jillian looked uncomfortably at the sky, but didn't say anything.

I slid away from Sarah, keeping my knees bent so I could look up at her. The one-G started to tell on my poor thighs, but I ignored it as she continued talking.

"Mom gets really nuts whenever anyone shows up."

"The Slump can do that to someone. Remember Brown?" Jillian asked. "She had a better thousand-click stare than any of us. And we'd been in combat ..."

I shook my head, still looking at Sarah. "Sarah-Bear, wh … why didn't you trust me?"

She blinked. "Trust you? Dru … Dru, I came out of the *closet* to you. Mom's part of a Catholic sect and Dad used to be in a Mad Men club! He had to get his nose replaced because he burned his sinuses out doing cocaine off of the tits of a high-priced hooker!"

"Whoa! Respect," Jillian said, her voice mock solemn.

"Jillian!" Sarah and I said at the same time.

Jillian looked abashed. "Sorry." She opened her mouth, as if to ask a question, then looked away, shutting herself up.

Sarah shook her head. "I just didn't want to add any more to your worry-tank."

I smiled at her. "Goof." I stood up ever so slightly and leaned forward, putting my forehead against hers. She closed her eyes.

Jillian coughed. "Now that we got that out of the way," she said, hurrying us along. "Can we move onto the main issue? We've got two days down, twenty-eight days to go before we both muster back into the service or go AWOL and the police come after us." She turned and sliced off another branch with the chainsaw, just to make sure that we didn't look like we were doing no work. "While this place has bandit problems, I'm guessing bandits don't have power armor, thousand joule pulse rifles, and rocket-propelled grenade launchers. Right?"

"Right. We only get those on the first Tuesday of the month." Sarah smiled, a bit of her old spark coming back. It bloomed. "How do we start looking for a way to keep you guys out?"

I opened my mouth, closed it, looked at Jillian. She shrugged.

I looked at Sarah. "I have no idea."

Sarah reached up and slapped my arm. "Then we hit the wikis!"

Chapter 4: Grasping at Carbon

4/5/2068

Republic of Quebec, Northern Reforestation Zone

T-Minus L-Day: 137

Midnight. My eyes felt heavy, like gravity was tugging at them harder than everything else on my body. The text I was trying to read—the endless reams of minutia printed about military codes of conduct over the decades—blurred. I rubbed my palms against my face.

"Ugh … I don't suppose you can fake homosexuality …" Sarah muttered, her head pressed against her desk as she used her hand to scroll through a collection of wiki-articles which were projected along the desk surface at a crazy canted angle so that she could read it with her cheek mashed against the plastic.

"You're reading cached wiki files." Jillian sounded too crisp for someone who had been scrolling through the blacknet for hours.

"I know … I ran out of up-to-date wikis …"

I closed my eyes. It'd be easier to read after I had closed my eyes …

Whap!

I jerked up, trying to figure out what had hit me. I saw that Jillian's arm was cocked for throwing, and a crumpled-up piece of paper had hit my forehead. As it lay on my lap, the paper quivered then poofed into perfect flatness, projecting one of its preloaded images.

"Wake up."

"*Wǒ xǐngle!*"

"*Tǎng zài líng hú,*" Jillian shot back.

"*Pouvez-vous parler anglais?*" Sarah glared at the two of us, picking her head up and off the desk. "Jillian, how is the criminal side of things going?"

"Well, most of this stuff is the kind of thing that the CAA government frowns on. To be fair, this entire enterprise is kind of a big naw-naw."

"It's pronounced no-no," Sarah said, pursing her fingers together. "No. No. You know what, screw it." She tapped her desk and the wiki she had been reading—adjusting itself for her head position—vanished with a faint whirr. She brought up another one. "Why don't we look at the illegal ways to get out of the army? If you guys are willing to sit the war out and damn what your country thinks, why not go for the illegal shit? You can desert, right?"

I rubbed my eyes. "Jillian, Evidence B."

"Evidence B ..." Jillian tapped at her tablet—well, Mrs. Cayer's tablet, borrowed for the moment—and held it up. The image was a crisp, high-rez image with hypertext and contextuals—all of which, Jillian shut off with a single tap. It showed five men hanging from a gallows near a collection of organic recycling machinery, with the US Capitol building (complete with the fresh smoking crater in the side of the dome) in the background.

"Emergency Acts of 2022, re-invoked during the current situation," I said. "They catch us deserting, they space us. And they *will* catch us, unless we want to run to the far corners of the Earth. Which..." I pursed my lips, looking at Sarah. Jillian's grin was all grim gallows.

"Hang us," she said, picking up a piece of paper and balling it up. "Spacing is too expensive down here." She started to toss the paper into the air, catching it as it dropped down.

"Firing squad, I'd imagine ..." I looked at Jillian. "I'd hope, at least. Hanging is so twenty-first century."

Jillian nodded, trying to match my nonchalance. "A good way to bum a cig, right? They give you those before you get shot."

"You don't smoke ..."

"I've been meaning to start," Jillian said. "Earther vices, baby!"

"Guys!" Sarah tapped at her desk. Her voice held a combination of irritation and excitement. "Stop saying dumb but adorable things—" and didn't that just get my heart fluttering "—and get over here!"

I stood from my place on the comfy chair (which Sarah had practically beaten Jillian out of to secure for my skinny butt) and stood next to Jillian. We looked down at the desk and saw that Sarah had patched up the wiki article on CAA conscription laws. She had been trawling through it, and had highlighted a section on grounds for discharge.

"Psychological?" I asked. "You want me to flunk me out of the war via *shrink*?"

"You could fake it." Sarah smiled at me.

Jillian grabbed the air above her neck and hung her head to the side, sticking her tongue out grotesquely.

Sarah frowned. "Listen, girls, you're going to have to break a law. Which is better: risk being punished for draft dodging, or risk going into space?"

"To be fair ..." I admitted. "I don't think they'd actually hang us just for trying to get clear on grounds of psychological issues."

"No, they might." Jillian leaned over, opening a tab on the desk and then drawing up a keyboard, typing up on the search engine. Within a few seconds, she had some of the latest psychoanalytic machinery on the view. Just reading some of the descriptions made me raise a few eyebrows.

"How true do you think some of this is?" Sarah asked. "You know the Mark Twain quote."

"What?" I asked.

Jillian and Sarah managed to say it at the same time: "You can't trust everything on the internet."

It took me a few seconds to work that out. I snorted.

Jillian sighed. "Seriously, though, I was in the hospital bay on the Forge. I got to chat a bit with God while she was operating on us—"

"Always knew God was a woman. Someone should tell Mom," Sarah interjected.

I grinned and put my hand on Sarah's shoulder. Jillian continued: "The way she talked about some of the neurofeedback machines ... they can practically read your mind."

"Well, VR exists," Sarah pointed out. "It causes vertigo, but if you're not inputting new data, just reading it, I don't see why there'd be any problem."

"Fantastic." I sighed. "Not only do we have to get out of the draft, we also have to lie to mind readers."

"Could be worse," Jillian said, but her quip was cut off by a yawn that could swallow whole stars. She didn't follow it up with any explanation *how* it could be worse. I walked back to my chair and thumped back into it, just to take some of the weight off my feet, off my bones. Even that didn't really help.

"So, along the list of things that we can't do, we can add 'lie' to the list: So, that's lying, maiming ourselves, having a genetic disorder that prevents our serving in the armed forces, running to another country, and claiming we're conscientious objectors. All out," I muttered into my hands.

Jillian nodded.

This felt like a late night math problem that just refused to resolve into an elegant solution. Instead, we were kicking at snarling equations and integers that didn't want to go away and variables that we could just shuffle around and never actually turn into a real number. A real chance.

I could literally *feel* the air around my head solidifying.

"All right, that's it." Sarah tapped the desk, which powered off. She wheeled herself around to face us, her hands working deftly to spin and stop. "We're not getting anywhere like this. Everyone to bed."

Jillian nodded, pushing herself off the bed and walking to the door. "G'night, you two."

Jillian stepped outside. Sarah's room had a great position in the house, angled so that when you opened the door, you could look down the corridor and into the main kitchen/eating area. That had the downside of making it easy for Mrs. Cayer to keep an eye on who came out of Sarah's room. She had made it really clear without saying a single word that I was to sleep in the guest room with Jillian, not with Sarah. Sarah pushed over to me, smiling up at me.

I looked down at her. I was at a loss for words.

Sarah patted my thigh. "If ... you have nightmares again, maybe you should tal—"

I shook my head. "I'll be fine!"

Sarah tugged me down and leaned forward, kissing my cheek. "I ... okay."

I kissed her on the lips.

You know, back when I hadn't actually kissed that many people, I had this weird idea that kissing Sarah would be perfect. That had survived exactly zero seconds on the Earth. Kissing her meant kneeling and leaning forward over her knees. It meant trying to balance against her wheelchair, which she locked into place so her hands could get all over me. It meant moving and turning my head, trying to match her movements, which caused all sorts of little ... bumps.

Her nose hit mine. Her lips overlapped with mine. Soft, slick noises that sounded silly instead of sexual rang in my ears.

And you know what?

It was the hottest damn thing I had ever experienced.

I drew back, panting, rocking onto my ankles. Sarah grabbed my shirt to keep me from falling onto my ass, her wheelchair scooting forward ever so slightly as my weight tugged her back.

"Good night."

"Don't go ..." she mouthed, her eyes shimmering.

I blushed, grabbing her hands, squeezing them, kissing her knuckles, then her palms. She bit her lip, eyes closing. I kissed her wrist, feeling her pulse.

"*Oui ... oui ...*" she gasped.

I leaned forward and kissed her on the lips again, then her chin, grabbing her shoulders and practically crawling onto her wheelchair, which groaned and complained.

"Ahem."

I and Sarah were on the opposite sides of the room in less time than it takes for a PPR to cycle. Mrs. Cayer looked from me to her daughter to me again, standing in the doorway of the room. She had moved so quietly that I hadn't even noticed her—I had been distracted, but damn—and she looked disapprovingly at me.

"Dru, do you need anything before you go to sleep?" she asked, her voice sweet as can be.

I shook my head, unable to actually make a sound.

"Then sleep tight, dear," she said, stepping back and letting me walk out of the room. I walked to the guest bedroom, which made up most of the 'newer' part of the cabin. I could tell, because the wood was a different shade and a slightly different cut and polishing. The guest room itself looked a bit similar to Sarah's room—rectangular, with narrow windows that were made to let in as much light as possible while also having a gridwork of wooden planks (reinforced by what looked like bulletproof carbon weave) that could be pressed over the window. There was a slot for a rifle to be braced and what looked like a little box for extra ammo.

But the soul was gone. No wallpaper holograms, no potted plant. The ammo box wasn't stuffed with a mixture of underwear, bras and caseless ammo bricks. There were no knick-knacks: No dayglow ponies, no posters of ancient movies whose actors were both long dead and long forgotten. No MP3 players with cracked screens dangling from bits of string, used to make constellations of junk. No ...

No Sarah. Just a bunk bed and a light.

Jillian had stolen the bottom bunk. I frowned at her.

"Hey," she said. "I got top bunk in space. Plus, you were having fun."

I smiled, wistfully. "Fun ..."

"Lights, dim," Jillian called out. The lights dimmed, obediently. In the darkness, Jillian shifted, rolling around and getting comfortable. I remained on my back, looking up at the ceiling.

I didn't get to sleep for a long time.

>+<

I jerked and then fell out of bed. There was a single moment of speed and then a sharp, hard impact that made me scream for a second before I clenched down on my jaw. I rolled to my side, grabbing my wrist, hissing in Mandarin. Jillian rolled out of bed and came up in a combat stance, her eyes wide and her shoulders tense.

She looked down at me. "Dru?"

"YES!" I shouted at her. "DRU. THAT'S MY NAME!"

"What the—"

The door opened and Mrs. Cayer burst in, holding her rifle. She lowered it, looking down at me. " ... did you fall out of bed?" she asked.

I lay on the wooden floor and let my head thump down. My wrist throbbed, because I hadn't fallen right: Weeks of training and practice at falling properly, all forgotten in a single drop. Damn it. But other things were wrong: I felt soaked with sweat, my arms trembled like I had been lifting weights, and I was shaking with adrenaline. I didn't quite remember my dreams ...

I blew out a sigh as Mrs. Cayer grabbed my unhurt arm, asking "Broken?"

"I don't think so." I moved it, wincing.

"I got a medical press. Let me grab it."

Sarah pushed into the room after her mom left, looking concerned. "Bad dreams again?"

"No, I was attacked by a ghost," I snapped, wincing as I rubbed my hand. Sarah frowned.

Jillian, who was dressed in her skinclothes and nothing else, sighed. "Well, I'm hitting the shower. Uh, which one was working again?"

Sarah pointed and Jillian nodded her thanks, walking past the both of us. Sarah pushed herself just a bit closer. "Dru ..."

I looked at her.

"Maybe you should steal the bottom bunk."

I managed a smile as Mrs. Cayer came in with a medical press, which she slapped onto my wrist, the thing adjusting shape to fit with my hand, immobilizing it just right and releasing a few dermal bone-bonding agents into my arm, along with contact painkillers. I closed my eyes, trying to stop my hands from shaking.

"Sarah, come on, we have to cook breakfast. Dru, while we're cooking, could you be a dear and take Jillian out to check the perimeter?"

"Mom—" Sarah started as her mom headed out of the room. Mrs. Cayer talked right over her.

"I was thinking we could cook them something tra—"

"Mom!" Sarah cut her mother off. Mrs. Cayer turned to face her. "I want to check the perimeter with Dru."

Mrs. Cayer frowned. "I need your help in the kitchen."

"Jillian needs to learn to cook. Dru needs to learn to cook."

I suppressed the desire to say that I knew how to cook. I knew better to get between bullets. But, I couldn't stop myself from putting my good hand on Sarah's shoulder and squeezing her.

"And," Sarah continued. "Dru's my girlfriend, Mom. We're going to spend time together, no matter how many times you give us separate chores. Deal with it."

Mrs. Cayer frowned. "Don't take that kind of tone with me, missy."

"Mom, I'm sixteen!" Sarah said, her hands squeezing the wheels of her wheelchair, her shoulder trembling and tense. "You—"

Sarah's words choked off when her mother thrust the handle of the rifle at her. Sarah took it, checking it over with commendable speed and efficiency for a civilian. Mrs. Cayer's voice was curt and to the point: "Dru, Sarah, check the perimeter."

She turned around and walked out of the room. I grinned at Sarah, who smiled at me.

Sarah let me hold the rifle. It was lightweight, but not quite as bulky as the PPR—mostly because it didn't have to hold all the focusing apparatus or the power source to create a dedicated laser—and I sighted a few times just to make sure I had a feel for it. Sarah rolled along the tracks of the farm, her wheels shifting and changing to suit the terrain she pushed over.

"God, Mom drives me crazy sometimes."

"Tell me about it." I bit my lip, chewing on of my old canker sores. I forced myself to stop. "I missed you last night ..."

"I did, too." Sarah smiled as we got to the fields, moving between row after row of genetically engineered, high-yield crops. The garish colors looked wrong, unhealthy, but Mrs. Cayer had said that they were all showing healthy indicators. We got to the very edge of Cayer land, where the forest had been cleared out to make a dirt path that connected to a paved road that led to the other homesteads. Quebec Arcology rose in the distance, towering and ominously huge even from kilometers away.

The mailbox was stuffed with anachronisms that made me stop dead and ... and laugh at just how silly it was.

"What?" Sarah grinned at me. "You're surprised to see actual paper mail?"

She pulled out a collection of envelopes.

"Yes, actually."

She sighed. "Aunt and Uncle Baston lost their whole fortune to a netwar attack twenty years ago. Since then, they have refused to use electronics unless they absolutely have to. Their whole house? Analog." She grinned and then held up a second bushel of paper stuff. "And these are the physical magazines that still deliver. The whole thing is run by for-profit transporters who popped up when the American post office died."

"Why use them and not the Québécois mail?"

"Cheaper, mostly," she admitted, shrugging as she shoved the letters and magazines into the container on the back of her wheelchair. "Come along, my darling Dru." She started to push back to get to the inside of the forest—the cleared out rectangle that marked the Cayer land. I walked alongside her ... and ...

Tried to enjoy myself.

But I kept having odd feelings. The way the dappled sunlight winked and flickered reminded me faintly of an alarm light.

CRACK!

I threw myself flat, one hand holding the rifle against my shoulder, my other hand grabbing at the floor, scrabbling for the latch that hid my breather. Instead of hard, smooth surface, I just felt ...

Leaves. I blinked and I was in the forest again, with Sarah looking around, frowning. "What? What is it?"

I sighed, a shuddering, stop and skip sound. Breathing in felt tight, like a belt was wrapped around my chest. My hand, still dug into the leaves, clenched, the leaves crinkling and cracking.

"Dru?" Sarah asked.

"Nothing ... it was nothing ..." I whispered.

"Okay." Sarah paused. "What was it. Actually?"

I closed my eyes. I could have sworn that was the sound of a window cracking open. Depressurization. Blowout. Admitting that sat on the tip of my tongue, just waiting for launch codes.

Instead, I shook my head. "Nothing," I said. "Tripped."

Sarah frowned. "Dru, don't lie to me."

"I tripped," I said, again. "*Tā māde*, I'm a terrible liar ..." Nervous laugh.

"Yes, you are, we should send you to night school." Sarah grinned. I ... wasn't sure if that was a joke or not. "But, seriously, are you okay?"

I brushed my hand along my thigh, knocking leaves off my hand.

"I thought I was in a blowout," I admitted, and it felt like pulling teeth.

The perimeter was fine. We checked it twice, which was something I could get behind. Then, we got to come home for my first "real" Earther breakfast. We had bought take-out Chinese food in the San Jose Arcology, so I was a bit excited to see what Mrs. Cayer and Jillian had cooked up for us.

I got a bit less excited when Sarah and I found Jillian leaning against the door outside of the kitchen, looking greener than I'd ever seen her.

"You okay, Big-J?" Sarah asked.

"Yeah. Just fine." Jillian's voice was pinched.

I opened the door for Sarah. I reeled backwards as the smell of breakfast slapped me in the face like a soaked towel. "Ugh!"

"Ooh, sausage!" Sarah pushed herself into the house, her wheels shifting to help her get over the lip of the door. I looked at Jillian, whose eyes were closed.

"You know dicks?"

"The ... people or the organs?"

"The organs. The things you'd like if you were sensible and bisexual."

I nodded, then tacked on a 'yeah' because Jillian's eyes were still closed. She continued.

"Well, imagine those but cooked and made entirely out of carni-meat. The *air* is greasy. I'm not even kidding, it's like being served marinated fat and human fingers." Jillian was starting to make me feel even queasier myself.

"What's the side dish?"

"Waffles. Those ... those actually looked pretty good." Jillian opened one eye. "But I'm waiting for the grease to get turned into concentrated chemical weapons."

"I ... think that the chemical plant under the sink is just for making it into a petrosim."

"Right." Jillian rubbed her face with her hands.

Sarah stuck her head out of the kitchen window, grinning at us.

"Don't tell me you two get sick at exotic food! You're … Spacers, you like live and die in a zero-G environment! This is what gets your stomach upset?"

"We'll be in in just a second," I said, looking up at Sarah, who pouted, but nodded and ducked back into the house proper, closing the window. I turned to Jillian, who had gone back to leaning against the wall.

"We're going to have to get used to this," I said, slapping her shoulder. "Come on. I'm sure after the first time, we'll get to really like it."

We didn't.

Chapter 5: Heaven

4/12/2068

Republic of Quebec, Northern Reforestation Zone

T-Minus L-Day: 130

One week.

One week was all it took.

First, the nightmares got worse. Before, I had just felt achy or sore or sweaty after sleep. Then, as each day became night and I crawled into the bottom bunk—Jillian had given it up the second time I'd fallen out of bed—the dreams became clearer and clearer. First, it had been figures zipping down corridors, surrounded by globbing spheres of red—blood in microgravity. There had been flashes of light, subdued booming noises.

After that, my brain moved onto reliving the worst moments of my life.

Again.

And again.

And again.

And again.

And again.

It didn't take a week for me to try and sleep as little as I could. I stayed up late at night with a tablet, tapping through webpages, reading articles about the draft, about the news, about the world. But every night, I still had to sleep, and then I had to dream.

And I had to see *them*.

Liam. His brains dragged through the back of his head by a screw.

Chuck. Turned into cover—*guǐ cover*—as bullets thudded against his dead flesh. I had hidden *behind* him. My friend. My ...

David. Quiet. David.

I had seen his spine snap at least three times, tossing around on my bed.

One week was all it took for me to grow to despise two words, whether they were in English, Mandarin, French or Swahili.

"You okay?"

"Yes. I'm abso-*tā mā de*-lutely fine." I shoved a pitchfork through a bundle of reduced fiber and hurled the stuff up and into the main recycling vat. Sarah looked at me sidelong as she tapped in the programming controls.

"You look like you haven't slept in a week. Are you and Jillian staying up all night?"

"No," I muttered and didn't respond to any other questions, focusing on just the chores.

>+<

"Nǐ méishì ma?"

"Tài hǎo le! Xiàng nǐ mā de bī!" I glared at Jillian, kicking the chair halfway across the room.

She held her hands up. "Okay, whatever you say, Corp."

She headed out of the room.

I glared after her, walked over to the chair that I had kicked away, put my boot up on it and started to tighten it before heading out to handle my chores for the day.

>+<

"Dru, *nous avons besoin de parler.*"

"I'm fine!" I turned to face Mrs. Cayer. I had only *just* gotten up today and people were already—

"I didn't ask if you were fine." Mrs. Cayer frowned at me. I noticed, a few seconds too late, that she was dressed for travel: boots, leather jacket, a rifle slung across her back.

"Oh ... I ... don't actually—" My voice cut off as I yawned.

"I'm aware of that." Mrs. Cayer crossed her arms over her chest. "I've armed Jillian and put her in charge of defending the farm while we're out. Come on."

"Where exactly are we going?"

"To a psychiatrist," she said, her voice flat.

"A ... a psychiatrist?" I asked, walking after her. She opened the front door of the farmhouse. I tensed, clenched my jaw, and then forced myself to relax. I didn't need a breather. I didn't need a skinsuit. There was no vacuum outside. "I can hack this."

"Hack this?" She turned to face me as I walked through the door. "What the hell does that have to do with anything?"

I rubbed my temples. "I can pull my weight. I don't need a godsdamned psych-tech telling me what I can and can't do. I'm ... not fine. But I can deal with it."

Mrs. Cayer frowned at me. "I'm your legal guardian, you signed that over to me. So, think of it this way: You go to a psychiatrist ... or I sign you back over to the Alliance. How gentle do you think *they* would be with your psych-eval?"

I was in the car five seconds later, glaring out the window as Mrs. Cayer drove down the road and out of the Cayer homestead.

I got to enjoy the view out the window. I hadn't really paid attention last time, because last time had been night and I had gotten the backseat and, under the cover of darkness and Jillian providing enough inane questions to distract the ever-present gaze of Mrs. Cayer, I had made out with Sarah.

Under the harsh gaze of sunlight and a sullen desire to not look at Mrs. Cayer, I could admire the trees, the other homesteads that the car smoothly glided past.

But the ride all the way to Quebec Arcology was too long—far too long for me to just sit here and pout.

I looked at Mrs. Cayer.

"I'm not a little kid."

"I know." She didn't take her eyes off the road. I noticed that there was a button on the dashboard of the car labeled 'auto'.

I wanted to go into why this was stupid, why it was stupid that I felt so ...

So damn confined.

And ... then ... it all clicked into place. Every time I talked back to Mrs. Cayer, I felt a tiny stab because she was the next best thing to a mom. I closed my eyes and rubbed my palms against my face. My mother ...

I looked back out at the window.

I could totally sit here and pout for the whole damn car ride.

We drew up to the outskirts of the Quebec Arcology, which was open at this time of day and supported a steady stream of cars zipping in and out, heading to the suburbs that spread around the base of the arcology, the spaces between the suburbs filled with trees. If you were curious what it looked like, just picture the San Jose Arcology and put it in southern Quebec's sprawling forests. Bam. Done.

The parking lot was automatic, with loads of shifting plates that could take cars into a hidden recess in the superstructure of the arcology proper. Despite being right there, Mrs. Cayer didn't drive into place just yet. Instead she parked and looked at me, frowned, and asked: "Drusilla, can I trust you to go to the doctor's office alone?"

I glared at her. "You can't even trust me with your daughter, so I'm—"

"I'm Catholic. A branch of Catholic, but still Catholic," she said. "We don't think gays are sinners anymore, but we still have to stick to fundamentals of our religion. Sex before marriage is *wrong*. Hell, if people could keep it in their damn pants before they filled the world up with pretty, precious little babies, then maybe we wouldn't have needed so many of them to die off during the Slump ..."

She paused, then shook her head.

"Drusilla, I know you think you are grown up. People thought they were grown up during the Slump. Kids who had been weaned on the internet and the media that Sarah finds so fascinating ... they were thrown into a *nightmare*." She closed her eyes. "Refugee camps, the civil wars, the fallout. In just five years, I went from pitying Americans for their spree shootings to carrying an assault rifle." She sighed. "Sometimes, I ... still can't believe we're all still alive."

I stayed quiet. It felt like talking would break a kind of spell that filled the car, a spell that held everything around us still. There wasn't a car waiting behind us to park. There was no doctor appointment waiting for me. There was nothing but the past, floating around the cabin.

Mrs. Cayer lurched on, putting the car into drive mode again. We whispered through the gates and into the parking lot.

"So, yeah, we all had to grow up really fast. The adults didn't know what was happening and the kids were all broke." She tapped her fingers on the wheel of the car as she took a turn. "I know what you are thinking. You miss your parents. You think the world is unfair. You want to just crawl back into the internet, into the video games, into my daughter, and just let the world go away ..."

She looked at me again as we came up beside the arcology's pedestrian entrance. The building loomed overhead, adding a bludgeon of literal symbolism to every word. "The world is out there, Dru. It never gets better just because you want to hide."

My hand slid along the door, finding the latch. I didn't trigger it right away.

"I am not hiding," I said. "I ... I'm not hiding. Okay. I'm fine." I looked at her. "I'm going to be fine. The shrink isn't going to find anything wrong with me."

Mrs. Cayer watched me, then nodded fractionally.

Silence.

More silence.

Even. More. Silence.

"You're afraid to open the door, aren't you?" Mrs. Cayer didn't sound judgmental which made it even worse. I tried to unclench my jaw to speak but couldn't. My knuckles had turned white.

I jerked the door open, blew out a sigh—not a sigh of relief, you breathe out before a blowout to empty your lungs before the vacuum can turn them inside out—and stood. Mrs. Cayer tapped the dash, calling out to me as the door closed.

"I sent you the directions. Be there, he's a family doctor," she said. "Call me when it is done. Good luck."

She drove backwards, her car whirring almost silently.

I turned and faced the arcology proper.

I could do this.

The Quebec Arcology wasn't segmented or partitioned vertically like the San Jose Arcology. Instead, it was set up on horizontal lines, meaning that I could look clear across from one end of the arcology to the other side, assuming a break in the crowds popped up. There were unobtrusive guide and transport utilities built into the layout, with slidewalks and turbo-lifts and all the other futuristic gizmos you'd expect to see in a city-building. I didn't use them, instead letting my collar guide me with a tiny voice in my ear, which I keyed to sound as much like Sarah as possible, with the mood set to flirtatious.

"Take a right, sexy."

I glanced at my sleeve, tapping on the shirt's interface, double-checking my volume settings. They were still on directed audio. I shook my head and listened to the breathy, seductive computer guide me left, right, right, forward and then into a honeycombed wall, each octagonal inset walled off with semi-transparent glass. I took a flight of unpowered stairs, tensed and barreled my way through an automatic door, and found myself in the antechamber of the doctor.

I took a moment to look around, spinning on one heel with my hands in my pockets—my finger tapping off the guide.

The office had the same futuristic look as the rest of the arcology, with the wallpaper set to a smooth, unobtrusive white and the floor plated with more plastic whiteness. Egg-shaped chairs sat around a table that had a few tablets for library access. A scanning light flicked across my face and a calm voice speaking in English, then French, came from all around me.

"Welcome to Dr. Abbe's office, Drusilla Zhao. Please, take a seat and wait for a few moments, Dr. Abbe will be with you in a few minutes."

I nodded, sat down in the egg-chair, and waited for it to shape itself to me. I picked up a tablet and tabbed to the news channels, finding the local news—I really could *not* deal with world news right now.

"And in latest news, a transhuman hacker going by the name of Lord Dagon has been found and captured." A smooth, almost genderless voice read out the news as the tablet showed a holo-gram of a sneering, bald-looking man of indeterminate age. He wore a leather jacket and had a series of little studs in the right side of his forehead, sinking into his skin like rivets. "Wanted on two hundred counts of data tampering and personal theft, Lord Dagon—real name Andre Perry—was apprehended by a branch of the Interfederal Netcrime Division lead by Investigator Elijah Tam with minimal casualties."

Hypertext flowed along the bottom of the screen. I tapped minimal casualties and got a text sidebar describing that Lord Dagon had had physical augmentations that had gone along with his mental implants. My fingers twitched and I set the tablet down, rubbing my temple with my metal fingers.

Thinking about Dagon—and Darren, the transhuman from a few weeks ago—made my skin crawl. What if Darren had tried violence? Would an augmentation or two have left Mrs. Cayer and me a bloody pile of twitching muscle?

I closed my eyes and tried to get that image out of my head. "Drusilla?"

I took my hand off my eyes, looking up at the doctor: Peter Abbe had more pigmentation in his skin than most people I'd met, with a wide, trusting face. He smiled at me and I managed a watery, tight lipped smile back. "That's me."

"Peter Abbe, Doctor Peter Abbe," he said, walking forward and offering his hand. I took it as I stood, trying to relax.

This was just a psych-eval. Nothing special.

But ...

The one thing that no one ever wanted to do was to get chucked to Heaven and become an angel. Heaven was the hospital station where every Spacer who had gotten limbs blown off or their organs flash-fried by a burst of hard gamma had gone to get patched up. Angels were the people who went because they flunked mentally. You didn't bad-mouth angels, but everyone had it in the back of their mind: angels were weak. Pathetic.

They couldn't hack it and they cracked, that was all there was to it.

"Come on, let's get you comfortable."

I had an image of what a psych-tech's office would look like: desk, comfortable couch, lots of books and diplomas in the soft sciences. Maybe a pill dispenser.

Abbe's office didn't look like that. He did have the desk, but there weren't any books—that made sense, after I had thought about it for a few seconds—and there weren't any hanging diplomas and there wasn't a comfy couch. There was a rather terrifying-looking chair with a gigantic mechanical spider hanging over it. The legs reached around and to the headrest of the chair, with a recess in the middle of the thing's bulbous body for someone's skull.

"Sorry about this old thing," he said. "I'm saving up for a more, uh, discreet fiberweave reader. Have a seat, please."

"A ... Aren't you going to ask me any questions?" I asked, sidling nervously over to the chair. I heard a whirr and a click. I spun around, looking for the source of the sound, my heart in my throat. What if—

No. The room was *not* depressurizing. I closed my eyes and when I opened them I was looking at the doctor. He stood behind the desk, a holographic interface popping up as he held his hands over the desk. I noticed his fingers had faint discolorations on them—haptic interfaces implanted into his fingertips, so every time he pushed a holographic "button", his finger tip would buzz. I could actually see the vibrations as he played around with the controls.

"A few ..." He smiled at me. "Drusilla ... do you mind if I use your first name?"

"N-No." I shook my head.

He nodded. "Drusilla, have you had a psychological evaluation before?"

"I've … seen movies."

He smiled. "Well, I'm going to have to let you in on a little secret … movies make things up."

"R- … Really?" I asked, my voice weak as I gaped at him.

He laughed an actual laugh— I could tell after having tried to force so many myself. "Really. This ugly thing will give me constant, up-to-date feedback on all sorts of biometric tell-tales. Uh, heart rate, blood pressure, skin tension, perspiration, microexpressions, brain electrical and neurochemical levels. That kind of stuff. I will ask you questions once I've started getting actual information so that we can start to create a picture of your mind."

I nodded, then sat down in the chair. I grabbed the arms and breathed in, in even more, then waited a few seconds before blowing it all out.

The spider legs tapped against my shoulders and extended, spreading the tips into suction cups that stuck to me. The recess closed around my forehead and I felt more things press against my skin.

"And … there we go. Feeling tense?"

I pushed out one of those forced laughs I mentioned before. "Me? Nahh."

"Liar." He smiled to show he wasn't angry. "Now, let's get a baseline set up … what is your name?"

"Drusilla Zhao."

"Very good. Who were your parents?"

I closed my eyes. "were Mary and Michael Zhao."

"Mmhm …" Dr. Abbe tapped a few buttons. "Where you were born?"

"The Hub, Earth-Sun L1, one point five million kilometers above the surface of the earth." I smirked. I could list that address in my sleep, it had floated through my head often enough. Every time I'd had stopped and reflected on the world, on what had been going on, I ... I had just remembered how far away I was.

And, stupid me, I thought ...

I thought that it'd be easier. That, somehow, life would just become something fuzzy and indistinct and better, not just another cycle of worries and concerns. I was an idiot.

"And," Dr. Abbe asked another question. "Do you have dreams?"

I frowned. "Yeah."

"What are they about?"

I closed my eyes, inside the helmet that wrapped around my head. I closed them and I tried to focus.

"Memories."

I felt a buzzing in my head—somewhere between a *feeling* and a *noise*. I wasn't sure what was causing it, but it made my nose itch and my head feel itchy and unsure.

"Memories of the war?"

I gritted my teeth. The buzzing thing had faded into voices. I could hear them, whispering at the edge of my consciousness. Familiar voices, I tried to stretch out my hearing.

"Yeah. Uh, Doc, I'm hearing some weird *lā shǐ.*"

"Hmm?"

"Shit."

"No, I mean, what weird shit, in particular, are you hearing?"

"Oh, uh, voices."

The buzzing noise came louder again, the voices fading into indistinctness. Instead, I started to feel a definite presence in the room. It was as if I could *sense* something looming nearby. My stomach twisted underneath me and I gasped. I felt fear. Anger. A desire to grab my PPR and just start shooting. I had to get to cover! I had to get into a suit! I squirmed and started to reach up to yank the helmet off my head, but stopped myself, not sure what that would do to my brain.

"Stop it!" The words ground between my teeth.

The buzzing noise shut off and Dr. Abbe sighed, his voice soft. "I have gained enough of a reading for a diagnosis."

The helmet slid up, the spider legs retracting and the whole thing vanishing mostly into the ceiling. I rubbed my face and realized I was sweating and my hands wouldn't stop shaking. I looked at them, then at the doctor.

"Zĕnme huí shì, yīshēng?"

"Please, English."

"What the ..." I paused. "What was that, Doctor?"

"I was attempting to provoke certain subconscious reactions through the use of infrasound. I apologize, but informing you ahead of time could have skewed the results."

I frowned, standing up. I clenched my fist, tight and hard, my body shifting into an MMA stance without thinking. *Trumped up technician thought he could just dick with my brain and not earn a boot up his—*

He held up his hands. "Drusilla—" He didn't sound nearly as scared as he should have been, considering how I felt at the moment "—I believe I can make a diagnosis, as I said. You have a form of Post-Traumatic Stress Disorder."

I blinked.

Then I blinked again.

"N-No, I don't."

"No, you do," he said, his voice a bit more firm. "It is a standard result of psychological trauma."

I realized that my hands were still up, halfway between grabbing my shirt to adjust it—the collar felt deadly tight—and a combat stance. I decided on the former, adjusting my shirt as I set my lips in a frown.

"I don't have PTSD. I was scared when I was fighting, yeah, but we're not fighting down here. At all." I frowned. "Spacers don't get PTSD."

"I can see that you have a strange idea about what does and does not happen to Spacers ..." he said, his voice slow, as if he was trying to pick his way around to a tactful answer. I bristled, but he went on before I responded. "I have read the psychological articles published by the few Spacers who practice, and I am aware of your cultural biases, but I need you to look past them."

I glanced aside.

"I am going to contact your legal guardian. If I get her permission, I am going to send this brainscan information to the Chinese-American Alliance Space Corps."

I snapped back to him.

Now, this is going to make me sound really stupid, but I had not made the connection until Dr. Abbe said that. I had not pieced together the two facts: The CAA draft was exempt under the extenuating circumstances of mental health issues. I had mental health issues. Or, at least, this overpaid psych-tech thought I had mental health issues—I was terrified, I didn't want ... I wasn't ...

I shook my head.

"You, of course, have certain rights when it comes to this kind of information ... but as your paid psychiatrist, I strongly suggest dealing with this before returning to the armed forces," Dr. Abbe said, reading my head-shake all wrong.

I held up one hand, my thoughts settling down.

I had PTSD.

That was a *problem*.

And that problem had a solution. I clung to that *fact* to keep myself together. But, and this made me want to laugh and cry at the same time, that *problem* also *was* a solution. Medical discharge. An escape route from sandcasters and railguns and hard vacuum.

"Send the info."

He nodded, but didn't send it. Not at first. At first, he started talking about the ways to deal with the issue—drugs, and if the drugs failed, VR therapy, and if VR therapy failed, something called targeted psychosurgery—and then he started suggesting times for a follow-up appointment and that I should discuss this with my guardian and so on and so forth. I paid half an ear to it, my mind coming onto an idea that felt as rational and sane as a four-sided triangle.

But ...

What was it that the ancient soldier had said?

Insanity is part of the times?

I walked out of Dr. Abbe's office, the idea still in my head.

Chapter 6: Patch

4/13/2068

Republic of Quebec, Northern Reforestation Zone

T-Minus L-Day: 129

I had kept my hands in my pockets for the past few minutes, to hide the fact they were shaking. I looked right at Sarah, trying to project cool. Confidence. Dru, laying out her plan to save her ass from the frying pan.

"So, that's my plan," I finished.

"I think I'm going to throw up." Sarah put her hands over her face, then shook her head. I blinked and looked at Jillian, then back at Sarah. She was taking this worse than I expected.

"No. No. No no. No. No. No no no no. No. God, no. Please, no."

I closed my eyes, trying to brace myself for the emotional sledgehammer had hit my chest. It was like being a spineless fish caught between a fire and a vacuum. I closed my eyes, opened my mouth to try and explain the logic, the math, the reason behind my plan again. It was all so logical, really. It should have been easy. I should have been strong and firm and laid it out again: Flush the pills down the toilet and let myself just stay crazy. Bite the mental bullet, rather than face a Loonie's.

Instead, I crumpled like a cheap solar sail under half-a-G of acceleration.

"I don't want to die!"

The words came out in a wail and I hit the ground, curling up slightly. I had waited a whole day, thinking about my plan—"I have an idea, but I need to think about it," those had been my exact words—and that had just given me time to wind my feelings up like a clockwork bomb. I covered my face with my hands and tried to speak. Sarah put her hands on my shoulders, leaning forward in her wheelchair, squeezing.

I managed to go from crying to breathing.

Jillian—who leaned on the corner of the room—took up the slack.

"Sarah, we went through the meat grinder. You grew up in the boonies, and yeah, bandit attacks are scary. But bandits, for the most part, don't have machine guns and power armor and grenades and combat shotguns." Her voice was calm. Cold. Surgical. "And bandits don't have the *kubwa* cheat that is defense in space. The defender has *all* the advantages. All the bases covered. They use sandcasters, they have fortified positions, they ..."

I saw her rub her face through my blurred eyes and my fingers.

Sarah nodded. "I get it." She didn't. "I understand it." She didn't. "But ... this isn't the answer." She shook her head. "Listen. Health care isn't something you can screw around with."

I looked at her, trying to come up with an answer. But I could see the difference between Earther and Spacer culture, stretching out between us as big and as empty as the space between stars. A sudden wave of uncertainty rocked my guts as I thought through her eyes.

Crippled by a war-plague.

Surrounded by the detritus of the Slump.

How many people had Sarah known who had been torn to bits by plagues and a lack of pills?

"There has to be another plan," Sarah said, again.

"Do you have one?" The question I could never ask, coming from Jillian. I could kiss her. I wouldn't. I could still only barely breathe. It took everything to just listen, and to not let my brain drop down into a lower, faster orbit. Debris floated there: *Die die die die die die die.*

"No, but ..."

I pushed myself up, so that my face pressed against Sarah's knees.

"It's ..." I trailed off, shuddering. "I-It's the only solution we have."

Sarah closed her eyes. Nodded. "How are you going to convince everyone else?"

I sighed.

Jillian shrugged. "Well, I can flush the pills. Or at least desynth them in the barn, your chemical equipment is pretty good. Then, Dru just claims to have taken them. That buys us at least a month, maybe two before they switch to a different pill. Dru can ditch those too, using the same method. Eventually, they'll try the other methods."

"And what then?" Sarah asked, frowning.

"We hope the war ends?" Jillian asked.

Sarah rolled her head back. "Arrrggh, this isn't a solution, this is putting a medi-patch on a slit throat. And not even a modern patch, I'm talking about one of those ..." She trailed off, shaking her head.

I closed my eyes, turning my face to rest myself against Sarah's knees. They were bony, hard, but they were still Sarah. Being near her was like dragging the contrast bar in an option menu way up, then lighting a supernova: The darks became cloying. The whites, the brights became blinding.

"It still give you time," I whispered.

Sarah stroked my hair.

Jillian crouched down next to me. "So, uh, while I admire you turning a mental problem into a way to sit out of a major war, but ..."

I looked at her.

She grinned, managing to hide her terror. Or maybe she was just a badass in a way that I wasn't.

"How do I stay out?"

I closed my eyes.

"No idea."

Jillian gently pushed my shoulder with her knuckles. I opened my eyes and saw she was still grinning.

"So, don't give up yet, or else I will have to pull rank and order you to keep on looking. Got it?"

"I outrank you."

She rolled her eyes. "Details."

Sarah made a strangled, furious noise at the back of her throat, like an angry cat. Her fingers—stroking through my hair—tightened enough to make me hiss.

"How can you joke at a time like this?"

"Joke or go crazy," Jillian said. "Oh, wait ..."

That was a bit much. I shot a glare at her. Jillian sighed, then mouthed an apology to me. Sarah did not look pleased. Still, she didn't have time to vent her displeasure. Neither of us had time to do anything for a while after that, because ...

It's funny. Small things. Small things can make a pretty damn big difference, from time to time. I chose to glance outside at that moment because I didn't want to look at Sarah or Jillian right then. A small thing.

And I saw the man in the forest. He had what looked like a modded hunting rifle, complete with handmade scope and printed magazine extender, all illuminated by a flash of moonlight. Then he was gone, shifting to a new patch of shadow. I hissed, "Bandits."

Sarah pushed to her desk and slapped open the interface, finding the emergency button. Jillian grabbed the shutter and threw it across the window as the lights in the house went from bright white to a dull-reddish color that wouldn't kill our night vision. Everything looked stained in blood ahead of time. I was already running down the corridor to Mrs. Cayer's room. She was out of bed and had her clothes on. She tossed me the rifle.

"You're a marksman, right? Get to the roof."

I grabbed the rifle before it even half-finished the arc. Mrs. Cayer had made sure that Jillian and I had gone through our rounds shooting the thing at trees and acorns. The kickback wasn't huge, but the rate of fire had something to be desired when I was used to fully automatic weapons. Still, I clicked on the safety, crooked it under one arm and went to the emergency ladder. I clambered up it and crawled onto the roof. I belly-crawled, something I had learned in Basic and never used until now, to the edge of the roof and shifted around the rifle, making sure that I had a good traverse. The roof was— like most parts of the house—designed to be a fortress. The edges were raised, reinforced with bulletproof weave, and had little compartments for ammo storage. Those were all empty— Mrs. Cayer was paranoid, not wealthy, this was supposed to be loaded in advance.

Ah, well.

I swept my gun-sights around. The bandits—I counted four to eight of them, the moonlight and the trees and the total lack of optical enhancement (Gods, I missed a helmet) making everything feel uncertain and confused, like the whole world was made of chaff.

"Count four, maybe eight," I muttered into the intercom woven into the wall.

"Same. Wait till they get into the open, then start taking shots. Shoot to kill." Mrs. Cayer sounded as coldly professional as any hard-bitten NCO in the service.

"You sure?" I bit my lip, trying to judge …

I had trained to make shots up to fifty clicks away—albeit with a scope and a directed energy weapon. I could aim for legs …

The thought of Sarah and my own tactical doctrine spoke at the same time: *Nope.*

They sure as hell wouldn't be aiming for the limbs. And if they got past me …

With a sudden blaze of static, the intercom cut off. "The—"

My gun autoejected the ammo block without me touching a thing, blaring and hooting loudly. The holographic interface that hung around the stock, bolt, and trigger mechanism blazed to life, red and glowing with skulls and crossbones. The few seconds of utter confusion almost killed me. A flash of red laser light in my eyes shook me out of my daze.

"Tā māde!" I swore, then threw myself as flat as I could. Silenced bullets started to piff and slap against the wood, zipping over my head and thudding into the bulletweave. The red dots of their laser sights waved about on the far wall, before flicking off. Silencers still were loud enough that I could judge their direction and rough distance—from the woods, the fields. They were keeping my head down in case their netwar attack hadn't disabled the rifle.

Oversight to not have some backup weapon, I'd have to bitch to Mrs. Cayer if we survived the night. The bullets stopped shooting overhead—pausing to reload? Or move? I didn't know.

I noticed something else. No voices, no hushed commands. Military sign language or they had some kind of other silent coms. I had to focus—and for the first time since I'd hit Earth, I was actually able to do that. I looked over the gun, trying to see through the haze of the holo.

There!

I slapped the deadman's switch and the rifle's electronics crashed and hard-reset. No holographic sight, or ammo counter, or specialized bullet carving, but the chamber had some mechanical backups. I slapped the magazine block back inside and worked the chamber.

Cha-Crunch!

The Cayers downstairs—and Jillian—hadn't started shooting. Their guns had to be jammed or they were suppressed too. I rolled onto my back, then onto my belly, facing the fields. I scooted forward, gun laid across my arms. I peered down the iron sights—those and the lever action made me feel like I'd fallen back into the *first* World War, rather than being caught in the third.

Wait, they used *bolt* action, not lever. I was back to the first Civil War. *Tā made.*

The bandits—eight, definitely—were in the toolshed. They were hauling out supplies as fast as they could, throwing them onto what looked like smart-sleds. I took aim, sighting at one of them—crouched at the edge of the field, firing with a bolt-action rifle at the house, the bullets whiffing and piffing into the window shutters, the glass already blown in.

I fired.

The gun leaped against my shoulder and the man pitched back, not making a noise. I worked the lever—harder than before, as I had to *force* the lever mechanism through the ammo brick to carve out the bullets and propellants. I sighted on another, one firing with what looked like a pistol wrapped in a lightweight framework to give it long-arm stability.

They had shifted their aim to me. Bullets zipped by my head. I fired. They twitched, but didn't go down. Didn't even *move*. I figured they'd have gone to better cover, like the others.

I worked the lever. Fired.

This time they went down and I felt the rush of a confirmed kill. Something in the boneless way they dropped, the knowledge that they'd gone down.

Not. Me.

The wounded-but-not-dead bandit started to get up, moving jerky and slow. I started to sight, but the ones who had gone to cover behind trees and the shed, opened up with every gun they had. I had to do nothing but bury my face against the wall and curl up and hope that the bullets wouldn't clip me. I felt one whine past my head, heard others thud into the bulletweave.

When the bullets stopped, I stayed down. Waited.

Nothing.

I stayed down.

Nothing.

Then I peeked over the edge.

The bandits were gone. They'd taken their dead with them, and pretty much every single thing in the storehouse. I closed my eyes. My heart was racing. My brain was focused. And ...

I felt a sharp shock as I realized it.

I felt normal. For a few short minutes—maybe four, maybe three, it was hard to tell, time flexed and warped weirdly in combat situations—all my instincts, all my training, all my tics and nerves, all the things that made me crazy ...

Made perfect sense.

Well, okay, not *all* of them. For one thing, my twitchy desire to stick my breather on didn't make a sense. The breeze wasn't a depressurization.

But still ...

>+<

Mrs. Cayer didn't let us go out until next morning, and by the time we did, I was buzzing with the aftereffects of adrenaline and a screwed-up sleep cycle. I had pulled double shifts patrolling the inside of the house while Mrs. Cayer took the roof and Sarah worked on unjamming the guns.

"Tracking and logging is all well and good, but I'm going to write my reps ..." she had muttered half the night, again and again. Either it was a way to remind herself to actually write her representatives—I didn't remember if the Republic of Quebec used senators or representatives or some other weird word for it—or she was really pissed off that the bandits had managed to crash her whole defense in a few seconds.

Apparently, the guns all had safety codes built into them to prevent random spree shootings—if they were fired in gun-free zones, they self-ejected their ammo and sent alerts to the local police—and the bandits had somehow managed to crack said codes. Which was supposed to be impossible.

We found out why they had gone to the effort in the morning. With Jillian covering us, Mrs. Cayer and I walked out. I had the rifle cradled in my arms, safety on and my thumb near the safety. It was still in deadman mode.

"Sarah is pissed," I murmured under my breath, not wanting Sarah—who I knew had to be hovering near Jillian, listening in to everything we said.

Mrs. Cayer put her hand over her collar, frowning and then murmuring back, speaking a slow and careful Mandarin. I was impressed; I hadn't known she was practicing. "She is my daughter. I will protect her."

"I know," I said, using the same language. "I ... kinda wonder what my parents would do to keep me safe, when I think about them at all."

Mrs. Cayer paused, then spoke, slowly, carefully, clearly not trying to screw this up. "They would have moved heaven and earth, if they could have. I know this."

Maybe it was the slow voice, the careful word choice, the attention paid to tone and pitch, but Mrs. Cayer's words sounded so solemn and truthful that I felt my eyes blur. I shouldered my rifle, groped for words, then just mumbled a thanks.

Mrs. Cayer ruffled my hair.

I hugged her, tight.

"Hey ..." Mrs. Cayer spoke in English. "We have to stay frosty."

I only vaguely knew what that meant, but I nodded, wiped off my eyes and resumed looking around warily. There weren't any bandits waiting to jump us as we got close to the battle-site. I saw the bullets that I had sent out—funny, I counted at least ten ... my memories of last night had been fuzzy, but I hadn't thought my count had been that far off.

I shook it off, kneeling next to a smear of blood and the marks of a body being dragged off. Footprints showed that at least two people had been dragging the hit bandit off.. Something about the blood was wrong ...

"I'm used to blood globbing and floating around you," I said, looking at Mrs. Cayer. "But still, something here is not right."

"It's the wrong color."

I nodded. "Sure that's not from the dirt?"

"Positive." She frowned. "And look at the footprints, the dragging. This guy weighed too much for a bandit, they go hungry more often than not. And, plus, he was only dragged away by one guy."

"And that means?"

"Either they were hopped up on some kind of stims or mite ..." She sounded grim. "Or they were transies."

"That'd explain the hacking." I sighed. "Are there ... really that many transies running around? After the Singularity Scare ..."

She rubbed her face. "When I was young, if you wanted a cybernetic implant, you needed a surgery ward, a few billion prewar dollar bills and a morally bankrupt cyberdoc. That's why only the Windrip administration ever actually *did* it *en masse*."

I nodded.

She looked at me. "Now, you just need raw materials, and a med-tech with a blacknet tutorial can jam a cybernetic into you."

"Is it that easy?"

"Well, no, surgery is always harder than it sounds and looks, but with autodocs ..." She shook her head. "The point is if you want to enhance yourself, nothing is going to stop you short of a ..." She mimed a gun, put it to her temple.

I frowned and decided to leave all the assumptions in *that* sentence for Future Dru to bring up to the heavily-armed survivalist. "I still can't get used to how out of control this planet is."

She looked at me. "I thought you lived in the wild-fu ... freaking west up there in space."

I shook my head. "There's lots of room, yes, but all your air comes paid for by the CAA. Makes it easy for them to watch what you're doing."

She nodded. "We'll call this in ..." She pinched the bridge of her nose, then called back to the house. "Sarah, help your friend catalog what we lost."

Sarah pushed out to the storage shed and I set the gun down near the door. Sarah winced, taking stock with a slow look around the room.

"They took all our 3D printer feedstock, the replacement parts we can't fab annnnd …" She leaned forward, slamming her fist against the wall, hitting the wood right above a yawning hole. "Our secret stash of ammo."

"You had a secret stash of ammo?"

She frowned. "Mom told me to never tell anyone, but … shit, it's the armor-piercing rounds and the hollow points."

"Hollow points?" I blinked, stepping around and looking into Sarah's eyes. "Sarah, those are banned! I know, I've actually *read* the Hague Convention."

"Mom had them left over from the Slump!" she said, holding up her hands. "She didn't want to sell them or just throw them out, so she hid them!"

I rubbed my face. "Godsdamn it."

Sarah put her hand on my thigh, rubbing it. We stood, silently, for a bit.

"Also, Dru …" Her hand reached out, tapping against the wooden, hinged door to the shed, pushing it shut with a finger. The hinges were whisper quiet and the melted locking mechanism clicked against the curled snarl of blackened metal that was what was left of the latch it used to connect to. "We have a problem."

"Yeah, some transhuman bandits just got their hands on military hardware and the stuff we need to keep the farm running through the winter!"

"No, a bigger problem."

That shut me up.

Sarah took hold of my hands, and then told me about Emergency Clause 44.B2A. It had been buried in the reams of thick, impenetrable legal text we had had to wade through over the past few weeks. Sarah translated the words to English.

"In the case of draftees with exceptional or special combat training that makes them somehow important or vital to the war effort, the government has the right to take you from your legal guardian and ensure your wellness with the most efficient and safe psychological treatment available." Her eyes shimmered. "Dru, they're going to take you away. And you just sent all the information they'll ever n-need to do it."

Tears started to roll down her cheeks.

I hugged her, eyes closed.

I felt like my suit had sprung a leak, air was billowing out into a vacuum.

And I didn't have a patch.

Chapter 7: Arrival

4/24/2068

Republic of Quebec, Northern Reforestation Zone

T-Minus L-Day: 118

There was one thing about impending death—or, in this case, impending kidnapping by the men in the lab coats with the psychopharmacological knives—that made the last week almost bearable.

It added a really fantastic, ferocious, desperate edge to sex.

I panted, my body glittering with sweat as Sarah crawled—gods she was strong—back onto the bed, laughing.

"Wow."

'Wow," I whispered.

Things, at first, had been awkward. But, see, Sarah and I had actually had a really long discussion about this. The kind of discussion you could *only* have with text, where you had time to think and bite your lip. Where you could take thirty or forty seconds to really process what you are typing, where you could write up a response and see how it orbited, then shave off a word here, there. Then send it.

We knew things would be awkward, going from text based erotic roleplaying (more dignified than crass cybersex, anyone could do that) to the nitty, gritty real thing.

So, we powered through it.

And ...

And save for the ...

The nightmares. Aside from the nightmares and my nerves and the other ... complications, things were good. Desperately good.

Sarah kissed me and whispered. "Mom is going to be pissed."

"Yeah ..." I closed my eyes. There had been a few awkward silences out in the fields or on patrol or when Mrs. Cayer told me to keep watch while she reported to the local police force or whatever it was called around here. Mrs. Cayer still had a way of saying a whole hell of a lot without saying much at all. The translation of her paragraphs came out to: *You shoot good, you're good in a fight. If you break Sarah's heart, you will be ghosted like* that *and no one will know where to find your body.*

I shivered. Partially from the memory, partially because of what Sarah was doing with her fingers.

She got to sleep before I did.

I braced, like I was getting ready to throw myself into microgravity. I closed my eyes tight and kept bracing until my muscles cramped and shook. What felt like hours later, my brain dipped ...

No ...

I wasn't in bed.

I was ... *watching* ...

My Star ghosted out over the smoothed sides of the Forge. The view danced down and up, down and up, the camera on Jillian's helmet taking in the solar panels that they zipped over, then back up to look at the rest of my Star. My Star. Where was I? I was inside. Safe. Watching through a wallpaper feed. My Star had gone off without me, because I'd gotten myself thrown into the brig. And they were doing what I should have been doing. Out there. Without me.

I hooked my feet into wall sockets, giving myself leverage. My fist pounded on the wallpaper, which flexed, then rebounded, unharmed. My mouth was open, but no sound came out. David, Jillian, Chuck, and Jason landed, their handheld cold gas jets spurting them down. Their boots contacted and I could practically hear the click of magnetic soles hooking up with metal walls.

There they were. Looking at their targets.

Sandcasters. Tubes of compressed nitrogen and ball bearings, big old space shotguns, banned by the Geneva Conventions and the Hague Conventions and the Articles of War and ten other agreements, and put on the Forge by the order of General Lau. I was in the brig because I tried to say no.

Jillian's voice sounded over the com. "All right, let's disconnect the guns."

I watched. I knew what would happen. My voice didn't— wouldn't—work. It would never work.

Three guns were detached and disabled, and David was working on the last.

"Lunar Separatist forces are on an approach. ETA, forty-five minutes."

Their attack craft were in range of the Sandcasters. The last one slipped around in its cradle, a silky-smooth motion. It'd fire, and the Loonies would get ripped apart and the debris would get caught in orbit. And we'd all be trapped up here as the orbital pathways became hopelessly unstable again, and the war would drag on and on. No retreat. No reinforcements. Nothing.

David knew that.

The built-in knife snapped out of his suit's knuckles, shining in reflected sunlight.

"No!"

The knife plunged into the compressed nitro tank. And the dream didn't end. It never ended. It didn't end until the blast of nitro caught that arm, that shoulder, and twisted him around three hundred and sixty degrees.

I sat up and cried out.

"David!"

Less than five seconds later, Mrs. Cayer exploded into the room with her rifle. "What? What?" she shouted.

I yelped. Sarah fell out of bed with a whump, taking the blankets, comforters and the parka that we used as a secondary comforter because no one else was using it with her. Mrs. Cayer covered her face with her hands, babbling apologies while backing out of the room.

If my heart hadn't been going fifty thousand klicks a second—

If I didn't want to scream and scream—

If I wasn't sobbing uncontrollably—

If I wasn't freezing cold in the pre-dawn light—

If ...

If all of that weren't true, I'd have laughed. I'd have laughed so hard the gun would fall out of my mouth.

Sarah hauled herself back onto the bed as Mrs. Cayer shouted through the door. "Are you two decent?"

"It's been five FUCKING seconds, Mom!" Sarah shouted, her arms going around my shoulders and hugging me tight.

"Shh, it's okay. It's okay."

I rocked back and forth, bumping against Sarah, my forehead against my knees. She kept saying the same thing again and again: It's okay, it's okay. It's okay. Eventually, I untensed (I didn't relax, not quite) and could actually breathe.

"It's okay." This time, I was the one telling Sarah.

"Okay," she murmured. "It's, uh ..."

She yawned and when she was done, she checked the clock.

"Uh, four in the morning."

"Balls."

She snickered, then pushed me onto my back. Sarah had an unfair arm wrestling advantage, because she spent all her time pushing herself around with her hands and arms. I could still win in a wrestle if I got my legs around her.

Found that out the … funner than I would like to admit way.

She shoved the blankets over me. "Sleep," she murmured. "I'll watch over you."

"And what about your sleep?"

She shrugged. "Coffee."

I made a face.

"It's an acquired taste."

"Yeah, I know, I'm just trying …" My eyes closed. I couldn't get to sleep, not with that image—David's head, lolling, useless—burned into my mind. But I could at least pretend to be sleeping. I breathed in, breathed out, and my body still felt like it was ready for a bullet to whack into it. Tense. Ready to go for the cover I had scoped out in this room again and again. Ears tingling for every possible noise.

Tingling. I could *hear* the silence between Sarah's breaths, between the creaking of Mrs. Cayer's feet.

Vrrrrrrrrrrrrrrrrrrrrrrrrrrrrrrrrrrr.

I opened my eyes. Sarah frowned at me. "Hey."

"No, shh … hear that?" I asked.

Sarah cocked her head and I rolled out of the bed while she wasn't focused on me, her hands sliding against my shoulders and then against the bed. I grabbed my shirt and tugged it on before tugging up my pants. I stepped to the window as Sarah dressed herself, my body feeling alive and focused.

I peeked out the window and saw a dark shape on the horizon.

At four in the morning.

The shape got closer and closer over the next ten minutes, with Mrs. Cayer kneeling by the window, Jillian sitting on the bed and checking the pistols. Mrs. Cayer frowned and murmured, "It could be the police, but they swept this place last week and they call ahead. The sheriff knows my particulars."

"Particulars?" Jillian asked.

"That if surface to air missiles were legal or easier to hide, I'd put them on my roof."

Jillian snorted.

I was starting to wish we had a SAM site too as the VTOL swept around, ducking low over the forest.

Mrs. Cayer grabbed up a set of magnifiers and put them to her eyes. The optics whirred and clicked and she tapped an interface on the top of the magnifier. The image piped to Sarah's desk, a slightly grainy view of the VTOL writ large.

I recognized it from tactical briefings and from the nightly news: A classic CAA ground support troop transport. It could shred tanks as easily as it could carry them. Two swept back wings with two ionic engines, long triangular nozzles that made that annoying *vrrrrr* noise that buzzed through one ear, along my jawline and out the other ear. Black shapes dropped out, rappelling down black lines that dropped into the forest.

I tapped on the image and the desk brought up a simple image manipulation interface, one that was pretty similar no matter where you were in human space: the old triangle, square, double bars interface. I hit the double bars, then spooled around with the frame-selection bar that sprang up on the bottom, trying to find a frame with a good, clear image of the people going down.

There.

The soldier wore what looked like the power armor that I had donned up in space. It had felt futuristic and video-gamey then. Now, I knew what power assist arms could do to bones and flesh. The armor was skinned black and mottled green, the pattern shifting around between frames—not quite an invisibility cloak, but it would make them damn hard to spot in the forest proper. I spotted at least one shoulder mounted weapon blister—rockets? Grenades?—and a rifle slung over their back.

The noises we heard ...

The range finder said it was about four kilometers out.

But over those kilometers, we heard the noises that would have sounded more familiar to me in an enclosed corridor: The pop pop pop of rifle fire, with the occasional bang and whump of grenades.

The sound stopped. The VTOL collected the men—the magnifiers showed them zipping back up on their lines, then remaining there as other lines—attached while they were on the ground, most likely—dragged up body bags.

The VTOL turned off and then whirred away, zooming off and over the horizon.

It had taken about twenty minutes.

And Mrs. Cayer spoke up. "Dru, Jillian, stay here. I'm going to check that out."

"Ma'am." Jillian looked at her. "I don't think that's a good idea."

"That's almost on my land." She frowned.

"Yes, but we're both at least *in* the military. If anyone's left behind, we at least have call signs that will get them to stop shooting and ... hey, the worst thing they can do is throw us in the brig." Jillian smirked. "Plus, you and Dru got to check out the bandit shootout. I want my chance to snoop."

Mrs. Cayer frowned.

"I don't suppose you're even going to consider—" Sarah started.

"Dear, that's four klicks of hard forest," Mrs. Cayer said, not looking away from the window.

"I have smart wheels, Mom!" Sarah bristled.

Mrs. Cayer responded with a torrent of Québécois French. Sarah shot back with her own tirade, in the same language, with pretty much the same tone. The two of them shot back and forth and I kept trying to find words to slip between them, but both of them ignored me.

After five or maybe six eternities, time enough for the sun to grow bloated, red, then collapse into a white dwarf before being consumed by a passing black hole, Sarah got her sentence chopped in half by a single English command: "Sarah Marion Cayer, your room. Now!"

"THIS IS MY ROOM!"

"NOW!"

Sarah grabbed her wheels and shoved herself to the door, her chair practically flying as it hit a rise in the floor like a ramp. She landed with a thump, shot into the guest room and slammed the door, hard.

I moved to go to her, but Mrs. Cayer snapped at me.

"Zhao. Zhang. Check out the battleground, I'll be doing overwatch. Got it?"

I nodded before I'd even thought about it. Mrs. Cayer turned and headed for the ladder, smoke curling out from under her hair.

I opened my mouth, closed it, then looked at Jillian.

Jillian gulped. "I'm betting if we're not EVA in five seconds, she'll shoot us when we do get outside."

I grabbed the pistol, made sure the safety was on—the gun had considerably less computerization in it after a highly-illegal modification session in the lab—then went to the guest room. I put my hand on the door.

"Sarah, I—"

"I need time." Her voice came through hard. "Alone. Okay?"

I closed my eyes, pressed my forehead to the door. "I love you."

"I know."

She snorted a giggle, as if she could see my face. I *hated* that movie. She had to know I hated it. I grinned.

"Never change, Sarah. Never."

"Promise."

I stepped away. Jillian stood by the door.

We left.

Jillian had used the term EVA—Extra-Vehicular Activity—as a figure of speech. Same way I'd call Sarah after five espressos an outgassing comet. But the figure of speech felt dangerously literal as we got in among the trees. The early light was too little, too early for us. Thin streams of sunlight cut through the leaves and our breath came out in puffs of steam unlike anything I'd seen save on Earth.

The first kilometer was nerve wracking. We flinched at every cracking branch, twitched at every strange animal noise. The second kilometer got worse. Then, in the third kilometer, we had halfway gotten a feel for how to move in the forest like this. She would take up position behind a piece of cover, then keep her line of sight open as I headed forward to the next tree, moving low, crouching and jogging. It wasn't comfortable, but it felt safe.

We got to the battle site as the light moved from almost non-existent to enough to actually see with. The trees had been splattered with blood—going dark now—and bullet holes. I put my hand on a tree, my palm brushing along a long, jagged piece of metal.

"Fragmentation grenade."

"This looks like a shotgun blast. I mean, it's on wood instead of on metal, but the pattern is the same. Shotgun, shotgun, rifle, rifle ..." Jillian paused, then walked around to the other side of the tree, measuring a line with her eyes. "Entry wound, exit wound, entry wound ..."

She came back holding a bullet, tossing it to me. I caught it and eyed it.

"Ways to know your crazy MILFy survivalist hostess talks about guns way too often," Jillian said, leaning against a tree, her stance more relaxed—this place looked safely dead. I still felt nervous, my breath puffing out from my lips as I looked at the bullet. "Number One: You can identify a gun from a bullet."

I looked at Jillian.

"It's a CAA military rifle, caseless round, armor piercing tip."

I nodded, then dropped the bullet. "So, we know they were loaded for bear ..."

My eyes drifted from the trees to the actual clearings. Depressions in the bushes where people had fallen. Circles where fireplaces had been made. Tents, four tents. I opened one and saw the inside had electrical heaters and wallpaper. I stepped back, wincing: The wallpaper had been set to writhing, squirming masses of color that made my brain lock up slightly.

"Ugh."

"Dru, check this out."

Jillian kicked a bush which made a distinctly un-bush like noise. She looked at me. I looked at her. We both grabbed the bush and pushed back with a snarl of crackling roots. But they weren't roots. The camocarpet had been attached to the ground with a layer of dirt and some pitons, while the bush itself was mostly paint and scrap plastic. With that out of the way, we had a box: silvery, maybe a meter long, half a meter wide, half a meter tall. The front had a palm pad and a numerical key.

"Well ... isn't this interesting." Jillian grinned. "Loot."

"Dibs on any rare drops," I shot back.

Jillian looked at me. She sighed, then held up her hand.

"I was …" I sighed, deciding it wasn't worth saying that I was kidding. I held up my other hand. I threw rock. She threw laser. Laser cuts rock. I threw laser, she threw mirror. Mirror reflects laser. I threw rock, she threw mirror. Rock smashes mirror. Two out of three to Jillian.

"You get rare drops, then."

In the end, we carried the chest back. It had handles on either side so we could both haul it, though I felt a bit guilty.

"Hey, think of it this way," Jillian said. "Those guys were the bandits."

"I can accept that, I guess."

Jillian flashed me a grin. "So, what they stole is now free for us to take back. I bet the ammo and supplies they grabbed from Mrs. Cayer are here."

I snorted. "I don't think that's how this works."

Jillian shrugged, which made the box tilt so that the handle dug into my hand even more. I winced and then focused on the clambering and stepping over roots and branches and through bushes. When we got back to the Cayer homestead, Mrs. Cayer was still on the roof, keeping a steady watch. She was more visible in the morning light and she waved to us.

Inside, we heaved the box onto the kitchen table as Sarah rolled out of her room. Since Mrs. Cayer was still getting down the stairs, I stole a hug and kiss from Sarah, who leaned up and bit my ear, her hands keeping me low down for another kiss. Her mom walked into the room. Sarah kept kissing me, slipping me what I'd started classifying as a Stage Four Tongue: the kind of kiss you use when you're getting ready for some really mind-blowing sex.

Or were making a not-so-subtle point to your overbearing mom.

That was the thought that I managed to piece together in the next few minutes as I tried to rebuild my brain after Sarah made it explode over the wall.

Jillian—who stood next to me as Mrs. Cayer examined the box—elbowed me.

"Stop grinning like that, you're making me want to steal your girlfriend."

"Good!" Sarah grinned, looking smug.

Mrs. Cayer—who had been focusing far harder on the box than was really necessary—turned to face us. "This is definitely a bandit box. I recognize the lock, it has an explosive on the other side, designed to pulp anything inside if we try to force it. But ..." She slapped it. "The sheriff should be able to unlock it."

"That's good, right?" Jillian asked.

"No." Mrs. Cayer frowned. "Not if they have my ammo in there."

"Riiiiight." Jillian rubbed her palms against her face. Sarah frowned at her mother, who didn't look the slightest bit apologetic.

"Take it out back and bury it."

"Bury it?"

"Yes, bury it." Mrs. Cayer looked at me. "You do know how to use a shovel, right?"

"I think we can figure it out," Jillian said. "We took a physics course. A shovel's just applied physics."

"Everything is applied physics," I muttered.

"Just do it," Mrs. Cayer snapped.

"Can I come with?" Sarah asked.

"No."

"Too bad." Sarah pushed herself towards the door. "Guess what, Mom, they don't know where people do and don't go, they don't know how rain uncovers earth, they don't know how deep to bury something, they don't know where the game trails are or where to avoid dangerous critters. They're as clueless as arcos and if this crate gets found, you're going to jail for reasons that would be funny if it wasn't so sad. So, either keep me and go to prison eventually, or let me help my *girlfriend*."

I stepped behind Sarah and put my hand on her shoulder. Squeezed.

Mrs. Cayer kept her back to us. Her shoulders stiffened and I could practically read the expression on her face from the space between her shoulder blades. She jerked her hand up. "Fine."

We headed out. Sarah latched the crate to the underside of her wheel chair, the wheels shifting to accommodate it. She pushed herself down and off the porch, looking as driven as a Saturn V, her hands grabbing onto the wheels and shoving them along.

"Good job."

"Thanks." Her voice was clipped. She let herself trundle to a stop, then looked at me. She smiled. "I mean it."

I sighed. "This whole situation is messed up, but ... I mean, you can't let your mom keep you shut up forever, right?"

"Right." She nodded.

"And—"

I stopped talking. Sarah and I both looked up, silenced by the growing, whirring noise. A VTOL. I felt like a bug trapped between two window panes, an image that wouldn't have occurred to me a few nights before, and one that felt really apt and horrible right about now.

The Alliance VTOL we had seen early this morning whirred over the forest, causing trees to ripple and flutter, leaves going in every direction as it shot over the farm. Mrs. Cayer came jogging out, swearing up a storm in French.

"This is bad, isn't it?" I whispered.

"Yeah."

Mrs. Cayer ran to where the VTOL looked like it was landing, the arced wings and ionic engines brushing over the fields of crops, the wheels and landing gear pressing down into the track between the fields, digging in as the full weight of the thing settled. Soldiers trooped off, moving carefully to not trample *all* of the gene-fixed wheat.

Mrs. Cayer froze. She didn't have her rifle with her, so she threw the best weapons he had at the invaders.

"This is private land!" She watched, her face a mask of horror, as a trooper with shoulder mounted grenade launchers took up a defensive position on the right corner of the field, tracking his—or her?—rifle left and right. Another pair went to the small wall that the bandits had hidden behind last night, kneeling there and keeping their eyes on the forests. They were all wearing faceless masks, but their names were stenciled on their foreheads and chests: Wu, Tsui, Ho, O'Sullivan.

The last off was a woman wearing a standard CAA Army uniform: dark green with beige collars and a spread of medals. I flicked my eyes over it: she was a detached officer, a lower ranked one. 2nd Lieutenant, I think.

A cadet officer, basically. If I remembered the pay grade scales properly.

I threw her a salute, despite being off duty as she walked over to Mrs. Cayer.

"Lt. Kiprotich," she said, her skin tones and her hair cut making her definitely African stock, not a mixed breed. She had a perfect—i.e., unnaturally formal and forced to my ears—Mandarin accent, so she had to have been born in mainland China. "I was dispatched to deal with your class two bandits."

"This is Quebec, not China, ma'am," Mrs. Cayer said, arms crossed over her chest. "I'm a sovereign national and the legal guardian of everyone on this property."

Kiprotich held out her hand. She was holding a rolled up piece of paper, which unfurled. Mrs. Cayer took it, frowning as she looked at it—I saw that it had scrolling text and characters from at least four different languages on it.

Mrs. Cayer tapped the corner of the paper and the whole thing rolled back into a tube-shape, letting her stuff it into her pocket. Her face looked a bit like a mask, nothing moving unless it had to.

"I see."

"Now ..." Kiprotich stepped forward. "We have a secondary detail. Corporal Jillian Zheng and Corporal Drusilla Zhao are both needed for an extended special detail."

Special detail ... non-combat. Still, I bristled, my hand sliding over Sarah's shoulder. That drew the Lieutenant's eye, and she took in Sarah in a full glance. She paused, then pointed at the box. "First, let me take a look at that."

"That's—" Mrs. Cayer started. She stopped. I could practically hear the gears grinding in her head. If she claimed it as salvage or scavenging, then Kiprotich could and probably would make a fuss. And if she made a fuss, she had the guns to back up the Alliance's interpretation of salvage laws. "We found it and we were going to give it to the Québécois authorities."

"Well, that's why we left it at the bandit campsite," Kiprotich said, muttering in Mandarin—a quick, slangy dialect that was as far removed from my Spacer dialect as mine was from the standard Mandarin she had used earlier. Whatever she said, her soldiers understood it. Two hustled over and grabbed the crate from under Sarah's chair, causing Sarah to yelp and Sarah's Mom to open her mouth to complain.

The box hit the ground and some electronic doodad—an E-lockpick, doubtlessly—caused the lid to flip open, revealing a few prohibited automatic weapons, sleek data cubes, what looked like parts of a neural augment (all gray fibers and glittering lattices) and ...

The cubes of armor piercing and hollow point bullets from Mrs. Cayer's storage unit. Though I wasn't a CSI unit, I could practically see the fingerprints and forensic data all over it that would paint a big fat legal target on the Cayer homestead.

"All the bandit's, right?" Kiprotich asked, looking at Mrs. Cayer. "We should really turn these into the proper authorities, right?"

Let me take your wards, or I'll throw you to the wolves.

Mrs. Cayer clenched her jaw. She looked at me.

I nodded, ever so slightly. Out of the corner of my eyes, I saw Jillian shooting me an even fainter nod. Sarah seemed to be the only one left out of this—but she was catching up quick, a look of horror dawning on her face.

"I cede my wards to the needs of the Alliance," Mrs. Cayer said, speaking slow, awkward Mandarin.

"Well, then, we'll let the Québécois police pick these up." Kiprotich didn't look away from Mrs. Cayer.

Mrs. Cayer didn't nod or smile or say thank you. Instead, she gave Kiprotich a glare that would—even if I had had armor, guns and a missile-packing VTOL on my side—have scared the *mǐtiángòng* out of me. The lieutenant clearly had tougher skin than I did, because she didn't ... even ... blink.

"Get your kit, Corporal, Corporal," Kiprotich said.

Jillian and I turned, walking towards the house, numb.

"No ... no, no, no!" Sarah rolled after me. She grabbed me by one arm and jerked me to my knees, which hit the ground—mud, hardened by the night's chill, still caked my clothes. Sarah grabbed me and managed to get me into a position where we were eye-by-eye.

"I'm not letting you go. Not after getting you, not after falling in love with you *even* harder, you—" Sarah cut herself off with a kiss that almost drew blood.

"I'll be back," I whispered back.

Sarah shook her head. "I'm going to *find* you. Okay?" She squeezed me hard, hands calloused and roughened by her wheels. "This isn't space, and flying is cheap. I'm. Going. To. Find. You."

"Corporal." Kiprotich's voice had just a bit of warning to it.

I stood and walked to the house, nodding and grinning despite myself. I felt a bit drunk from that kiss.

And, more than that, I trusted Sarah.

Stuffing all the kit I needed into the rucksack took less than a few seconds. Being a Spacer really hammered home just how little you really needed, if most of your stuff was digital. But I still double checked that I had all my clothes, my collar clip—a bright red memento that I just couldn't bear to throw away—and the nine movie *Star Wars* chipset that Sarah had bought for me as a joke. I was tempted to grab something that Sarah owned, just to remind me of her ...

I didn't. I couldn't decide what to take, for one thing. And for another ...

She was going to find me. I knew it.

I slung the baggage over one shoulder and headed out. Jillian met me in the corridor, her bags as lightly packed as mine.

"Well, this sucks," she muttered in Spacer-Mandarin.

I nodded. I nodded two more times—once to Sarah, once to Mrs. Cayer—as I walked out of the house, down the patio stairs and across the warming mud. The sun continued to rise in the sky, and with it the whole world glowed ... the whole world save for the VTOL. Light vanished into it, swallowed by the metamaterials that made the thing nigh invisible on radar and LIDAR, making the wings and sleek edges seem more like an absence than a thing.

The door opened and I got in, the other troopers piling in behind me and Jillian. The lieutenant was in last, finding her seat near the front. The inside was ribbed like a whale, with seats hidden between the ribbing. Smart crash-webs snapped around the chairs, the materials able to find the hooking points on the armor by themselves, shifting and squirming like snakes. I forced myself to sit as still as I could, remembering when my skinsuit had been fitted to me. When the webbing solidified, a flex-screen closed around my head and patched me into the tac-net of the VTOL.

"All right, gents, prep for preflight prep." The pilot had an odd accent and brought out the double prep with the casual ease of someone used to a lot of bureaucracy. I couldn't place his accent, though. His face appeared in the upper right-hand corner of the view, framed by his name—Patrick Vane, Airman Third Class—but the rest of the flex-screen was dominated by a wraparound view of the whole VTOL. The same quantum-dot projection and recording technology that let wallpaper both record and project simultaneously let me pan a 360-degree view around the whole VTOL. I found an interface on the armrest and used it to zoom and focus on Sarah, who kept watching the door as it slid shut.

"Checking straps ... check. Feeds linked and synched, check. Stealthing activated, check. Barf bags and feed tubes, check." A faint chime sounded after each statement of 'check.' I rolled my eyes.

The VTOL started to rise. Mrs. Cayer put her hands on her daughter's shoulders and the cameras fuzzed out of focus, becoming blurry, multifaceted. Wetness trickled down my cheeks and I slammed my head back. The crash-webbing shifted around me, responding to cushion and hide the impact.

With the screen, and the webbing ...

No one knew I was crying.

"All right, you know the drill." That was all that the LT said over the com that was sent to everyone. A private window popped up, using text rather than video—even without the coms, someone sitting next to her could hear a mutter, the engines weren't that loud—and started to peel out.

Lt. Kiprotich: *Here's the drill, Cpl. The VTOL scanners try and identify hazards, but tangos have a nasty habit of throwing up com-camo, enough to confuse even a sturdy AI. So, keep your eyes open on while you are on shift. When off shift, review and prep for your landing.*

Guest: *frtg. Shit. Sorry, keyboard. Got it, sir.*

Lt. Kiprotich: *Any questions?*

Guest: *Yes, sir. What is the secondary detail?*

Lt. Kiprotich: *Sending briefing file.*

The next few hours alternated between dull and duller. The ache of being ripped from Sarah got smothered under the same kind of muffling pillow of boredom and I had to pull in every iota of my experience reading pointless military jargon just to keep myself hooked through the whole briefing. That was the dull. The *duller* came when I was on shift and had to watch the reforestation zone zoom by under the VTOL.

Still, I managed to slog, then rest, then slog, then rest.

The briefing was to the point—in military terms: I was being recalled for psychological evaluation. At the same time, I was also going to be involved with what the briefing described as a: Military Tribunal Witness, Minor.

I connected with Kiprotich with a few taps. Or, more accurately, I requested a contact with her and waited for her to reconnect with me.

Guest: *Sir, permission to speak freely?*

I managed to repress a smirk at the idea of this counting as 'speaking'.

Lt. Kiprotich: *Granted.*

Guest: *Do you know what this tribunal is about? The briefing doesn't say.*

Lt. Kiprotich: *Need to know.*

She cut the communication, curt and final as if she had walked out of the room and slammed the door. I frowned and tried to think of what I'd be a witness for. It'd have to do with ...

Daniel.

Lao.

The name echoed in my brain. I hadn't had much time to think about him during the farming and the chores and the *being* with Sarah. No, the time to think about him had been in the hanging midnight hours, where my brain stalled in freefall and didn't let me sleep until I had thought through the fights, the tactics, the decisions that had led to most of my command getting shot to pieces.

My *command*, like I'd been an officer.

I shook my head.

General Lao had ordered the use of sandcasters.

I knew, intellectually, that using them would have made me just as culpable as the Loonies. They were a war crime for a good damn reason. Setting off even one made the orbital pathways that we used to move cargo and valuable space borne resources that much more dangerous, that much harder to clean up. But at the back of my mind, the sneaky traitor of a thought remained: If I had used them, then the Loonies would have been turned into so much little giblets and everyone would still be alive.

Well, everyone I cared about.

I frowned and tried to not think about what that said about me as a person: It's okay to turn people into tiny giblets so long as I don't know their ...

Jorge Freedman. With the name came an image: one of the Loonies who had tried to surrender on the Forge. Instead of being taken prisoner, he'd been turned into hamburger.

Shut up, brain. I did not need to think about that right now.

The landscape beneath the VTOL continued to zoom past. It was disconcerting how much changed and how fast—that took care of the dullness pretty quick. In orbit, you could watch clouds change and the Earth spin, but the raw speed of it had a way of giving people screaming vertigo. Which ... really made sense, when you thought about it: in orbit, you really *were* falling a thousand miles a second. That's what orbiting was. Falling so fast that you never hit the ground.

But here, we were moving at a fairly sedate (relatively) pace, which gave me time to pick out the elements of civilization that grew up out of the forests. It helped that the VTOL's computer was busily scanning for any hidden anti-aircraft guns and enemy fortifications and popped up helpful indicators, circles, boxes and other tags that reminded me comfortingly of the computer in the helmet of my GISS. Still, most of the things that the computer tagged were harmless: tractors, farmsteads and the like.

Then we moved out of a reforestation zone and into a suburban blight zone.

It was less dramatic than it sounded at first, if only because natural reforestation happened whether we wanted it to or not. So, for a while at least the forest just seemed to thin and the computer spat out an increasing fog of tags before I started dialing back its identification filter so that I could see what was actually out there.

When the tags dropped away, it felt a whole hell of a lot more dramatic.

We were flying over a vast graveyard of rotting houses. The roofs had once been uniform and standardized, like in the old pictures, and there were sprawling masses of asphalt and other road surfaces, winding twisting loops like the guts of some fatally stabbed man. Now, roofs fell in or exploded outwards as plants reclaimed them. Abandoned cars were left to rust in their places. I could see people scurrying through the ruins—some in groups no larger than ten, carrying hand tools and pushing carts laden with salvage. Then we started to fly over the biggest salvage teams: huge, spindly-looking frameworks that spread out to encompass whole city blocks. Suspended between them were what looked like all-purpose fusion torches: The kind that people used to turn alloys and complex collections of elements (like, say, a rusty car) into a haze of particulates that could be sifted and shaken and put into containers and turned into the new kinds of things that the human race could use.

It was ...

Awe inspiring and filled me with a kind of quivering, cold anger.

These cars had been built to *fall* apart within a few years of their construction. These houses had been designed—either intentionally or without foresight—to bleed heat and need complex air conditioning and heating systems. Everything here stank of excess and ...

Obesity.

Now that wasn't a word that I had a lot of experience with. In space, dietary AIs and state mandated physical therapy kept everyone pretty close to the middle of the scale. Oh, some people had more padding than others, but it was nothing like what I'd seen in old pictures. Now, I had been taught all the mitigating reasons: the terrible food, the sedentary life styles, the poor understanding of human biology when acted on by complex chemicals and hormones. All that stuff added up to a generation of people who had dropped dead like flies when the power started going off.

But there was still a nagging, judgmental voice in the back of my head—a voice I wasn't sure I liked all that much—that whispered: *Lazy, selfish bastards.*

That voice had a megaphone as we zipped around the suburban blight.

The VTOL stopped off for refueling (no remassing, we weren't in space) at the arcology that marked the center of this blight zone. I couldn't be bothered to look up our location or the name of the arcology. Once we refueled, we took off and headed southward.

I dozed. I re-read the briefings. I figured out how to chat with Jillian, but we didn't have much to say beyond 'this is sure boring, eh?' and other filler. The time between my shifts started to feel like a deranged still pics of the landscape.

Urban blight.

A huge lake, ringed with algae processing facilities that pumped out plastics.

A forest zone.

A plain, covered with brittle-looking brown grass and herds of brown shaggy creatures that picked their way around rusted out shells of tanks.

A small city of cloth structures with a herd of horses nearby. People dancing around a fire and singing ancient songs.

I closed my eyes.

When I opened them again, it was to the sound of our pilot.

"All right, gents, we're entering the Mormon Republic of Deseret's airspace for the next three hours. There should be a quick flyby of their air force, but it should be nothing to worry about."

I frowned, connecting to Jillian.

Guest: Jillian, the ROD is an ally, right?

Guest 2: Well, we have nukes, they don't. We surround their territory. We outnumber their citizenry by something close to 1.9 billion people ...

Guest: *Right, right. I'm bet they're super glad we're flying in their airspace.*

Guest 2: *Overjoyed, I'm sure.*

I smirked and, sure enough, a few minutes later a Deseret VTOL moved to flank ours. It was a little bit pathetic: Their VTOL lacked the advanced materials that wrapped around ours, making it look both less and more fragile. While it did have a proper metal color and a hard edged, bulky look to it, I knew that it was still an aircraft. That meant that what looked hard was actually thin and wrapped around toothpicks, or else it wouldn't have flown.

It waggled its wings, its engines crude jet or ducted fans to our ionic lifters. As the wing lowered, I could see the golden beehive of the little Republic.

Our VTOL wiggled as well.

The Deseret VTOL banked off.

We needed fueling again by the time we were out of the Mormon Israel, and so the VTOL stopped at an Alliance military base that just so happened to sit at the edge of the territory ceded to the Republic of Deseret in 2039—what had once been Utah and some of the surrounding states. This time, though, the fueling didn't just involve sitting around waiting for a gauge to fill up. Instead, the screens slid away from my face and I blinked, like a baby crawling out into the light for the first time ever.

Crash-webbing slipped back and the LT started barking orders to the soldiers. She herded them out, then told us to wait here. The door closed and I took the chance to stand and stretch. "Ugh, I'm going to get all soft and fat in this thing." I glanced at Jillian, trying to grin.

"My eyes feel like they've been sand papered." She rubbed them with her knuckles.

"Hey, think how I feel."

We both turned. The pilot had cracked open the door that separated his pod from the rest of the VTOL. That was the right word, not cockpit. He wore a skintight suit (complete with cod-piece) that was studded with little sockets and nodes for him to plug in more directly to his ship. I recognized it as a fancy tactile response suit. It combined all the fun of haptic controls (if, for example, the fuel was getting low, the suit could cause his shoulder to itch or something that would warn him without him needing to take his eyes away from the screen) with the joy of being able to pilot for a few hours straight without having to get up and go to the bathroom.

Spacers didn't use them. In space, travel time was so long that, unless you were just going to cut to the chase and use a sense-dep tank and some fancy drugs (tempowhatsit, that had been what my doctor had called it), you might as well wear normal clothes and just take breaks like normal people would. After all, if anything went wrong so fast that it required the kind of instant response that a tactile suit would allow ...

Well, in space, that kind of thing meant you were already seven different kinds of dead.

Jillian and I saluted him as all these thoughts shot through my head. Airman Third Class Patrick Vane smirked and saluted back, though he added. "Airmen don't actually outrank corpo-rals. I'm E-3, you lot are E-4. Well, actually, E-4a."

Jillian put two fingers to her temple, then pointed them at him. "Let me guess. The A indicates—"

"We've got something strategically important. We're cigar carriers." I crossed my arms over my chest.

"Whoosh!" Vane made a gesture that I think indicated some-thing went over his head. Even Jillian looked confused. I sighed, arms tightening.

"In the Civil War—the first one, that is, the one with mus-kets and slavery. That one?" They nodded to show they knew which Civil War I was talking about. "In that one, a whole army's plans were written down and wrapped around a cigar box. It was found by some lucky private on our side and, boom, we knew the orders."

Jillian looked at me funny. "How the flying *Gāngmén dìyù* did that you know that?"

I looked at her, hooked her eyes with mine, then flicked it at the text-pads on the armrests. I'll tell you later. She seemed to get the gist of that and nodded, smirking. Vane shook his head.

"I like the historical allegory, and it's just about correct." He rubbed his face with his gloved hands. "This VTOL's going trans-pacific. We're going to have to land in Japan, which isn't going to be fun."

"Why not?" Jillian asked. "Their sexy cartoons—"

"Anime," Vane and I said at the same time.

Jillian somehow managed to encapsulate an ellipsis with a single look.

"The Japanese Defense Force hates the Alliance military with a fiery passion they normally reserve for ... actually, no one. They don't hate *anyone* more than us."

"But the rest of Japan is fine?"

"I don't know, they don't matter. The rest of Japan doesn't have super-sonic fighters and anti-missiles and nuclear weapons." Vane shrugged. He had a bit of a point. "Sides, the only thing that I'll have to worry about is some hostility, snippy air traffic controllers—"

"Perilous," Jillian said, deadpan.

"I just said it wasn't going to be fun, not tha ..." He shook his head. "Listen, the LT will be back on soon once she's done giving her GROPOs back to the base. I just wanted to ask: Why the hell are you guys so important?"

"No idea," Jillian said.

"I actually think I might know," I said. "I'm not sure I'm allowed to tell you. So here's why." I smirked at him, taking some petty revenge for being ripped away from Sarah. Tiny.

Petty. Still went for it. "I think they're going to hang General Lau."

Vane raised his eyebrows.

But before I could expand on that, the door started to open again. We snapped to attention as Lt. Kiprotich stepped back onboard. She was followed by a bald woman with a Major's collar tabs.

I didn't know it right then.

But that bald woman—a tall, ethnically Indian woman with a knife-thin body and a jawline that could slice metal—was the most dangerous woman I'd ever meet.

Lt. Kiprotich stepped to the side and saluted the woman as well.

The woman saluted us all back, then dropped her arm. She didn't say anything after that, she just walked straight back to the end of the VTOL, sitting down and letting the crash-webbing weave around her. The screen snapped into position and a series of images started to flick across it. Two ... no, three things unnerved me.

Firstly, the images that popped up—though they were inverted from my perspective behind the screen—went by so fast that there was no way that anyone could read them. Secondly, I didn't notice her hands or fingers move to access the controls that normally manipulated the screens.

And finally, I ...

I had the weirdest idea that she was reading through dossiers and brainscan images and maybe this was just the paranoia speaking, but I could have sworn I had seen my own reverse reflection appearing at least once or twice on the screen, the kind of dorky image that graced identification photographs.

But still, as the VTOL lifted off and we started heading towards the coast, I was able to slowly talk myself out of the sneaky feeling with a simple truth: I wasn't that important.

There were six billion people on the planet Earth, and a few million more in space. The important people stood out pretty clearly against the background radiation of the planet. I … just didn't. I was just a teenager from space with a slightly marketable skill in today's climate: I could kill people and follow orders.

And even those two weren't all that great, not enough to stand out.

A soft chime sounded, alerting me that I had received a message. It didn't pop up as an IM, though. Instead, the words just appeared flat in the middle of the screen, imposed over the view of the California countryside.

She's reading your brainscan
Feels a bit revealing … doesn't it?

"The hell …" I whispered. My voice was caught by the screen and piped to the rest of the ship.

"What was that, Zhao?"

"Nothing, LT," I said. "I thought I … saw something."

She didn't respond. The words had vanished from the screen. I blinked a few times, hoping that I had just...no, wait, which was worse? That someone was sending me secret messages or that I was going crazy?

We're all just a little bit crazy, D.
And if you ever want to contact me again
Just ask for K.

Chapter 8: Iron Sky

4/25/2068

Chinese-American Alliance, China, Xin-Shanghai

T-Minus L-Day: 117

Iron Sky. It was a term that I had heard before. I'd even seen pictures, vids, holodeck recreations of it. I had never actually gone in for those, mind you, because they were crushingly depressing and not exactly what one needed for unwinding. I had spent my crèche time in enclosed tin-cans surrounded by freezing-burning vacuum, I didn't need to spend the free time I had around that in recreations of something like …

Like this.

The VTOL had landed and let me step off and I still couldn't move. Jillian had the same look on her face. Even Lt. Kiprotich took a few moments to look around and really soak it in.

Xin-Shanghai wasn't just an arcology. It was four arcologies and the urban sprawl that linked them and the vast second layer that stretched between the arcologies and the urbanation built over that as well. We approached it with the sun setting behind it, so the whole megacity looked like it was on fire, with blazing red light shining through and around the spires and buildings, competing with the neon signs and the holographics and the rest of the lights that blazed from every single window and street-side.

The VTOL had dropped us off at a military base that sat at the very edge of the city proper. The base itself looked like a finger of green and black metal that rose out of the ocean, studded with defense weapons. I wasn't an expert, but I could recognize laser weapons. And if this one was the mold that the others I had spotted in the flight towards the city had been stamped out of, then the whole city had a pretty hefty anti-missile defense network.

To be honest, if I had been trying to house all the refugees who had to be yanked out of the western provinces after the whole Kashmir situation, I'd have put up as many anti-nuke weapons as possible. Just to relieve people who still remembered what mushroom clouds looked like up close and personal.

As that thought occurred to me, I noticed something else, something I'd never noticed in any of the holodeck sims ... and the fact that I was surprised by this made me feel like a royal idiot. But still ...

It was freaking *cold*. Breathing in made my lungs ache, and wind continued to blow and whip across the roof catching at my clothes and tugging like a load of little fingers. My eyes started to sting as well, filling with tears, turning the view into blurred mess.

"Corporal Zhao!" A man's voice called out. "Corporal Zhang. Over here!"

I staggered in that direction and felt something press into my hands. I figured out what they were pretty quick—goggles! I slipped them on and blinked away tears, the stinging no longer an issue. A young man wearing the same goggles as I did and a uniform I really should have recognized from my courses on military tactics waved at me as Jillian forced her goggles onto her head. The bald-headed major had already left, vanishing so quickly that I didn't even see her on the roof—which itself only had two entrances to the lower levels, in the forms of a large cargo elevator and a small outcropping that looked like it had a twin set of stairs and a proper elevator.

"I'm Petty Officer Third Class Gimhae Kim Geon-u," he said. "Missile Defense Force."

I nodded. "Sleepy job?"

"Not really," he said. "Texas lobbing an ICBM at us last month has gotten everyone really twitching but that's not really here nor there."

At least I think that's what he said. His Mandarin was kind of slangy, with odd accents and pronunciations. Part of me—even if it sounded a bit racist—really hoped it was because he was a Korean and not because that was how they talked around here.

"Still, thanks for the goggles," I said, switching to English, hoping to drag the conversation into something slightly more pronounceable.

He shrugged. "They're standard issue; we get a lot of pollution run-off over here. Follow me."

Again, this was just my best approximation of what he said.

Who said English was a standard language?

Idiots. Idiots said this.

Then I blinked. "Wait, pollution? Don't we need breathers?"

But he was already off. I decided to not breathe deep.

The inside of the stairwell didn't make me feel hopeful about the rest of Shanghai. Then, after ten steps down the stairs, I reminded myself that not every single part of the city was exactly like every other part. Still ...

The walls were made of crude, recycled metals and the pollution that blew in from the mega-city worked into the metal, staining it strange colors in circular patterns, condensing down from the ceiling. It was like nothing I'd ever seen before, and it felt decidedly scummy. But by the time we hit the third switchback in the stairs, the discoloration was long gone and we were just walking down slatted stairs, lit from overhead and to the sides by dull lamps.

"There's an autocar waiting for you two down at the bridge," Geon-u said, glancing over his shoulder, as if to make sure we were still following him. "It'll take you to the city proper."

I nodded. Jillian, though, had an actual question, asked as she tapped her finger against the wall and wrinkled her nose at the faint residue that rubbed off on her finger tip. "Where's the wallpaper?"

"The MDS—the, uh, Missile Defense Headquarters, that is—is old. Like, Slump old," Geon-u explained as we headed down and down and down, the only break in the green-gray walls being the occasional exposed conduit that hadn't been closed up by whatever tech-crews worked around here to keep things running properly. "Do you know how much additional infotech has to go in to support even basic wallpapering systems?"

I nodded. "Yeah."

"Well, that stuff didn't exist until about ten years ago." He shrugged. "Moore's Knife."

"I've heard of Moore's Law, but not—" Jillian started.

We got to a switchback. Geon-u turned to face us, taking a breather. "It's just the latest way of saying Future Shock. Things change too fast, and big projects have inertia. The old Republic made this place to protect it from any nukes fired by the United States, and they didn't have time to update anything more than the most essential, backbone computer systems. Moore's Knife stabbed us in the back." He shrugged.

We continued on down and I amused myself trying to spot the security that the place did have. Because, while a wallpaper was a great way to keep tabs on everything, there were still at least half a dozen other methods that the Alliance could use to make sure their MDS was secure.

I spotted at least five cameras, which meant I was probably missing at least twenty.

The stairs let out into a collection of musty cubicles, each one stuffed with a set of computers and holographic projectors. A few MDS petties and techies were sitting around at their stations and I felt a tingle of familiarity: They were working on what looked like orbital calculations ... no, suborbital. Intercontinental stuff. You didn't have to get a nuke into orbit to get it to a city on the other side of the world.

Funny, I'd have expected more stuff based around fighting Loonie orbital attacks, but the Loonies hadn't used their orbital advantage yet. Maybe those ops were being handled in a more secure room deeper in this already secure facility.

Maybe the Loonies didn't have the capacity?

Then again, the 'capacity' required to make an orbital attack was to A) have a big rock and B) be willing to throw it at the ground. And that was a big issue, because orbital strikes were edging pretty close to weapons of mass destruction, especially if it was a big rock or a fast rock or, worst of all, a big *fast* rock.

A few of the techies turned to watch us walk past. They looked caffeinated and slightly spliffed—a kind of expression you'd see on a technician anywhere in the world from any time in the past century: the expression of someone who hadn't been outside and had been doing math problems. These people were the kinds of people who had the combination of patriotism (or at least, the desire to not get nuked) and the love of mathematics required to work in the MDB, and even they looked like they were sick of doing math problems.

So, I was actually a bit glad to provide a bit of a distraction.

We got to the front doors and I felt a rush of tension and fear, part of me shouting for me to get a breather. I slid my goggles on instead and the gesture—so close and yet so very different—did little to calm my nerves. It didn't help that I had real things to worry about now, too.

The doors opened onto a broad bridge, which was blocked off by a sturdy-looking gateway, which opened to let in any of the traffic that had to come to the missile defense site. I turned my head and looked up. The spire shot into the sky, looking so very tall from up here. And in the background, I saw the very edge of the Iron Sky proper and ...

And I felt something inverted, something backwards. Orbital vertigo, but in reverse. Rather than fearing a fall down into a spinning Earth, I felt a crushing terror of the sky falling on me. I would stay still and that vast, steel gray mass would come crushing down ... down ...

I looked down, trying to put it out of my mind as Jillian murmured in my ear.

"No wonder these people need fusion reactors."

"Yeah." I closed my eyes, trying to not think about how desperately the CAA must be hurting for power. A lot of the deuterium shipped from the Moon hadn't been immediately chucked into the fusion reactors. Lots of it had been stored, under a paranoid 'we must never let the Slump happen again' mentality.

How long could it last?

The autocar that waited for us was colored a nice teal shade, and it hummed its way out of the missile defense post with the smooth elegance of a hover-car in some spec-fic vid. The engine had to be electric from how little sound it made, and the autopilot was thankfully light on inane conversation. That left just Jillian, me, and the wall for conversation partners. She sat on the other side of the rounded interior, buckled in and leaning back.

"I am so godsdamned sick of being in vehicles."

I closed my eyes. "Jillian, I ..."

I could tell through closed eyes that Jillian was taken aback. Call it a sixth sense, the kind of thing you pick up going through the meat grinder with a fellow Marine. "I was kind of setting you up for some snark, Corp."

"I'm trying to think of how to ask you something without sounding crazy."

"Well, the best way to start would be to say what you're thinking and trust me to not call the crazy card until you start drooling and biting the heads off live halibut."

I snorted.

I looked out the window, and Jillian gave me time to marshal my thoughts. In the time it took to get my mind sorted, the car zipped from the bridge to the city proper. We shot past a blur of Chinese symbols arranged in slangy ways, surrounded with the occasional English or Hindu word, springing out of the neon haze like exclamation points, like targeting icons thrown up by a confused, bedazzled AI. The car didn't slow or change course, slotting in and out of traffic that pushed through the streets at speeds that made me want to close my eyes and pretend it wasn't there.

"I was sent a message."

Jillian nodded.

"It said ..." I chewed one of my well-worn canker sores. I wanted to go back in time and smack my younger self, the one who'd imagined that living on the Earth would mean I would have less stress, less of an impulse to chew on my lip, less of a reason to leave the inside of my mouth with more craters than a Loonie's lawn. "It said that the weird, bald major was reading my brainscan."

Jillian frowned.

"And it said that if I ever needed help, that I should just ask for K." I glanced around the car. "Think we should tell anyone?"

She shook her head. "I figure it's either someone pulling some lameass stunt or ..." She shrugged. "Or something we should treat with the same level of urgency and attention as a rip in a space suit."

I nodded.

"Say, do you think this car is bugged?" Jillian asked.

I slammed my hand into my face.

"Hey, what's the worst they're going to do?" she asked, grinning. "We have constitutional rights."

She paused. The cynicism detector encoded into her brain clicked once, maybe twice. It was the only sound in the car, save for the faint whirr of the electrical engines and the hum of other cars shooting past the windows.

"Tā māde."

The taxi ended up taking a few extended stops when we finally got to the arcologies proper. It turned out that there were interior tube-ways that could lock around the smoothed shapes of the cars and then send them hurtling upwards, either through some pneumatic trick writ large or some other fancy piece of technology. It didn't really matter, because the pipes created traffic jams.

I'd actually done an entire mathematics project on traffic jams while in the crèche. Not traffic jams like this—this was just a simple bottleneck issue, the kind of thing anyone with access to the Lag-Net could understand—but the old Earth sprawl, pre-Slump traffic jams. Those had been mathematically complex far beyond what you'd imagine and they'd been entirely unautomated. There had been nervous, twitchy, poorly evolved human monkey brains behind the wheels of every single one of the billions on billions of cars that had driven around the pre-Slump sprawls.

That mathematics issue dogged me as we waited for the tubeways to spit us out in whatever location they were shipping us to. Not the solution ... the problem. Millions of human beings, each one making minute decisions at a case by case basis. Sometimes, it ended with a crash that would wrap a car around a tree or a lamp-post or another tree. But the vast, vast majority of times, it had simply led to a continual, arterial spurt of cars.

Seeing all these people—the windows had views of the clear parts of the tubeway, which opened out in the sprawling foot-traffic of the arcologies main layers—had spun off an odd thought.

Wars are the traffic accidents of human history.

Well, that was freaking trite.

I tried to empty my brain of all thoughts. That just left room for missing Sarah.

The tubeway opened up and the car didn't waste any time, zipping out across a vast ...

Holy.

Hells.

This is the kind of thing you see from orbit and think you feel awe, then you see it from the window of your autocar and you really realize what *awe* means. It means being terrified and impressed and humbled all at the same time.

The Iron-Sky of Shanghai had a bright top. Miles on miles of glittering, gleaming, glowing surface, shimmering with intense heat and sizzling sunlight stretched out in every direction, almost to the point where the horizon started to curve. The only things that rose above it were the mirrors—massive, curved parabolic mirrors that caught the sunlight from the surrounding countryside and aimed it straight at the collectors. The solar panels were striped, though, every five hundred meters, with tiered high efficiency agriculture, each one zipping past with a hypnotic regularity:

Solar cells.

Tiered, high efficiency agriculture.

Solar cells.

Tiered, high efficiency agriculture.

They were growing rice. Trillions of tons of rice, enough rice to feed the billions of citizens that clustered on the coast of China to escape the blighted regions left behind by the Paki-Indo nuclear exchange.

"I feel so very communist right now," Jillian whispered, pointing at the window. "Look."

In the distance, far enough away that even going this fast, we could admire it, I saw a huge mansion rising out of an ugly, black spar. It was easily the size of the entire Hub storm cellar, with a ludicrous European castle look and flapping flags and everything. When I saw that, I saw the others.

There had to be at least a thousand of them, dotted around, maybe more if distance and heat-waves acted like a kind of low-tech chaff for my equally low-tech eyeballs. A thousand of the world's most wealthy citizens, building on the top of Shanghai ... not because it was the best place to build their buildings, but because it was the most *impressive* place to build their buildings.

Which made me wonder, for a moment ...

"Why is this roadway on the roof and not through it?" I looked at Jillian.

Jillian frowned and we started to toss ideas back and forth.

"Wastefulness?" That was her first suggestion.

I shook my head, slightly. "If this was 2015, maybe."

"Oversight. They realized they needed maintenance when the thing was finished and so they hurried to make a way to get to places fast?"

I frowned. "Why not just use VTOLs for that?"

Jillian tapped her knuckles against the car. "I don't suppose you know?"

The car didn't answer.

We were getting closer and closer to a building. It rose up out of what I felt was the exact middle of the solar-roofing, but I had no way of proving that. It looked a lot like the missile defense stations at the edge of Shanghai, though quite a bit shorter. As it swelled, I was sure of it: The blisters of X-ray laser stations, the circles that had to be missile launch ports and the hardened composite material that could take hits and keep on ticking.

VTOLs shot in and out of the defense complex, many of them painted civilian colors and carrying what looked like repair and farming equipment—"Well, that eliminates one possibility"—but more than a few had military colors and weapon pods.

Then, with an abruptness that felt almost fatal—we shot into the defense station. The car slowed, then drove into a lighted garage. The doors opened and we stepped out. Inside, the air felt air conditioned and the light only came from ceiling lamps that dangled from the ceiling. Still low tech.

A man jogged over to us. He was about my height but easily twice my weight, so where I was spindly and delicate and almost elfin, he was stocky and muscular. He wore a uniform, but he had pips and a badge I didn't immediately recognize.

"Judge Advocate Mike Sawyer-Joo," he said. I snapped a salute and he saluted back, laughing. "Don't worry, I'm not a huge stickler for the regs. So, do you know what the JAG is?"

It clicked.

"We're Marines, sir," I said. "We got the whole of Basic even if we were in space."

"I actually heard they hustled you out half-done. Not that you didn't kick ass, take names, and introduce a new generation of Loonies to their ancestors." Sawyer-Joo's English was properly accented, enough that I was able to understand it and catch the actual tones underneath. They were nice tones. I managed a smile as he turned, leading us out of the garage.

"Yeah, but we still had plenty of reading material," I admitted. "Judge Advocate General, right?"

He nodded. "You two were the witnesses furthest from the trial who could actually be physically here. The only people further than you will have to Skype in."

"S ... Skype?"

He looked at me and Jillian, stopping as he did so. We both look confused.

"I'm so damn old," he muttered, even though he didn't look that much older than Mrs. Cayer. He shook his head. "They'll have to telecom in."

I nodded, then moved to follow him as he headed to the exit door. The door opened and led us into a corridor. He kept up his explaining as we moved around other soldiers with tablets and handheld computers hurrying here and there and wherever.

"So, we got a big clump yesterday and they got briefed, the same briefing you're going to get. But to save some time, the basic gist is ... we're pressing charges against Daniel Lau, formerly General of the emergency Alliance Space Marine Force."

I stopped dead.

He turned to look at me. "Hence why we flew you in across two continents and threw our weight at the Rock—"

It took me a few seconds to realize he must have meant R.O.Q, or Republic of Quebec—

"—and so on. You're the prize witness."

I grinned.

Sawyer-Joo led us through the interior of the defense fortification—which looked a hell of a lot like an office complex, the kind used back before Slump, considering how many tiny computer cubicles there were and how everyone looked completely dead inside—and gave us what felt like a well-practice spiel.

"So, I want you two to completely forget everything you've seen on the Net. The judicial process isn't nearly as dramatic as it is shown to be on the vids." He flashed us a grin. "This makes my job more about making sure that the evidence we collect is filed properly than giving stirring speeches to a jury. Which is good, I'm awful at that kind of thing." He shook his head. "So, while you're technically witnesses rather than pieces of evidence, the actual difference is a bit ..."

He paused as we came to a door that was stenciled with falling letters. They, unlike the slangy, Earther Mandarin I'd heard walking past the cubes and the corridors of this place, were easy enough to understand: *Medical Facility.*

"Academic." Sawyer-Joo found a word that fit his desires.

"Why?" Jillian asked. I nodded to back up her question.

"Well..." Sawyer-Joo leaned against the wall beside the door. He made a few false starts, then snapped his fingers. He pointed at me. I realized he was gesturing at my hands. I held them up and his finger refocused to my cybernetic replacement fingers, which glittered in the fluorescent lights of this place. "Those. And VR. I'm betting both of you are pretty good with VR, right?"

We nodded, though Jillian looked a bit green around the gills. Note to self: Rag her about that later.

"The ability to inject images into someone's brain and suck out their nerve impulses so that it can change a computer program? That also gives us a pretty darn good idea of how to ..." He paused, then shrugged. "Well, do the next best thing to mind reading."

Jillian made a scoffing noise. "Dude, if we could do that, then the Loonies shouldn't have been a problem!"

I glanced at her. "You can't kill someone with a mind reading machine."

"No, I mean, we just grab a Loonie, shove him into one of these things, then yank out the information," Jillian said. I wasn't sure if she was ignoring the Alliance's constitution or just assuming that the powers that be would ignore the Alliance's constitution.

"I said next best thing." Sawyer-Joo patted the wall next to the door. His fingers must have tripped something, because the door swooshed open to reveal a curved room, about twenty meters long and stuffed with sleek, comfortable-looking beds, each one surrounded by a haze of highly-advanced-looking machinery. "It's still not *that* good."

I recognized some of the machinery—the spidery headsets of the Québécois psychologist's office—and inferred that this place had to be some kind of psych ward.

"Why the hell do you have so many angels here?"

"Well, I always did say this was like NERV ..." Sawyer-Joo said, shrugging as he led us past the beds. A lot of them were occupied by men and women in the missile defense uniforms. I glanced at Jillian. Jillian shrugged and looked as confused as I did. Sawyer-Joo continued. "I'm guessing that angel is a Spacer aphorism for someone with mental health issues?"

At my nod, he continued. "Basically, the entire Missle Defense Force suffers from what we call Doomsday Syndrome. Spend your entire workday behind a computer screen working on anti-nuke defense contingencies, it has a way of making people go a bit siggy."

I guessed if 'angel' was our aphorism, then 'siggy' would be his. Still had no idea what a NERV was, but I guessed that it would just remain a mystery for now—lost amid the sea of far more important things happening right now.

"So, the top brass shoved in a big old centralized mental health facility right here. It works out great for my purposes." He shrugged as we got to two beds. "The infosec here is crazy good. Good enough that I don't think even the best Tibetan hackers could get through and tamper with your evidence."

He turned, grinning at me. "So, who wants to plug in first?"

Chapter 9: Privacy

I stepped into my quarters on the VA level of Shanghai's first, last, and best defense against sudden, catastrophic nuclear attack. I stretched, letting my back pop, my joints aching thanks to the trembling tension that still burned through me after the first hellish day of "submitting evidence."

If you've ever been in public VR, you know the dislocation and the faint nausea that can come from a poorly calibrated headset. Imagine that, except the calibration never sets in, and you get forced to relive the worst memories of your entire life.

Yeah.

I cannot put enough airquotes around the word *fun*.

And, with my hands rubbing my face, I said something that would confuse the hells out of anyone who might be snooping in on me.

"All right, K ... you here?"

I smirked, sliding my hands off my face. I wasn't smirking because I felt particularly happy or amused. I smirked the kind of tired, wan smirk that came easy to me after getting my brain grabbed, thrown against a wall and kneaded into place, like in Basic.

Wait, I hadn't *smirked* much then. I think I had mostly curled up, crying myself to sleep and writing Sarah long emails. Smirking came with age. Cynicism.

I was only sixteen. By all the hells, I knew for a fact that my older self would look back on right now and smack me upside the head for thinking things like: Age. Experience. Cynicism. I'd read enough books and seen enough vids to know that was the expected arc of teenagerdom. But no matter how much genre awareness I thought I had, that didn't change what I *felt*.

To distract myself from feeling and thinking, I rooted around the room, looking for a terminal—thinking about Basic led straight to the all too appealing idea of emailing Sarah. I found a cot, a patch of wallpaper that looked like it had its interactivity routines turned off, and a cruddy, old-style terminal built into a desk.

I tapped it on after finding the old-fashioned symbol for power on—a circle with a bar through the top. The screen flared to life and—rather than showing the comforting view of the standard OS for military terminals—it showed a simple black screen with a thin spray of greenish text.

You rang, D?

"Godsdamn it," I muttered, slapping my hands over my face.

And here, I had thought that maybe I had just gone temporarily insane. When I slid my hands off my face, the text hadn't changed.

"Who are you?"

A friend.

"Thanks for the cryptic, useless shit." I cracked my neck. "Can you act like an email service?"

Yes. But I won't.

"Then right now, I'd rather have a regular OS, not some creepy wanna-be white hat sitting at an autobus stop with a handheld!"

I'm not at a bus stop.

"Then at a coffee shop," I snapped. "Or somewhere else with free wi-fi."

Everywhere has free wi-fi.

"This is stupid." I glanced aside. Wait. It *was* stupid, but not for the reason I had originally been thinking. Here, I had a mysterious, well informed super-hacker friend and I wasn't taking advantage of it! I looked at the screen. "What is your name?" I asked, figuring he'd give me the same letter as before.

K

"Right." I rubbed my face. "Who was the bald woman and why was she looking at my brain scans?"

Colonel Mary Singh was checking to see if your fingers were a fluke.

I looked at my hand. Come on, Dru ... it wasn't that hard to tell that the only fingers anyone would ever be interested in would be the cybernetic ones. What had her uniform been?

I closed my eyes. I didn't remember her having anything other than a simple, navy blue uniform, with major pips.

S3TA. If you were curious.

"I've heard of that branch ..."

My eyes widened. The first-in rescuer of the Forge, the man who had used a shotgun and had worn sunglasses even while inside a space suit. He had said he was S3TA.

"Space Special Service." I cracked my knuckles. "Tactical Analysis? Tactical Attack? Never could figure why they had that last bit, though."

That's not what TA stands for. But I have to go soon. Before I do, I need you to know something.

I leaned forward, my heart going a little bit faster. This was all going a bit fast for me, and all these other questions were bouncing around in my head, kicking me for asking such idiotic ones for my first run.

Never go unarmed.

The screen winked out and when the image flickered back on, it was the normal OS, not my little black screen of dubious helpfulness.

"Great," I muttered. I'd been told that my treatments would be happening once the last bits of evidence had been reconstructed out of my brain scans, earlier if my PTSD got any worse. To be honest, I hadn't felt any effects recently, but that might have to do with the fact I felt halfway in a combat situation, with lots of hurrying here, there, and almost no sleep.

I managed to bring up an email service and found an email from Sarah. It was, unexpectedly, rather short, and the header didn't provide any real clues—it was just called "!!!!", one of Sarah's favorite methods of titling.

I opened it.

I'm coming. Love <3 Be there on Friday.

I slumped into my chair, eyes blurring with tears. I laughed, throwing my hands up, but I didn't manage to scream in pleasure, just because my throat felt completely choked up. I closed my eyes and leaned back in the chair, kicking away from the wall.

For a little while, it felt like I was spinning in space, out of control.

Privacy meant I could spend some time being a girl, without anyone around to raise an eyebrow. That meant I could jump around, squee, and generally act like an idiot. That is, I could squee until the door hissed open. The noise sounded dangerously close to air hissing out of a room, and it sent up alarm bells in my brain. I hit the deck.

Jillian blinked. "Wow, it isn't locked," she said, taking her finger away from the door buzzer—which acted as a door opener when the room wasn't locked. "Sorry."

She walked inside a moment later. She still looked really green. Her normally hard, focused face was pale and almost fish-like. All the signs of someone coming down from a *nasty* case of sea sickness—or, considering the situation and what we had just gone through: VR vertigo.

"Dru ..." She sat down on the bed and hung her head forward, breathing. I stepped over to her and then grabbed her hair, sliding it back behind her ears, so I could see her face. She had let her hair grow out a bit, not much but enough that if she upchucked in that position, some might splash all over her. "Dru, how in the hell of hanging upside down while being skinned alive did you manage to get through all that so fast and how can I copy you, you cheating bitch?"

I smirked. "Well, it ... I ..." I paused. "I actually have no idea how I ever got used to VR vertigo. I think I just beat my head against a brick wall—a metaphorical brick wall," I added, because Jillian had tugged her head up, looking hopeful. "I just kept using it until I didn't throw up anymore."

"Great." She closed her eyes. "See, I was actually kind of ... not crazy before the war. I didn't bash my heads into walls just so I could use VR, especially when there was a perfectly good holodeck with perfectly good augmented reality to enjoy."

I nodded.

"And ..." Jillian opened one eye. "I didn't make the mistake of having an Earther girlfriend. That's why you did it, isn't it?"

I nodded again, blushing a bit.

Jillian chuckled—it sounded partway to a groan. "Hey, if I had *known* she was that cute, I'd have fought you for her. And I could have won, I'm a sneaky bitch when I want to be."

"Just keep telling yourself that," I said, slapping her back gently. "And, hey, perk up. This is just the baseline stuff. The trainer stuff."

"Huh?"

"Well, they had you run around in the floating white maze, right?"

She nodded.

"And shoot the demons with a shotgun?"

She grinned, ever so slightly. "That part was actually kind of fun."

I nodded. "That stuff, and take this from an old VR vet, is the stuff that you can use to ease yourself into having your brain hijacked by machines for fun and profit. The ... demon bit is actually based off one of the earliest video games ever, back when they didn't even have polygons, let alone fully realized sim-voxels."

I realized that, from the glazed over look on Jillian's eyes, I had starting going full Swahili on her.

"So, yeah if you can hack this stuff, it'll be easier when you get to the actual construction. I ... got to do some of that today." I frowned.

The techies had been overjoyed when I had told them that I was pretty well versed in VR. They'd done a quick warmup to test me out, then launched straight into the rebuilding memories and recording them. That had been the really frustrating and wearing part, as I had to run a headache-inducing double game: reliving the experience in virtual reality *and* providing running commentary and answering questions.

The embarrassing part was how much I got flat wrong.

Turns out, the human brain is absolutely terrible at memory. We have to shift and strain out reality with our eyes and our ears and our skin and our noses. The memories of those straining efforts gets jumbled, confused, crossed around and connected to the wrong thing entirely, especially when you compare the fallible human mind to a machine.

The machine, in this case, was the Hub's recording systems, the notes taken by Scribe—even months after Basic, the memory of Scribe, the punishment list program from Basic, filled me with a cold, murderous fury that had actually caused a few techies to ask me, nervously, if I was leaving something out about my recollections—and other assorted, impartial machine advisers.

Jillian dragged me back to the present by laying back on the bed. "It's still a drag. I'm used to being *good* at things. I aced Basic."

"I know."

"I aced being a Marine."

"I know." I looked at Jillian—about to tell her about how I missed being a Marine, missed belonging. How I never wanted to go back. How I wanted to punch myself for trying to weasel out of my tour. Instead of saying any of that, I felt my stomach pull a queer flip in my gut, like it had just hit a road bump (an analogy that never would have occurred to me before 2068) as I noticed something. Something that picked the *absolute* worst possible time to crop up—and yet, powered by hormones and dislocation and chance...did.

Jillian was...really *hot*.

Her shirt had ridden up on her belly, exposing her taut muscles. Her breasts rose against the thin surface of her shirt and as she breathed, they moved in ... interesting ways. I had *ogled* girls before, I had drooled over them, I had even had embarrassingly frank and to the point dreams about them.

But that had all been *before* I had gotten my hands on Sarah.

And hell, Sarah was coming. Right now! No other girls! I jerked my eyes away from Jillian.

What was *with* my brain these days? Did all teenagers have these stupid, conflicting desi- yes. Yes, all teenagers had these stupid, conflicting desires and dumb thoughts and uncertainties. That didn't make it any easier to *deal* with them. I closed my eyes and laid my head back against my cot.

"Ah well ..." Jillian sighed, then started. "Oh, this might sound crazy, but ..." She paused. "Did you get into contact with K again?"

"What brought that up?" I asked, cracking an eye open.

"Well, just thinking this is the first time you've had alone."

I found a canker sore, familiar and well worn, and chewed it. I waited until the silence got just a *little* bit awkward before, finally, I nodded. Jillian's eyes were still closed. D'oh.

"Well, did you or didn't you?"

I rolled my eyes—mostly at myself—and sighed. "Yes, Jillian. I did."

I traded the story back to her, explaining what K had said. Jillian took it well.

"You're an idiot, Corp. No offense. This person's obviously got a serious link to some equally serious black ops BS I'm talking about ..." She glanced around as her voice trailed off for a bit. "Oi, K, is anyone listening in on us?"

I looked at her like she'd gone crazy, which was a lot less worrying than how I'd been looking at her before.

"How does he talk to you again?" she asked, looking at me.

"He uses the screen." I waved my hand towards the screen and Jillian stepped over to fiddle with it. She frowned.

"No response. Hey, Corp, what do you think is worse, going to war or going to a detention camp for giving up state secrets?" she asked, looking at me over her shoulder. I met her eyes, then judged the issue in my brain. My brain wasn't exactly the best place to really judge such things, so I tried to step back and really look at options. Yes, at the front, people would be trying their best to kill you in the cold, sucking vacuum of space. But ... considering what I'd seen down here on merry, old, civilized 'recovered from the Slump' in the most sarcastic quotation marks I could possibly freaking manage ...

"The front."

"Damn." Jillian frowned, tapping her fingers against the desk. For a few moments, that was the only noise that filled the entire room, or so it seemed to me. "I hate this."

I nodded.

"No, I mean, I *really* hate this. I hate not knowing who's listening or why or what they might be thinking. I don't know if we've got a meme-tech analyzing every sentence we say for hidden nuance or if we've just got a dumbshit subroutine on a security AI that sends up a red flag whenever we say things like treason or … or … "

She trailed off.

I rubbed my temples. "Hey, just remember, we're not important enough for a meme-tech."

"We're star witnesses in the public crucifixion of one of the CAA's highest ranked generals, no matter how much or how little he deserved that."

I let that spin around in my head.

"Wait, deserved the ranking or deserved the crucifixion?" I asked.

"The rank," Jillian said, casually. "War crime is a war crime is a war crime."

I frowned. "If you could go back and bring back David and Liam and … .all of them, by wiping those Loonies out with the sandcaster, would you say the same thing?"

"Yes," Jillian said, her voice holding a fierce snap to it. Then, before I could even try to respond, she added, "No. I don't know." She shook her head. "Ask me an easy question like how to solve world hunger, or something, Corp?"

I sighed. "I've been kicking around impossible choices for so long, it's starting to get routine."

Jillian chuckled.

We didn't have anywhere to go from there. Any and all conversation options ended poorly. It was like being caught in a sadistic bastard of a MUD's dialog tree, the kind of MUD that was a direct descendent of the old Mario hacks that had turned archaic games into sadistic mazes of flying monsters and instant death traps.

"Do we get any leave?" I asked, finally settling on something safe. Ish. "In Shanghai, I mean."

Jillian shrugged, turning to the console. A few minutes of silent searching around—well, silent save for her muttered curses at terrible GUIs and slow response speed and a few exasperated repeats of the traditional computer handler's prayer of Garbage In Garbage Out—and Jillian had an answer.

"If we log the leaving, we actually *can.*"

"Really?"

"Yeah." She turned to face me. "We're not on duty unless we're getting our brains dredged."

I nodded. "Perfect."

Chapter 10: Balcony

It was midnight in Shanghai and Jillian and I were holding hands. It wasn't due to anything romantic, but rather, because to do anything else would mean getting dragged under and devoured by the crowds.

When leaving the defense base, this had seemed like a really good idea, but out here in the messy jumbled up press of humanity that was Xin-Shanghai's four main arcologies, it didn't seem like a bad idea. No, it seemed like the worst damn idea in the history of the universe.

Every step brought me into contact with things so far removed from space or Quebec that it stunned me, made me want to stand and just gawk. And if I had been allowed to do that, I'm pretty sure someone would have just stolen everything I owned and left me to die of exposure. Fortunately, Jillian's hand and the pressure of the crowd kept me moving.

Kept me stepping.

Step.

Glowing neon holograms, showing a naked woman, writhing and dancing around a pole, with words in English and Mandarin, blurring into a confetti of meanings: HAPPY SUPER FUN TIME! Men, sitting around a cargo container that had been cut in half and put in the side of the corridor, like a gravity well in a stellar dust cloud, causing the crowd to flow around it. They were playing cards or dominoes or something. There were men and women leaning against walls in dead end alleyways that sprouted from each corridor like arterial veins. There were shops, hotels, brothels, factories, parlors, restaurants, musicians, street performers ... it was all so much, all jammed into such a tight space that things overflowed and intermixed into each other: brothels that served food, places where you could get yourself tattooed and—if the sign was to be believed—modified with cybernetic prosthesis. Not that they came out and *said* that, but I spotted a few glittering arms and bald spots— the bald spots that showed where someone had gotten a brain implant of some kind—lurking around those stores.

It was madness.

Jillian and I got shoved—partially due to her instinct and partially due to the pressure of the crowds—from an interior area to an external area, where the hallway turned into a balcony, with a view at the co-urbanation and the other archologies and the steel sky and—through all that—the blackness of horizon and distant promise of a currently invisible ocean. The sun had gone all the way down, and that just seemed to make the megacity even brighter.

We could actually talk now. The wind was fierce and the crowd noises were omnipresent, but they had faded just enough, and our ears had become just deadened enough, that we could hear something beyond the drone, the buzz, and the thrum. And, unlike in the possibly-bugged room we'd been given, this place was private; private thanks to the noise and private thanks to the comforting cloak of a dialect so different it might as well be a different language entirely.

Jillian put her hands on the railing. She grinned, looking at me and nodding. I put my hands there and felt warmth flow through them. Now, that was nice, I'd thought it'd be as cold as the rest of everything else, sitting out here in the fierce winds.

"Can you hear me now?" I asked.

Jillian nodded. I managed a grin, even though it had been Sarah who'd shown me that meme. Jillian, though, had let her smile fade away, leaving a face as intent as a statue.

We stayed in the not-silence of the balcony for a while, watching the co-urbanation writhe with the lights of traffic and the flicker-stutter of window lights winking on and off, like the stars seen through a hazy, imperfect atmosphere. Finally, Jillian hung her head forward and spoke.

"So, you know how you sent me into the DOTtie we raided. The *Hope*? To police it?"

I did, but it took me a little while to wind my gears back, to our first engagement—our first battle. It'd been burned into my head, yeah, but I hadn't expected to be shot back to it while on a balcony in Shanghai. It took only a few moments to remember it all like it was still happening: The Hub, low on supplies, had sent half trained kids to capture. It had even been called the *Hope*, for maximum maudlin irony. I nodded.

Jillian sighed. "I went in to check the back and Lau telecommed me directly—the whole way, everything micro'd as if he was a Korean at a Starcraft competition."

That was odd. The light lag between the Hub and the Loonie freighter had been big enough that any orders given would have been delayed so much as to make them worse than useless.

"He told me that I was the best girl for the job. I think it's just because Cao Cao started sucking on vacuum five seconds into the op." She shook her head. "Anyway, they sent me back and I got to a door that had been welded shut. Now, the nice thing about a PPR is that it takes maybe five, six seconds to turn the thing into a pretty good cutting laser." She smiled, wanly. "Got the door open, and when I went inside ..."

I waited. Jillian closed her eyes, her mind wrestling with what she was about to say—I could see it, plain as a solar flare on her face.

"I found two magnetic bottles."

Those were not exactly the words I had expected to hear. Jillian looked at me and grinned. Grinned like a skull.

"You know those fusion reactor diagrams we learned in the crèche?"

I nodded.

"Well, imagine a fusion reactor, but there's no central fusing chamber, no shielding beside what the bottles have, and the bottles are hooked up to a mini-nuke-plant. The whole thing weighed about a ton and had no markings on it at all, save for some CAA colorings. It did have an RFID chip, but the thing pinged my suit with a 'do not have authorization code' thing."

I imagined the device—two spheres, a brooding atomic battery between them. The image came, but I couldn't for the ...

Jillian's face was haunted, drawn, the grin far, far gone. I remembered her sudden, fierce cynicism when it came to the Alliance using sandcasters just a month later. She had been eager, ready, to disobey orders, and with her and me of the same mind, everyone else had gone forward with it. I shifted to look at her.

"Jillian, it was listed on the manifest as—"

"I know." She cut me off.

The sound of the crowd, the whistling of the wind, it didn't seem enough to cloak what we were talking about. I leaned forward, hissing.

"Why didn't you tell me?"

"Orders!" She laughed, bitterly. "I was just following *niúbi* orders."

We were silent for a while.

"Plus, I was scared and shaken. It was the first time I'd ever been shot at, and here was our CO telling me to keep my mouth shut and ... and ..." Her voice shook. "And I had just gotten out of Boot and I just did what he said. And when I did it the first time, it was so damn *easy* to just not talk about it again. Then not talk about it again. Then ..." She shrugged. "Then it was too late and it didn't matter."

AM storage. The words had been on the manifest, a mystery in the back of my mind, bugging me for a week while we were stationed on the Forge. Then the Tiananmen Station fiasco and the attack on the Loonies and the slow, grinding retreat ... all of that had taken that little mystery and stomped on it, hard.

Anti-matter. The Hiroshima shadows of the 21st century. The Big Shiny, named after the only place where an AM bomb had been set off in the Earth's atmosphere, in what had been called Arizona before Deseret shifted around the borders. The crater didn't glow with radioactivity, it glowed because the area had been turned into shockingly pure glass, and that was just a test zone. There were no anti-matter reruns of Hiroshima or Vicksburg or Bombay—thank the Gods. But there didn't need to be, not for my imagination.

"How big were the bottles?" I asked, breaking the silence.

Jillian blew out a long sigh that came out like remass from an engine, billowing out into the open air before the balcony. She didn't respond for a while. "About five cubic meters. No telling how much of that was vacuum, or containment, or the magnets."

I nodded. "Still, let's say ... about five hundred kilograms if it was all anti-matter? So ... enough weaponized anti-matter to crack the goddamn moon in half?"

"I'll have to check your math on *that*." Jillian smirked.

A man stepped up to us, interrupting this discussion of illegal weapons being made by our lawful government and the fact we had been hung out to dry to cover it up. And the reason for the interruption was so mundane that it almost felt like we had been yanked into a parallel universe. He asked us for directions. At least ...

I think that's what he asked us. His Mandarin was peppered with English slang we'd never heard before, words like Slossin or flabble. We both gave him shrugs. He gave us the middle finger and kept walking. I wondered if that was the norm around here—but from the irritated glares sent his way by others who walked past and cycled through the balcony's open space, I guessed not.

Jillian and I didn't have much to say, and by silent, unanimous agreement, we headed back into the crowds. We had gotten leave for two hours of exploring Shanghai's various arcologies—a task similar to being given a squirt gun and told to use it to fly to Mars—and we'd eaten up a lot of it just getting to the balcony. Getting back to the car-tube took up most of the rest. Once there, we keyed into the car-tube's system, the computers that ran the thing finding our identities through several unobtrusive and slightly creepy methods: eye-dent, gait recognition, facial scans and the RFID tags that had been clipped onto our necks for "ease of transition" through the city.

Still, with our identities confirmed, it only took a few moments for the section of the car-tube we stood by to open, a waiting autocar sitting against the side of the tube. We got in and the autocar zipped along the car-tube, back up to the surface of the solar level.

Once there, Jillian got to go on ahead to her room—and, in an hour, to another one of our evidence collection sessions. But I got stopped, stopped by a ping on my sleeve. I looked at it—

the uniforms that we wore had computers woven into them. They were pretty terrible, so the most I used it for was checking the time. This time, though, my wrist seam was glowing and a series of Chinese letters flicked past the area between my wrist and my elbow: *Cpl. Zhao, visitor waiting in guest room 3.*

I nodded to the guard at the front desk, then spoke to the wall. "Guest room 3."

The wall shimmered and a glowing square appeared, projected from the wallpaper. The square slid and slid along the wall guiding me down a series of corridors. I wondered who was waiting for me ... maybe one of the other Spacers? Maybe ...

My eyes widened. Then, grinning, I stepped to the door and opened it a crack. I saw a flash of blond hair.

I overcame my nerves about opening doors, beat down the voice that screamed at me to put on a breather ...

And I tackled Sarah Cayer to the ground.

Chapter 11: Routine

4/26/2068

Chinese-American Alliance, China, Xin-Shanghai

T-Minus L-Day: 114

If Sarah hurt, she didn't let it on. She didn't let it on for the whole night, because we definitely saw enough of each other to make any bruises on her back or legs obvious. So, I guess the tackling had been—at the very least—expected. Plus, it helped that I wasn't exactly the heaviest person in the universe, and I hadn't gained much weight while on the Earth, despite having to work a third harder at everything thanks to the upped gravity.

We didn't say much that made sense. Everything from the first tackle on seemed like a bunch of half-sentences, endearments, and the sounds of kissing. No discussions, no weighty topics.

No, we waited for midnight, for the ticking over from Wednesday to Thursday, to get into that kind of stuff.

Sarah slid her fingers through my hair and I panted, my head lying in her lap. She had used her hands, not her legs, to position everything properly, and it was shockingly comfortable. Her fingers twisted and twined and she grinned.

"It's going to be hard to get used to this freedom."

"Mmm ... yeah ... I'm waiting for your mom to burst into the room."

Sarah's fingers stopped moving. It was funny, I could almost picture her face just from the movement of her fingers. Like turning a bunch of Xs and Ys and Zs into orbital elements, I transformed a swirl, a casual caress into a nervous look, a worried glance. I cracked open one eye to confirm my suspicions. Just as I thought, Sarah's head had turned away. She looked at the wall, frowning a bit. She didn't bite her lip—that seemed to be my job around here.

"Sarah?"

"I ... Mom's not coming."

"How did you ..." I pushed my hands under myself, moving until I was upright and could look into her temple. I reached up and tilted her head to face mine. "Sarah, how did you *get* here?"

A load of information that I had filed in my brain as *stuff I never needed to worry about* came tumbling out. Things like: passports, transport security, the cost of taking a suborbital flight from Montreal to Shanghai. It was easier to get around on a globe than in orbit, but that didn't mean it was *easy*.

"Well, it started routine," Sarah said, using her hands to scoot forward, so she could lay all the way back. "Arguing about what I could and could not do. Then I said that I ... I needed to see you. That you were going to be at some big mega-city, having Gods knows what happen, and you'd need my support because I love you and can shower you with all this affection I've stolen."

I grinned, looking down at her.

"And, well ..." She shifted around. "Mom and I got into one of those big-huge arguments that mutates. It starts about you, then becomes about farm labor, then about you *and* the church. Then ... it got mean."

"Like how mean?"

Sarah belted off at least three paragraphs of flowing Québé-cois French. She moved fast, striking syllables like atomic bombs, her eyes focusing at the ceiling as she repeated the whole thing verbatim. I didn't catch more than a word or two, and both of those were the more vicious curse words that Sarah had taught me. The ones that profaned their God and His symbols. I winced.

Sarah trailed out of French and into English. "Like that mean."

I nodded. "So you went AWOL?"

"Oh yeah." She nodded, her eyes shining slightly with unshed tears. "It's about damn time too. Stupid, stubborn jack-ass ... " She blinked, then closed her eyes. I slid my arms around her and squeezed her as she started to cry. It was the kind of shuddering, shoulder wracking cries that should have made her kick, but she was rooted to the bed. I had cried like this, in orbit.

I hadn't had someone to hold me.

It didn't make me feel heroic, or anything. I didn't feel like a good girlfriend, I just felt like ... like a sandbag trying to save Miami during the Slump. Still, I did my best as the waters poured over me. The crying—unlike the Atlantic—subsided. Slowly, but it did. Sarah and I didn't say much.

I figured that was for the best.

>+<

I had bad dreams. No, I don't want to talk about them. Don't want to think about them. Don't want to describe them. *Tā mā de.*

>+<

I woke up and Sarah was still here. For a few, confused seconds, I didn't know why or where I was or if Sarah was someone trying to strangle me or not. Then, I realized what was up. Up became up, down became down, and having Sarah became amazing, not scary.

I squeezed her, she kissed me. We had bad breath, and we didn't care—or at the very least, we pretended not to.

And then the door thumped, loudly.

I got out of bed and padded over to the door. Sarah started to wriggle into her shirt and her pants.

"Who is it?"

"Corporal Zhao, this is PFC Cho. Do you have the guest civilian Sarah Cayer in your room?" The voice sounded male and ever so slightly annoyed.

I glanced at Sarah. She had gotten the pants on and was working on her shoes and socks, starting with the latter.

I opened the door and nodded to the PFC.

"I do."

"Begging your pardon, Corporal, but the CO sent me here to escort her off the grounds. This is still a secure facility."

I blinked, opened my mouth to bitch. Then, remembering, this PFC had the weight of the commander of this place behind him. And the CO—who I hadn't met—was ranked high enough to get the command of one of the biggest anti-nuke bunkers on the Chinese coast.

I nodded. "I wasn't aware that she had to leave."

The PFC shrugged. "Security has been merry cobbed by all the shit we've got to deal with. It's no biggy, I'm sure the CO will just send a minor rep-memo to you."

I could figure what merry cobbed meant by the context. "Putting up a bunch of Space Marines is really that disruptive?"

He shook his head. "No, it's all the external meme-techs that are ..."

He paused, seeing that Sarah had gone from socks to shoes to wheelchair. "Ma'am," he said, speaking over my shoulder and to Sarah. "An autocar is waiting to take you anywhere in the city."

Sarah frowned. She didn't complain, I figured she knew that it wouldn't be a good idea.

She looked at me. "I'm in a hotel … " She named the coordinates and arcology, a list of numbers and letters I immediately started running through in my head as fast and as often as I could.

It meant I didn't say goodbye. It meant I didn't even notice she was off, down the corridor with the Private First Class until I had gotten the address fixed in my head.

It hurt.

The door closed, automatically, and I leaned against it, forehead first. True to form, a few seconds later, I got the warning memo. My desk chimed. I went to it, sitting down and tapping on the screen. I wondered how scathing it would be.

They're getting complacent. Imagine, S could have been a Loonie terrorist.

My gut lurched. K.

This time, I'd ask good questions.

"Can you keep this room from being bugged?"

Yes. No. E-bugs are subverted, but an ear against the wall …

I nodded. So, K had his fingers—or thought he had his fingers—suffused through the Alliance's security.

You are being tested.

With my mind full of images of snoops being aimed at the door, laser-light bouncing off the metal, reading the vibrations that would give away every word I said … I didn't speak. Instead, I splayed my fingers out and typed on the keyboard.

By who?

Whom.

:|

Interested parties. Who do you think?

CAA?

I thought you told J you would ask good questions.

I scowled.

I'm beginning to realize that things are really complicated down here. There's a big picture that isn't forming for me. The pieces I have, though, are enough: A major is looking at my brain scan. A general is being tried for using sandcasters—while the CAA makes weaponized anti-matter. And you, Mr. K are some kind of super-hacker who has decided that I deserve some extra help. But what is it all pointing towards? And don't get cryptic on me, or I will turn my chatlogs in to the Alliance.

I delete these chatlogs once they're done.

Duh.

I sat there, with my arms crossed over my chest. I didn't want to dignify that with an answer.

The Big Picture?

The big, single reason for why things occur?

Childish.

The Chinese-American Alliance is a super-federal government imposed over the entire North American region—with the exception of Quebec and Deseret—and the entirety of China—with the exception of the rad-zones. This includes Texan revolutionaries, arcology dwellers, forest punks of various persuasions, and so on. It has an armed forces created of an amalgamation of two of the largest imperial forces of the previous century. It has—

I cut into the diatribe flowing across the screen with a few key punches.

i get it i get it

Good. I was worried for a second.

But if you want another piece of the puzzle.

The meme-techs reading your brain are not just gathering evidence.

They are testing you, as I said.

And you have already passed.

Cyber-affinity. Research it. But not on this terminal.

The light winked out and the regular OS returned. The memo chewing me out—or not chewing me out, I never learned for sure—went unread. I leaned back in my chair and thought … and thought.

I didn't have much time to think. The routine we'd been put into was as inflexible as any other law of physics. I had a dead space, a time where there weren't enough minutes to get food or talk to someone, but there also wasn't quite enough time to actually get up and go. It was just a few minutes where I just had time to sit and stew. Cyber-affinity. It sounded like something a transie would say. That just made me feel even more unsettled. Finally, the dead space had passed and I got out of my room. Others were leaving their rooms at the same time, including Jillian. I moved to walk alongside her.

She grinned at me. "Soooo …"

I nodded, blushing a bit.

"Had fun?"

"Yeah."

My grin was as goofy as it should be. Despite the … despite everything, I was still sixteen and in love.

We got to the evidence chambers and I looked over everything with new eyes, K's warnings echoing—as much as text could echo—in my head. They were testing us. But it couldn't just be every single person on the team. Could it? If it was the entire team, then it meant that the conspiracy was deep and good at hiding. Or maybe it was just the government and *I* was the conspiracy.

I was the one talking to mysterious uber-hackers.

I shook my head and focused on what I had to do. Just standing here would get people asking questions.

The VR booths we used were top of the line. The flat cots that I had thought we were going to use had been replaced with tubes that sat at a canted, forty-five degree angle. They had comforting foam on the inside and could mold the interior to suit your body. Add to that a full life support and cooling fans that kept you from getting too hot or too cold, and you had something that would have been great in space, when my only access to the Earth was the holodeck. Down here ...

Well, it was hard to enjoy the finest in vid-gaming equipment when you had to use it like *this*.

"Corporal." A meme-tech saluted me as I came over. He was a civilian contractor, given away by the color of his jumpsuit and the badge on his shoulder—and, of course, the fact that he saluted with the wrong hand. "Are you ready for more ground-rigging?"

I rubbed my palms against my face, then nodded.

Ground-rigging. It was, as far as I could determine without a degree in memetic engineering, a slangy term to mean screwing around in VR to get things to work proper. The tech had explained it like thus: "We'll put you through some simulated brain trials, basic psychosomatic stuff that'll dredge up various thought patterns and mindforms that we can then check against what we have from your record, and what our psycho-statistical analysis has determined to be proper responses to stimuli. Then, we'll start using that groundstate to begin the mnemonic retrievals and back checking against IRL vlogs."

He had then smiled, a kind of nasty smile that made me think he knew that it had all gone right over my head, and said, "See. Simple."

I got into the tube after swallowing a pill that was handed me. I relaxed into the VR tube, tried to not grit my teeth as the inducer snapped into place around my head, and let myself fall into virtual reality.

Another round of memories.

Another round of screaming and panic and blood.

>+<

Afterwards, Jillian and I got lunch at the mess hall. The Spacers were separated from the rest of the mess, which was full of off duty MDS people. They didn't pay us much mind. Hell, we didn't pay ourselves much mind.

"You look like shit."

Jillian looked at me. She did. Her eyes had bags under them, and the red marks from where the VR headset fit snugly over her scalp were imperfectly covered by her hair, which itself was mussed and dirty. She looked like she had been digging around in her friend's guts. Since we had both been taken through the final bits of the siege of the Forge, that made sense.

"You look just as bad."

"Let's look bad together." I reached out with a fist and bumped it against her fist. Our movements were slow, sluggish. We spent a few minutes just spooning rice into our mouths. Once we had gotten slightly more food into our bellies, Jillian sighed.

"Going to visit Sarah?"

"If they let me out." I grinned. "Want to come with?"

Come with, and I can tell you about K's latest infodump.

Jillian shrugged. "Sure. Should we bring one of these other Spacers?"

I looked to the left. They had been people wounded before the big fight, who'd been hiding away with the civilians while the Loonies and my defense force—a pang of guilt swelled up in me—and so, the only thing we had in common was the fact we were in the Marines and the fact they all looked like everything was thirty percent too heavy.

Which it was.

I didn't have to strain myself too hard to look at Jillian and shake my head.

Getting leave was harder this time.

We arrived at the CO's office after submitting our requests and he sent us the ... rather ill-omened response that he wanted to see us. The office itself looked like it had been cut out of the same cloth as the rest of the bunker: square, metal walls, a faintly humming fluorescent light source, and a decidedly 2020ish retro look to the computers. The CO, now that we could see him face to face, looked a hell of a lot more like an office administrator, with a rounded, chubby face and a pot-belly that would have gotten him thrown out of the airlock in space. He wore a thin mustache and kept his hands clasped together while he talked to us.

There was just one problem.

He spoke the Mandarin—and only Mandarin, no English intermixed in there—of Shanghai. The other people in the base were easy enough to understood if we stuck to English and simple concepts, but the CO seemed to think that if Mandarin was the mother tongue, he might as well stick to it and only it.

But I still got the basic gist of the issue: The meme-techs didn't want people wandering around while they were providing evidence.

"I believe—" I think he said, "—that they want to be able to keep a tab on you, and are worried that the stimulation/stimuli/stimusomething in Shanghai will throw their readings off and mean we have to begin at the start all over again."

We nodded. "Yes sir."

What else was there to say to a major? Even if he was the next best thing to a Coast Guard officer, he was our CO for this stint.

"Permission to speak freely, sir?" I asked, careful to stick to Mandarin and to speak slowly and carefully.

He nodded, waving to me.

"Can I have an extension on visits from my SO?" I asked. "Significant Other?" I added.

He shook his head.

Yes sir. That was the only thing we could say.

When Jillian and I walked out of the room, Jillian muttered. "Stupid meme-techs."

"Yeah," I said, looking at her. "Say, you know the view we had from the balcony in Shanghai Arcology Four, right?"

Jillian looked at me as if I were crazy. I kept walking, hands behind my back, and looked back at her, trying to indicate she should go along with it. Something in my nearly frantic eyebrow waggling got through to her. She nodded.

"Yeah, they were pretty great, why?"

"Well, I was just thinking about what you said, and thinking that sometimes, I wish I could say something similar." I shrugged. "But ... you know ..."

She grinned. "Corp, are you hitting on me?"

I blushed and started to splutter, my attempt at subterfuge—piss poor as it was—clearly a failure. Then I saw her wink. Gods, I'm an idiot. I kept spluttering a bit, more to cover for myself than anything else, and we got to our quarters. We had an hour of R&R before the next VR shift. I opened the door, gesturing her inside. "If you want," I added.

She shrugged and followed.

Once the door closed behind me, I said to her, "We're private here. Private-ish."

"Oh ..." She bit her lip. "Were you actually hitting on me, Corp?"

I turned and looked at her. I felt an odd turn in my stomach, as if it wasn't sure if I was falling or flying. "Wh-What?"

"Well, you know, inviting me into your private room and making it clear that we've got privacy." She grinned at me.

I scowled, picking up the pillow off my bed and chucking it at her head. She ducked as smooth as could be and the pillow thumped to the floor.

"Seriously, though, what's up?"

"K contacted me. He was, as per usual, mystical and obfuscating and just scary enough to keep me up at night. Or at least, he would be if he hadn't called me in the morning." I sat down on the bed and rubbed my face. I laid out what we'd gotten.

"Cyber-affinity ... that sounds like something out of a game," Jillian said, frowning.

"I'd have heard of it, if it was," I said, shrugging.

"MUD-snob." She grinned. "You played MUDs, not actual games. Those things are basically like glorified chat-rooms with rules."

"Yeah, I know, that's exactly what they are. Chat-rooms with rules."

Jillian rolled her eyes. "I'm talking about *actual* games. Games with graphics and stuff. Is it safe to search on the net? K said that the room was bug-safe—"

"Actually," I corrected her. "He said it was safe from electronic bugs."

She nodded.

"I think that includes searching too. I mean, he did *tell* me to look it up."

Jillian cracked her knuckles and sat down on the desktop. She started searching around, partitioning the screen into a few dozen smaller windows, each one holding a search tree that she found her way down. It was a bit dizzying to watch, the kind of thing Yolanda would have done—would still be doing, actually—as a programmer-at-arms. I felt a pang, I hadn't seen or heard from Yolanda in what felt like forever.

Jillian opened up one of the windows. As she did so, I remembered that K had explicitly said for us to search for cyber-affinity on anything *but* this console.

Tā māde.

"Aha!" She turned around in the chair, grinning at me. "Cyber-affinity is a game term, from an old game. A classic, actually." She gestured. "*Cyberpunk 1999.*"

I stepped over and leaned down to look at the screen, trying to convince myself this looked like an innocent historical search. I did see something comforting: The root search hadn't been the term "cyber-affinity", it had been "cyber-punk video game pre-Slump."

The end result of the scan showed screen shots from a game so ludicrously primitive that rather than using voxels *or* polygons, it used what looked like drawn sprites, splayed out in a crude mockup of a three-dimensional view. It was like ... like Doom, that kind of oldness.

"Really makes you feel the history, doesn't it?" Jillian said. "This is System Shock. It was one of the first First Person Shooter/Role Playing Game combos. And ..." She paused. "It was basically a big old Singularity Slasher film made almost sixty years early. I know. I played it."

"Any good?"

"Punishingly hard. But that's neither here nor there, what IS here AND there is cyber-affinity: an in-game statistic for measuring how good you are with cybernetic prosthesis." She turned to look at me. She looked oddly smug. "And now, I have managed to pull an old reference out of my brain to rival Sarah's My Little Pony one-liners. Hah!"

I gently whacked Jillian upside the head, the kind of gesture you did to reprimand someone for being ridiculous without actually hurting them.

"What the hell does this have to do with anything? What does it tell us that we didn't know before?"

She rubbed her hair back into place—my hand had done more damage to that than to her head.

We were silent for a moment. Jillian broke it.

"The top secret transhumanist conspiracies that hold our government in their cybernetic grasp are run by huge nerds?"

Chapter 12: Deathtrap

I could barely believe it.

I was out. I was free.

Sure, I was stuck in what amounted to a deathtrap in cloth—the utterly moronic, outdated dress uniform for a Marine—and I was five minutes away from having to go up on stage and swear on books and all the other things that seemed a lot less scary when I watched them on the vid-screen. I fidgeted left, then right, pacing back and forth in an antechamber to the courtroom.

The courtroom—the courthouse, and the entire building it was situated in to be exact—was a delicious breath of fresh air. Like stepping into a hydroponics bay after a month in a suit. And after the month I'd spent in the bunker, this was amazing. The walls were made of paneled wood, for one thing. Plants hung from curved planters and traditional Chinese artwork—as tacky as it was probably fake— were placed at strategically effective positions to cover up any signs of high technology as unobtrusively as possible.

The whole building was like that, right up until you got out of the endless cubicles for administration and data-wrangling and into the hardened exterior. This building, from the spiel that Sawyer-Joo had thrown our way, was one of the central administration hubs of the Alliance, not just Shanghai. That explained the automated machine gun turrets hidden in the ceiling, the drone closets waiting to pop open and launch out mobile response units, and what looked like not-so-subtle armor plating on the outside of the building.

Ugh. And here, I thought *I* was the paranoid one.

I looked at Jillian. She, along with the other waiting witnesses, sat against the wall. I wasn't the only one pacing, though, there were a few technical advisers who weren't Spacers who would be providing their testimonials in the upcoming trial. One of them actually smoked an electronic cigarette, an affectation and an addiction I'd seen in movies and vid games more than I'd ever seen on the Earth. And ...

Frankly, after a month with only periodic visits to Shanghai, I had to wonder why. Even after the good, hard whack that the Slump had been, this city still put out enough pollution to make me wince. And I wasn't even an eco-nut. Still, I figured that was what the climate control sats were for: To counter for a species that was just too numerous and too in love with industrial by-products like comfortable living and not having to do everything with shaped metal and horses.

I shook my head. My brain was jittering from thought to thought: pollution, Sarah, the trial, Sarah, Shanghai's crowds, Sarah, that guy's goofy E-cig, Sarah.

"Hey, maybe the leash will be a bit shorter," Jillian spoke up when my pacing brought me back to her.

I looked at her.

"I figure, once we give our testimonials and the evidence is submitted and everything is all proper and shit, then we'll go back to leave until they want us back in the Marines again." She shrugged.

"I hope so," one of the other Spacers cut in. I think his name was James Ho? I hadn't really tried to learn other people's names during our time in the bunker. That had been more due to my natural inclinations towards finding a social hole and hiding in it than any lack of interactions, we'd all been crammed together pretty close.

But, hey, I'd gotten to sixteen years up in space without making more than a few friends. Most of them didn't hold a candle next to Sarah. Archaic? Yeah, but I actually *liked* candles. They were warm. They weren't at home in the cold vacuum that was space. They were Earth, through and through.

I wanted to think more about candles.

Jillian nodded, but her look to me was loaded down with extra mass.

The whole ... conspiracy thing made the days crawl sometimes.

But there was something, as stupid as it might sound, that made everything go that much *slower*. I could actually, through some trick of the human brain's infinite ability to be more concerned with minor day-to-day things than the huge, looming, uncomfortable truths that face us, forget the very idea of a conspiracy. K's mysterious warnings and Jillian's confessions would fade into the background radiation of my day and then go unnoticed.

That left the one thing that never could fade, at least, I hoped never could.

Sarah. She kept that fire bright, because she'd send an email whenever she could. She wasn't being supported by her mother and when I tried to send her back pay, she refused it with an assertion that she could make it on her own. And, amazingly, she actually got a job. As a recycling vat scrubber.

She claimed it wasn't that bad.

"All right!" A voice jerked our attentions to the far side of the room. Standing at the wooden door that led out of here and to Gods know where was Sawyer-Joo, hands on his hips, looking very official. "Now, most of you have never done this before, so here's the basic protocol. Pay attention." He stepped slightly forward, letting the door close—the hinges were automatically powered. "You will be taken before the tribunal judges. There will not be an audience for this, but there *will* be a media presence, mostly in the form of camera drones."

"Isn't this a general court-martial?" That was one of the techies, the man with the E-cig. He twitched it in his lips.

"Yeah, but would you rather a controlled media bleedoff or someone sneaking a drone camera in and putting it all on the blacknets? At least this way, we'll have an official story to counter what the conists—" a slang word that I'd heard once or twice, I think it meant 'conspiracy theorists' "—will be spewing. Now, once you're in front of the judges, you'll be asked to swear you're telling the truth and so on. Say you do. After that, it's just a set of questions from any of the tribunal members who feel as though they have a reason to ask a question. Once they are done, I and the other JAG for the defense will get to try and disqualify anyone we think might hurt our case. For that, you get to sit by the sidelines and answer any question we throw your way. Got that?" We all nodded.

Sawyer-Joo ducked his head, checking his sleeve, which glowed faintly. "Now, we're going to be leading with the Spacers' evidence first. Open Source?"

He spoke the name without asking if it was real. The boy—dear Gods, his time in Basic had to have been hell—raised his hand and stood at the same time. The JAG took him off, through the doors, which shut behind him as automatically as they had opened.

I rubbed my face. "You know, I wish life had smash cuts. Just cut, we're there."

Jillian nodded, looking morose.

"But then again," I added. "That'd mean actually *getting* there."

"Smash cut to us on Hawaii, drinking wine while beautiful women and men dance in the background," Jillian murmured to me.

That was a cut I could agree to.

>+<

Life did not oblige. After a few hours of torturous tedium, I was out there.

In the court.

The room didn't have the harsh metallic lines that I was so used to, but it also wasn't the same kind of comforting wood and faux nature shit that filled the areas between the armored exterior and here. Rather, they had gone for something faintly traditional.

And in China, there were more traditions than you could shake a stick at, but two overwhelmingly powerful ones survived the Slump and to this modern age: Imperial China's long stability and Communist China's promises of equality at the price of a few million dead. Both of them had their issues, but it's funny how looking back smooths away the bad parts of things, leaving you with just the stuff that was nice.

Like, right now, I'm missing the tight confinement of the Hub.

The room took after Communist China, with tall walls, the wood blending into harder plastics and ceramics, so the whole place felt as monolithic as the Alliance wasn't—considering how the Alliance was a patchwork of religions, races and languages so confused that I was having a pretty hard time even talking to my fellow countrymen just because I was born a million kilometers away from them.

Wait, actually ...

The front of the room had a curved desk that met the wall, leaving a bulge behind which sat the tribunal council or whatever the hell they were called. Their seats were raised and they looked down at me, from a higher orbit. And they had all the rocks—metaphorical rocks—to throw. My eyes flicked from person to person, looking at their chests rather than their faces, at least to begin with.

Now, I kind of figured why they wore frilly, easily torn, un-insulated, itchy, *zāogāo* uniforms. The colorful pinnings on the front, once translated through what I'd learned in Basic, turned into a constellation of places and wounds and command commendations.

The tribunal was stacked with veteran combat soldiers. I wondered if that was normal.

A functionary wearing a LT's thin bar and star stepped up, holding a framed tablet containing the CAA's bill of rights and every single holy text from the Bible to the Communist Manifesto. I put my hand on it and he spoke, in English that sounded trained, because he had the same "newscaster" accent that everyone seemed to understand: "Do you swear by the articles contained within that you will tell the whole truth and nothing but the truth?"

I nodded. "I do."

My throat felt dry, it made my voice sound funny. I tried to not show I was gulping, but I was pretty sure it was obvious as a thruster in space.

"Do you swear by the articles contained within that every mnemonic collection that you give has been made as accurate as possible considering the limitations of the human brain and human spirit?"

I nodded again. "I do."

The man stepped back.

I waited for an onslaught of questions. The judges looked at me, then looked down. I heard a few taps from those of them who preferred turning pages on their screens with a tap instead of a drag—which was usually pretty silent.

"No questions," said the judge in the middle, an old man with a face built like the surface of the moon.

Sawyer-Joo didn't ask me questions first, as he was the prosecutor and I was one of his witnesses. The other JAG, a fit, trim-looking woman who looked pure Han, stood and asked me, point-blank.

"Corporal Zhao, is it true that you are suffering from Post-Traumatic Stress Disorder?"

Since I figured she had my brainscans, I nodded. Plus, under oath and all that. She waited, and I realized I probably needed to speak up. "Yes, ma'am."

"I request that this witness be removed due to a potential mental instability. Mnemonic evidence cannot be relied on if there is even a chance that the witness psychological state is less than optimal."

"Sustained," the lead judge said. I thought someone had to say 'objection' for that, but maybe I didn't know everything I thought I did. I glanced at Sawyer-Joo, who stood with casual ease and a relaxed stance.

"Corporal Zhao has been under intensive psychological analysis for the better part of two months. In this time, she has shown nothing that indicates a psychological state that is beyond the parameters set by ..."

And then ... words started to come out of his mouth. They went into my ears. They made an impression. But I'd be sucking on vacuum if I could tell you that I understood what the *hells* he was talking about. Dates, times, court decisions, people, people's names, and other assorted legalistic minutia went here and there and it apparently convinced the judge, because after the haze passed, I distinctly heard the word: "Sustained."

If you asked me what was sustained, what had been objected to, and what in the nine hells was going on, I'd have had to ask for a blindfold and a cigarette, because you'd be shooting me before I answered the question.

And, just like that, I was led out. A different functionary—not Sawyer-Joo, but rather a bored-looking middle-aged Han man with JAG stripes on his uniform—took me aside and laid everything out with a dull, plodding precision.

"Now that your evidence has been submitted, it will be reviewed more fully. Once it has been completely cleared, you will be called to the stand to testify." He sighed. "Any questions?"

"Yeah," I said, speaking slowly and carefully. Just so I'd be understood, though I felt like I was starting to get a better hang of the dialect down here. "Firstly, why do I need to testify? You have my brain scans. Secondly, do I have to stay somewhere secure or do I have—"

He cut me off, waving his hand impatiently.

"Context and a hotel room has been selected for you and paid for by the People's Commissions for Military Affairs. You are not sequestered, but you may be required to be if any further intensive psychological examinations are to take place."

I nodded, rubbing my palms against my face. After I had rubbed the grit from my eyes, I asked: "Question ... this 'context' *shì shénme guǐ dōngxi?*" I looked around for my lawyer, hoping he'd have an answer.

Sawyer-Joo was already around the corner.

But I didn't leave for my hotel and whatever waited for me there. Instead, I stood in the bit of corridor that stretched between this side of the courtroom and wherever the rest of the building was. The functionary who had dragged me aside stood there as well, arms crossed over his chest. He tapped one foot on the ground, frowning at me.

"Are you going to leave?" He asked after a few incredibly awkward moments.

I shook my head. "Waiting for a friend of mine."

"If he is a witness, he will be sent to the same hotel. If he is not, then he will have to meet you elsewhere. This is a secure building, you cannot simply loiter here because you're a witness in a trial." He pointed his finger down the corridor. "Keep going straight that way."

I shrugged and headed out. The corridor led past what looked like a few techies working on the guts hidden behind the wooden paneling of the wall. They all wore white, with white billed caps. The guy with gloved hands deep in the wall had swarthy skin, which wasn't *that* unusual, but his facial structure wasn't really Indian, per-se. I stopped and watched them curiously.

He was Hispanic. That was it. Not a mix. Not any of the weird ethnic groups that had cropped up after the Slump. That was weird enough for a glance, but not weird enough for a second. I shook my head and turned to continue down the corridor, following the course set for me.

I got to the hardened outer shell of the building. My face was scanned and my fingerprints were examined by two flying, disk-shaped drones with underslung optics bundles. As they flitted around my head, the security guard who oversaw the whole shebang looked over at me from the patch of wallpaper he had set to follow his commands, grinning ruefully.

"Sorry, ma'am," he said, his English accent sounding like glue in my ears. "Just need to make sure you're not a shapeshifter."

I snorted.

>+<

The hotel wasn't that bad, but it sounded like Heaven—the possibly made up Heaven, not the space-station Heaven—compared to what Sarah was going through.

"Do you know how stupid my job is?" Sarah asked me, her voice crisp and smooth, as if she were right next to me. She wasn't. That made it worse. I kept my eyes closed, so I could pretend as I lay on the bed and listened to her complain through the wallpaper. But it was the kind of irritated, lengthy rants that she had thrown at me before we'd really fallen crazy-go-nuts in love.

They were actually kind of fun.

"So, okay, get this, these tanks are supposed to do three things: fixing carbon dioxide, producing petrochemicals, and then their runoff also is sent to the nutrient processing facilities. Which SOUNDS fine. But can you please tell me who thought it was a good idea to recycle *bodies* into it? I mean, I know, some jackhole prolly saw Soylent Green and went, PERFECT!"

She sighed.

"But did they think about the sheer chemical logistics you have to go through just to break down a human body into something worth eating? Let's not even touch on the prion issues, or go into the whole ... digestive tract issue thing. Let's just think about the fact that most of the people who are both poor enough to will their bodies to resyk and dead enough to be worth recycling are from the lower levels of Shanghai. Now, it doesn't take a freaking rocket scientist to figure that these people have sucked enough pollutants, drugs, or bullets that they're barely worth reducing."

She paused.

"I'm not boring you, am I?"

"Oh, no, I find it really interesting." I grinned. "It's actually ... nice. Gritty. The kind of problem you can whinge about and not feel like the world is *wándàn.*"

"Honey, I'm talking about recycling bodies for food."

I opened one eye. She was grinning through the wallpaper at me. I smiled back.

"Yeah, but at least they're donated bodies," I said, shrugging. "You actually forced me to watch that stupid movie. Talk about unsustainable."

"I think that was the point. It was one of those social commentary things."

I nodded, waving my hand. "Tell me more about how badly the system is designed. That way, I can feel superior for being from space."

"No, no, I want to know more about your time in the big black box. Half the emails you sent out had huge hunks of them ripped out."

I frowned. "How could you tell? They didn't ... they don't still have those black bars anymore, do they?"

"Oh, no, but their handle on how you write is awful. It's really obvious when there are huge skips and gaps in what you're talking about." She smiled, a bit sadly.

I bit my lip, chewing my familiar worry-scars, the raised bumps that waxed and waned based on how much stress I was feeling. I rolled onto my back, then closed my eyes.

"Before I start talking, and before they cut this feed for me talking about things I'm not supposed to, can you tell me one thing?"

"Mmmhmm."

"Are ... you still not talking to your mom?"

She nodded. You might ask how I knew without opening my eyes. It's a gift.

"All right." I sighed.

I wasn't sure how I felt about this. On the one hand, it was Sarah's life. And I supported her decisions, because she was Sarah and that was how things worked: Sarah and I made up a two-legged, four-armed, wheeled monstrosity of a shared life, mostly sustained through the internet and IM.

I didn't say anything more. That turned out to be the right instinct, because Sarah started talking all on her own, in a soft, sad sighing voice that I didn't like to hear as much as her angry and running off about something stupid. She always sounded like she knew—in the back of her mind—how to *fix* things she was mad about. That was what made her dissertations on bad fiction so entertaining.

This?

"She's just so convinced that I can't make it. And ... I ... just ... can't take it anymore. I can't take being told that I'm *not* able to do something without even trying it for myself. I mean, I'm not stupid, I know there are things I can't do as easily as other people. I can't grab stuff at the high shelf, but ... like, in the job I'm in right now, I have a long, adjustable pole for making vari-ous cleaning motions, and for everything else, there are robots. It's mostly a maintenance watch, and the only thing that having a wheelchair does to that is it means they can use the stool nor-mally at the maint bench for somewhere else. But ..."

She sighed.

"Mom just doesn't see anything except me as a baby."

"I think most Earther moms are like that," I said.

"Yeah, but that doesn't make them right. Most people used to think it was a-okay to own people because they had the wrong skin color, that doesn't make them right. Most people—"

"Sarah." I opened my eyes and looked at the screen. "Your mom being overprotective is not the same thing as slavery."

"Godwin, godwin ..." She waved her hands, as if to deflect the entire fallacy with her palms.

Silence.

"Still, I'm doing just fine," she said.

I looked, for what felt like the first time, at the wall behind Sarah. There were tiny clues that what was being fed my way wasn't from a wallpaper—the frame of the screen, the resolution of the image, stuff like that. And the wall behind her didn't have any wallpaper either, instead it was a flat steel bracing. A tiny rivulet-stain worked its way from one corner to the ground, making rust where unpainted steel had been before. The door, which I could see only the corner of—looked like a solid brick of metal too.

"Sarah, what do you normally eat every day?"

She shrugged. "Same as what everyone else does, I guess."

I shifted from my side to my knees, actually sitting up and looking at her. "Sarahbear ..."

She glanced aside. For a moment, I was sure I could see her cheeks and neck turning green. I literally thought that was just an expression. She put her hand over her mouth, shifting her weight around in her chair as best she could.

"Reprocessed starch, uh, artificial veggies and protein soup. It's ... actually really filling, I managed to nick some of Mom's spices before I ran away, so, when I douse them in those it almost starts to taste like food."

I pursed my lips.

"Sarah, one of our first non-nerd related conversations was about you blasting a restaurant for having food that had been refrigerated improperly. You're a total foodie!"

"I know." She let herself look miserable for the first time ever. She'd looked sad before—both when we'd been chatting in orbit and when I'd been at the farm. But this was the first time she let loose with *everything*. Her eyes screwed up and she sagged her head forward, putting her heads in her hands. "I could take it if the food wasn't awful! I could take the pollution and the gangers who keep trying to sell me slice and crack and retro-AIDS. I could take the gross freaking job and the crappy bay, the shitty bed, and the cramped, awful elevator. I could … I could even take not being able to fall asleep next to you, but I c-can't take the food. How pathetic is that? How …" She trailed off into a series of Québécois French that sounded more incendiary than most banned munitions. "I'm sorry, Dru, I—"

"You're used to it." I grinned, slightly. "And we're more used to this." I gestured to the space between us, encompassing the foot or so between my wallpaper and the bed, and also the kilometer and then some of cabling and wire that connected wallpaper to screen. "But you've gone hungry how many days in your life?"

"Once …" she admitted. "When I was six and got lost in the woods."

I blinked. She'd never told me this story. And …

"You were six years old when you got the war-pox, weren't you?" I asked.

She shook her head. "It wasn't because I was lost," she said, smiling. "After my mom found me, she scolded me, and almost didn't let me go on vacation with her and Dad. I caught it at the airport. Bumped into a guy who was infected and didn't know it, I think the scanners missed him." She shrugged. "Bioscanners mess up sometimes. I got off better than half a dozen other people at the airport."

I nodded.

"But still, even the hospital had good food," she said, grinning weakly.

I shifted, getting off the bed, waking over to the wallpaper. I pressed my cheek against it, eyes closed. The quantum-dot camera/projectors that made up a wallpaper could scan at this range and project. I didn't know if the screen showed anything but a vague blur, but my voice still came through.

"I love you. And And I'll give you something tasty to eat when you—"

Sarah's giggly, snotty snort—which sounded as grotesque as it was absolutely adorable and heart melting—cut me off. She put her hand on the screen. I put my hand on hers and felt the faint buzz of touching a live feed.

We didn't need words after that.

Chapter 13: The Incident

5/22/2068

Chinese-American Alliance, China, Xin-Shanghai

T-Minus L-Day: 88

When I woke up the next morning, after fitful dreams and concerns about Sarah's well-being, I thought a seal-alarm was going off. I rolled out of bed, scrambling around for a mask to cover my mouth and protect me from sudden decompression. But then, with a flush and a cough, I realized that I was on the ground, in Shanghai, and that the hotel room I was in had an open window that looked out on the vast sweep of the mega-city. So, even if I had a breather …

I shook my head. The alarm was a call coming through the wallpaper.

I got dressed in my skinclothes as quick as I could, brushed my slowly growing hair—I really needed to get myself another hair-shot to get it under control—and answered the wall with a curt, "Yes?"

The wallpaper projected a slightly grainy holographic image, showing that whoever was calling had access to one of those clunky 3D booths. Those things had gone out of fashion a few years ago, when wallpaper become cheaper. But still, I sent a quick hand gesture to the wallpaper, to indicate I'd prefer a 2D image. The man—who had been really getting close to my personal virtual space snapped against the wall and looked like he was just in a camera phone.

He was a middle-aged man with slightly swarthy skin and straw blond hair. The left side of his face looked like it had been hit by a mid-powered laser weapon and hadn't been fixed properly by surgery or gene-grafted skin. Instead, he had some kind of synthetic grafted over the bone and skin, giving his cheek a kind of cross-hatched gridwork that flexed and moved as he spoke. His left nostril had been cut open and reshaped to give him clearer air passages and his upper lip had a serious cleft, like an upside-down V, exposing his teeth.

It was ...

Really grotesque.

It was also a face I'd seen exactly once before and it had given me nightmares almost four years ago, when Sarah and I had been sharing informational facts about our families.

"Hey Mr. Cayer ..." I said, trying to not stare.

"H-H ... He ... Hello D ... D ... Dru," he said, stammering. I didn't know if the stammer was because of what had happened to him during the Slump—he'd been outside of Los Angeles and had been evacuated to Salt Lake City literally the day before the transhumans tried to memebomb it, so I was pretty sure he blew my "woe is me, how unlucky can I get?" quotient out of the water.

I wasn't jealous in the slightest.

"Uh, are you calling to ask me about Sarah?"

He nodded.

I sighed, rubbing my face—which had the useful side effect of letting me not look at Mr. Cayer. "Well, um ..." I rattled off everything that Sarah had told me, figuring that Mr. Cayer deserved to know what Sarah thought, not just what Mrs. Cayer thought Sarah thought Mr. Cayer should know. Yeah, that made sense.

He listened silently, and since I was unable to keep my hands over my face the whole time, I had to look at his face. And, really, I was shocked at how much emotion he managed to get into his eyes without moving the rest of his face. They were the most adorable puppy-dog eyes that I'd ever seen, and focusing on them made everything else seem to shrink. They were hopeful, then worried, then glimmered sadly.

"I … I … I …" he stammered. "I w … wu … wo … worried this w … was … g …" He closed his eyes.

I bit my lip. "Uh, Mr. Cayer, if it makes you feel more comfortable, I can … we can go to a text box." I grinned, weakly. "Does your I/O device have a keyboard, haptic or otherwise?"

He nodded.

"Let's do that," I said.

I really, really hoped he didn't think I was just doing this to get away from looking at him. I was. But either way, the screen winked off and I spent a few nervous minutes working up a holographic keyboard with the wallpaper. As I handled that, I used my verbal commands to try and call Sarah, but she was already out.

I got the text box up just as Jillian started knocking.

"Hey! Dru! Are you awake yet, you lazy no-good excuse for a sergeant?"

M.Cayer: *I was worried this was going to happen. Susan can be very …*

He trailed off as I called back at the door, "I'm not a sergeant anymore."

"Pff, that's just some organizational screwing around and you know it. Come on, open up, we can get some breakfast before the court starts up."

"Just a second."

M.Cayer: *I think that Sarah needs to do this. She needs to find her own independence. I hope that Susan can figure this out. I will go to her, as soon as I can. Thank you, though, for telling me that Sarah is doing—if not well—then a-okay. I will deposit three thousand credits in your account, if you will let me. Use them on Sarah, if you can. If not, then save them.*

I blinked. Three thousand credits wasn't anything to sneeze at. It wouldn't get me one of those sun-bathing castles that the megarich could build on the roof of Xin-Shanghai, but it almost doubled my checking account.

D.Zhao: *Thank you. I will take care of Sarah, even if she'll stab me in the throat if I ever say that to her face.*

M.Cayer: *She is very like her mother. Don't tell her I said that. :)*

The smiley made me queasy, because I was thinking of him smiling. I shook my head, trying to stop being so-

"This is way longer than a second, so you know."

D.Zhao: *I have to go, Mr. Cayer. I will tell Sarah about you calling, k?*

M.Cayer: *K.*

>+<

Jillian and I got out of the vertical tram and carefully picked our way through the throngs. "I'm *starving*," Jillian groaned. "Let's get something quick."

"I think we shouldn't eat—" I started.

"What are you, a nutrient AI?" Jillian asked.

We both paused in shared recollection of those evil devils. If Satan and the million and one screaming damned souls of the ten thousand hells of China could be combined into a single artificial intelligence, it'd be ... well, okay, it'd be Scribe—the punishment AI for basic training—but the nutrient AIs would be one step below him. I shook my head.

"No, we *should* eat. Just, you know, not until eleven hundred. That's only twenty, thirty minutes off, and that's when Sarah gets a break-shift. I figure, we ambush her down by her work-site and drag her to a V-tram and get food together?"

Jillian pursed her lips. "Think we can afford a V-tram?"

I nodded. "Sure, Sarah's dad dropped three kilocredits into my bank account this morning."

Jillian turned to face me as we stopped to let what seemed like an endless stream of crèche-going school kids walk past, all in identical uniforms. Other people waited around us—most of them dressed in the shabby coveralls that typified this level of Xin-Shanghai for some unknown reason.

"Sarah has a dad?"

"... yeah."

"I ..." Jillian blinked. "I guess I never asked. Or, well, I figured he was dead or divorced or something."

I shook my head. "Want to hear the nitty-gritties while we head down?"

The school kids finished filing past, letting the through-traffic start up again. Jillian nodded.

"From what Sarah told me, he was American, and her mom was French-Canadian. Because back then, there was a French-Canada instead of the R.O.Q." I shrugged. "They didn't actually meet until after the Slump was partway through, when she'd been in the Québécois militia for a few years and he'd ..." I bit my lip, chewing on my canker sore as I tried to think of just how to put this into words.

"What?"

"He was in Los Angeles." I figured bluntness would be good enough. We stepped from the main corridor to a vertical tram waiting station. We didn't have long to wait, as the V-Tram whirred down from a higher level, then squealed to a stop, opening up its door as escalators descended from the bits of the tram you couldn't just walk into. People filed on, and as they did so, RFID scanners dinged their personal electronics and subtracted funds. Those who tried to tram-hop with jammers or having non-electronic clothes were detected by the biometrics.

I saw two of them—punkish, pink-haired boys with loads of studs on their faces—try and hop over the line. A saucer-sized drone detached from the wall, blurring the air with its ionic thrust, an under slung double-barreled taser on its belly. It flew to where the two boys were trying to find cover—the crowd hurried away from the two of them—and unloaded taser darts by the barrel full into their chests. They writhed on the ground till transport security dragged them off, whacking them a few times good with truncheons.

Jillian and I didn't bat an eye. Something about bringing up the world's biggest Singularity Scare since Singularity City itself made everything else seem 'not that bad'.

"Jesus."

Jillian paused, then seemed to decide that that wasn't enough.

"Jesus, Mary, and Joseph."

She paused again, then added a few dozen more names from every faith that the Alliance boasted to the list as the V-tram started rumbling down. Out of the corner of my eyes, I saw two women in shabby coveralls with ball-caps high fiving one another, a small boxy shape attached to both of their hips. Their jammers had actually worked ...

"How bad is it?" Jillian asked.

I put my hand over my right cheek. "All of this? FUBAR."

She whistled. "And they can't fix it?"

"I figure, when someone gets hit by a freaking ..." I glanced around, then whispered. "A freaking nanophage, the doctors don't want to touch it. Just in case."

"So, that's why he doesn't hang around ..." Jillian frowned. "How the hell did he get Sarah's mom knocked up if they're that worried about him?"

"Well, remember, this was before the proper Singularity Scare. It was before the first transies started going *completely* psycho, before the nanophages spread out of Los Angeles. Hell, they barely understood what *happened* to Los Angeles, let alone how dangerous it could be. So, he had a few months of peace and quiet before the Scare happened and the crackdowns started." I shrugged. "Why didn't you ever ask Sarah this?"

Jillian shrugged. "I figured that, since there weren't any pictures of him, it would be ..."

The V-tram shuddered as it came to the next level down. We waited, patiently, for the next set to leave.

"Still, at least he has money to burn."

"Yeah, he remote organizes and directs the major salvage operations in Delta City." I grinned. "Sarah says he still sends her salvaged bits and pieces that he fixes up. They all have to be metal so they can be disinfected."

"Huh."

We watched the vertical cityscape rush past—most of it was an insane confusion of tube-wall and the occasional opening into complex honeycombs of metal and steel and carbon composite—and Jillian asked the question I really didn't want to answer.

"So, uh, what if we're late to the trial? I mean, they said be there at oh-one hundred, and it's almost eleven hundred, and this thing isn't the fastest mode of transport in the city."

I shrugged. "You know, I know there are pretty serious repercussions if we don't show up ... but I don't give *gǒushǐ duī.*"

She smirked. "And you think if we screw things up, we might get kicked out of the Marines? Because I'm pretty sure that won't happen."

"Well, maybe. But it also has to do with something that happened last night." The V-Tram shuddered to a stop at the right level and we stepped off. "I was talking to Sarah, and I realized that she basically got herself away from her parents and into a new job in record time. She lost herself in a city of a half a billion people, that was the trick." I grinned. "If they get too mad, why don't we get ourselves lost too?"

Jillian shrugged. "Better than your PTSD idea."

I frowned.

Sarah's work level wasn't exactly a pretty place. It was near the bottom of the arcologies, where the urbanation between them was actually built onto and into the ground. The sewage system of the old city had been expanded and even turned into hyper-cheap apartment blocks, then expanded again. There wasn't much actual dirt down here, just more steel, more carbon composites, more metal. More electric lights. More impossible, desperate humanity.

The more I looked around, the more gut-punch sick I felt. People down here wore threadbare outfits that barely looked like they would hold together to the end of the hour, let alone last them for a long time. The lighting flickered every other corridor, and there were half-open doors, whose hydraulic and pneumatic systems had long since failed, the rooms beyond darkened, empty skeletons ... full of dark, empty skeletons. Not literal skeletons, but the people who watched us as we walked past were dead in everything but the condition.

Graffiti tags sprouted on the walls, and Sarah's workplace entrance was guarded by two goons—as in, actual goons who were clearly a private security foundation and not any form of municipal police force—with heavy armor and riot shotguns in their hands. I really hoped they were loaded with smart beanbags and gas, not flechettes. But you never could tell ...

"Are you sure this was a good idea?" Jillian whispered as the goons eyed us—though that was a bit hard to tell, their heavy armor included face concealing helmets.

"Nope."

What had been just a nice, romantic idea was rapidly turning into a movement into hostile country. Then a buzzing klaxon sounded. The door opened and a streamer of slightly less skinny, bedraggled workers came out, still wearing huge, thick, rubberized gloves on their hands. Most of them had just shaved themselves bald, while more than a few had their hair cut short, and the remainder had long hair tied and pushed under hairnet covers.

In the middle of the streamer—which broke off beyond where we waited into dozens of smaller groups, but no group was smaller than four people—was a single girl in a wheelchair.

It wasn't Sarah.

Then, pushing around two other people to join the girl in the wheelchair, was Sarah. She managed a laugh, speaking to the other girl in the *other* wheelchair.

"Sarah!" I shouted.

Sarah snapped her head around. She gaped, wheeling over to me. Then, she punched me in the thigh, laughing. "Dru! How ... the ... flying ..." she spluttered.

I knelt down, grinning and catching her cheeks in my hands, feeling the delirious blaze of joy I had expected. I ignored the smells clinging to her and kissed her. She pushed me back—or tried to—and kept kissing me at the same time. It seemed like a cross purpose to me, but what did I know?

She jerked her head back, gasping softly. "I smell awful."

"I know."

I kissed her again. Harder this time.

She jerked her head back, again. "I am starving."

"I know!" I grinned, but this time didn't kiss her. I stood, then gestured to Jillian. "We're going to take you to a restaurant."

Sarah opened her mouth, closed it, then said, stiffly. "I can't afford that."

"Sarah …" I knelt down again, my knees creaking slightly in the Earth gravity that still felt just a little bit too heavy sometimes. "You are an outstanding, amazing, powerful *woman* who has done braver shit than I ever will. I mean, I'd rather go to war than face your Mom down, and you didn't just face her down, you went off and did your own thing. And you're surviving. But!"

I held up one finger.

"That doesn't mean I can't want to buy you awesome things. And … if … we ever …" I coughed. "If we ever get married—"

Sarah's eyes widened.

"If!" I said, hurriedly. "I s-said IF!"

Sarah's eyes narrowed. "You know qualifying it *that* much isn't that flattering, goof." Her smile and her tone kept the words from being accusatory.

I coughed again, which I actually needed down here. "If we ever get married, we'll be sharing our money anyway, so you might as well get a little bit used to me paying for *some* things, eh? Now, come on."

I stood and let her push herself down the corridor. Jillian, though, was keeping her eyes up. She'd noticed that the other wheelchair girl had gone on, because I was startled when I didn't see her.

"Who was the wheelchair girl? The other one?" Jillian asked.

"Her name is Niho and she's a fresh worker like me. Of course, she didn't lose her spinal function because of the warpox like me, she … she got shot in a ganger fight." Sarah gulped. "A-and now that you've offered to pay me to take me to a restaurant, maybe we can go somewhere where the police actually patrol?"

We didn't laugh, even if Sarah managed to turn the last half of the sentence into something that sounded a little bit like a joke.

The V-tram let us off and we found a restaurant that would suit Sarah. I blew a slightly embarrassingly large amount of my paycheck on pampering Sarah, but the results were worth it: food that did two things that completely blew me away. One, it actually tasted like fresh seafood from the Hub, and two, let left me feeling incredibly—and I do mean incredibly—full.

Nutrient AIs never let you feel full. The eggheads who built the awful things claimed that that was a psychological and sociological quirk, unique to a small percentage of the population.

But we'd expect *them* to claim that.

I sighed and leaned against Sarah, closing my eyes as I let myself lounge and fill out as much of the curved bench that we shared. Sarah leaned against me and closed her eyes.

"I think I can face the rest of the day ..." she murmured.

"Good."

Jillian sighed. "I don't mean to break up the little romantic interlude here, but I did kind of sort of have this ulterior motive for getting all three of us in the same room."

I opened one food-laden eyelid.

"What?"

"Sarah, did you bring a weapon with you to Shanghai?" Jillian asked.

Sarah nodded. "Yeah. Legally. The Second Ratification of the Second Amendment applies here. Actually, the guns were the easy part, one of Mom's neighbors is a serious gun-nut and he built me two pistols as a favor. He called it his little contribution to my private revolution or something crazy like that."

Jillian nodded. "How much ammo do you got for them?"

"Uh, four magazines each, all non-lethal. Why?" Sarah looked concerned.

Jillian breathed in, then breathed out. "Dru, permission to speak freely about K?"

I glanced around the room we were in. The restaurant tried to ape an old cowboy saloon sort of place, but the wood was obviously fake and could easily be hiding any number of surveillance tools.

I sighed. "Granted."

Jillian laid it out, quite a bit faster and more efficiently than I could.

"And," she started to wrap up. "One of K's less cryptic warnings was that we should be armed all the time."

I only faintly remembered that.

"You don't think something is going to happen, do you?" Sarah asked. "We're in the middle of CAA territory. And ... well, you guys can't be watched *that* closely because they let you head down into dross-hound territory, but still, you guys spend your time at the courthouse, right?"

I nodded. "And the courthouse is built like a freaking battle onion."

Jillian mouthed the words 'battle onion' like she couldn't believe I had actually said them. She shook her head.

"I don't really want to put my life on the line without at least having something ..."

I sighed. "Well, since we can't really *get* something, we might as well get used to it."

Sarah leaned in on the conversation. "Why don't you tell someone? Like, you don't have to mention the whole—" Her voice dipped in volume, becoming a soft whisper, as if that would help. "—secret messages sent by an unknown conspirator. But you can still say you have some concerns about base security. I mean, even if they don't listen to you, at least you'll have done *something*."

I nodded, patting her belly under the table. She grinned at me.

Jillian frowned. 'There's just one problem with that. If we cry wolf, they might ask why we thought something was wrong in the first place. Then they'll ask us where we got our information. Then, if they haven't already gotten suspicious enough, they'll investigate all the surveillance they have on us with a fine-toothed comb and ... while I would love to mock our government for incompetence, I don't think we're the kind of superspy badasses who could get away from the panopticon enough to be scot-free."

"Doesn't that mean you should be safe, then? If they can spy on all of us *that* much ..." Sarah said. "They'll just spot the bad guys you're worried about. Right?"

Jillian laughed. "Oh, hell no. The global surveillance state isn't about security, it's about control. The people you're thinking about, Sarah, the ones we want them to watch aren't in the cities or the airports, they're out in the wilderness, the same way every terror organization ever has been ever since the end of the 20th century. Spider-holes and darknets."

"A blind spot," I said. "You could have just said they had a blind spot, Jillian."

"Hey, sure, I could. But I like being the center of attention," Jillian said, grinning. "Now—" Sarah cut her off with a yelp.

"*Tabarnak!*" Sarah pushed herself away from the table. "I'm going to be late, see, this is what your windy conversation does to a working woman."

Jillian looked apologetic.

>+<

As the V-Tram rode up towards the court-house level, I checked my sleeve. A message had come in from the administration of the trial that security would be going up two levels—so from passive to active to invasive scans.

"I bet they're bringing in Lau."

I looked at Jillian. She had just looked up from her glowing sleeve as well.

"Tā māde," I muttered.

"Why *tā māde?*"

"I don't want to have to look at him again ..." I said, shaking my head. "Especially knowing what he told you to do."

Jillian smiled. "Well, think of it this way. If this trial goes the right way, he'll be going into a deep, dark hole for a long long time."

I frowned. That didn't make me feel any better. In fact, I realized, it made me feel worse. Lau had had his orders, and the more I stayed in Shanghai—with its towering castles overhead and its crushing slums far below—the more I realized that the Alliance had enough rotten parts that even one man couldn't ...

Wait.

Wait. That little voice in the back of my head spoke up. It was a voice that was oddly smug, and I realized why it was smug.

The whole weight of the chain of command was on your back, telling you to do what you know, what we both know, was wrong.

I hadn't bent.

Tears stung the corners of my eyes as the V-tram came to a stop and the doors opened. I could pretend it was from the smog that seemed to be blowing thick through this part of the city. I could pretend it was from the sudden temperature shift as chilly air outside mixed with the warmer air inside. But that would be a great big whumping lie.

That little voice shut the hell up, because my decision in space had butchered every single person under my command—David, Chuck, Jason, everyone. They were all dead. Maybe I deserved the accolades—someone had mentioned a Star of Valor for me, though I hadn't heard of any actual ceremonies being set up—but I sure as hell didn't deserve a chance to be smug.

Jillian led the way, walking with brisk confidence, towards the courthouse entrance we were using today. The structure rose overhead like a pillar of strength amidst the co-urbanation, its austere decorations beating back the neon and holographic sign-work that surrounded it through sheer, bloody minded monolithicness. Every other building was shared with dozens if not hundreds of offices, homes, cookeries and who knows what else, but the courthouse was a single thing: a symbol of the Alliance's legal might. A few thousand years of legalistic Chinese tradition.

We weren't about to forget that, looking at it.

Level Three security stopped us cold dead. Rather than just waking past nearly invisible seams in the corridors, there were drones actively whirring around: Everything from a disk drone the size of someone's face which swooped down to do retinal scans to at least two hulking, four-legged riot-control drones that looked like oversized headless dogs, armor plated and ... weirdly cute, when they looked right at you. Their optical scanners made faces, like this.

o____o

But even that was ruined when we noticed the pods of 60mm smoke grenades mounted on the back, or the fact that each one had a small, snub-nosed machine gun slung under one belly, which could track around to shoot at pretty much anything in a hundred, hundred fifty-degree arc. I assumed it was loaded with rubber bullets ...

I hoped it was loaded with rubber bullets.

But those two hulkers weren't even the main guards. There were humans, three of them at our security checkpoint. Two of them wore body armor and had holstered pistols, while the third had a complex toolkit that he used on both of us in turn. The first tool looked like a large brush, though the tips glowed.

"What is this?" Jillian asked as the brush slipped along her sleeve, then between her fingers.

"Microbug sniffer," he said. "Also doubles as an EM detection and snooper kit, though it works best in microgravity."

"Really?" I asked.

"Yeah!" He sounded weirdly excited about the chance to talk about his gear. I was starting to regret asking him when he started on me, because by then he had gone through all the minute differences between each spool-line and EM sniffer and snooper and buzzer and every other bit of infosec machinery he had in his toolkit. The two guards were starting to look like they were a combination of annoyed and fearful that their security technician was going to start revealing state secrets or something when he wrapped up his spiel with a: "And can you believe, this is all bought in bulk from civilian retailers? Yeah, we don't even get fancy military tech. It's amazing how far and how fast this stuff has gone from being top of the line to being cheap in bulk ..."

"Fascinating." Jillian spoke the words through clenched teeth.

The tech opened his mouth to start enumerating the ways it was even more fascinating than we could possibly imagine.

A loud hissing snake-noise broke into the world, like something you'd hear while playing a really immersive fantasy MUD. I threw myself to the ground and my eyes blurred. My skin tingled and I started to spasm, my muscles twitching and convulsing.

For a few horrible seconds, I was absolutely sure I was going to die. My heart beat a thousand times too fast, my lungs couldn't draw in, and wracking pains shot through me as I twitched and flapped around like a fish yanked out of the water. My eyes were completely whited out now and I could only hear chaos.

Another hiss THUMP!

A shout of mangled Cantonese—not Mandarin—and then another hiss THUMP!

Groaning. No, screaming, screaming that came in between hacks and coughs.

"I can't feel my legs!"

The tech!

I managed to get my arms under me and grabbed the front of my shirt, dragging it over my face. I could see now, blinking my eyes to clear the tears and the haze out of it. Through the shirt's fabric, I saw dark shapes.

The tech, laying on his belly. Jillian, twitching. My own leg kicked and almost sent me flying forward to smash into the deck. My whole body writhed and squirmed, my muscles triggering and spasming and *twitching*. Twitching, twitching, twitching.

I heard footsteps and a language so out of place that it didn't even register as words until the bag went over my head.

Spanish!

Then the bag was over my head. It deadened sound and sight, the seal closing around my throat with a whirr, the entire thing becoming plumped out as fresh air was filtered in through the collar, a small motor built into the thing keeping my atmosphere from clogging with CO_2. I breathed in the air as a hand grabbed me roughly by the collar and shoved me forward.

I stumbled and felt the twitching subsiding. We were out of the gas?

That had been riot suppression gas, had to be. What was-

"I can't ... I can't feel my legs."

The tech sounded more desperate. I heard a quick exchange of Spanish, most of the words going straight over my head. It truncated with the tech screaming something in Cantonese—he understood something I didn't.

A gunshot made me fall to the ground all over again. The tech wasn't begging anymore.

Two more gunshots rang out and then a foot kicked me in the gut. If I hadn't had this godsdamned bag over my head, I could have done something about it, rolled with the impact. As it was, I curled up and bit down hard on my teeth, eyes closed. *I will not throw up, I will not throw up.* Another kick.

"Get up! Get up, *puta!*" The voice spoke in accented English.

A hand grabbed me by the collar and shoved me forward. Other sounds became clear to me.

Alarms.

Screams.

Gunshots.

And, underneath it all, a series of rattling thumps. As if every single door in the entire place was slamming shut.

A command was given. I was pushed off to the side. And, from the sound of cussing and questions, I could tell that Jillian was being pushed off to the side too. I felt my shoulder hit something very similar to a doorway. Then, wham! My back was against a wall.

A very gun-like barrel pressed against my chest. I stayed perfectly, completely still. With the gun against my chest, I heard a muffled order.

"Hands behind your back! Turn around!"

I turned. Zip-cuffs slapped onto my wrists and pulled themselves taut.

A finger pressed the collar and the black fabric shimmered, then became clear. Sound came back, louder than the distant, muffled noises I had been hearing before. We were in what looked like an office, though whoever normally worked here had run as fast as they could when the alarms started. I wondered, very academically, how far he'd gotten.

The people—the person—who had escorted us here looked like a normal, every-day technician, wearing a jumpsuit and work vest, studded with tools. But some of those tools were missing. It took a moment—a twisting of my perception—to see that they'd been fitted together into a sleek, one handed sub-machine gun, which itself had been stuck to a curved bracing, so that it could be used as a longarm with some chance of actually hitting a target. Slap some rifled bullets of the right make into that, and it could be as accurate or as spraying as you wanted, for the situation.

At this range, it didn't matter which way it was formatted.

At this range, Jillian and I were one wrong step from becoming so much carni-meat. Just, instead of being a clean formation of proteins and false-fat, we'd be twitching, shuddering piles of skin and bone and pulsing organs. The thought kept me very very still, looking at the two terrorists.

Wait, hadn't there just been *one*? I blinked, but no, there were definitely two.

Their faces, their gender, their eyes, everything that made them a human being, was hidden. Hidden by a thick, rubberized gas mask—they put me in mind of a soldier in an ancient war—it was impossible to tell just who was holding us at gunpoint.

"Names, ranks, ID numbers!"

I glanced at Jillian.

"We're not at liberty to reveal that—"

"You see a uniform on me, chink?" The man—it sounded like a man behind the mask. "Answer, or we'll leave you both face down in this room."

I closed my eyes. "Drusilla Zhao, Corporal ..." I rattled off my pay number. Jillian did the same.

The man paused, as if considering. I noticed his throat—one of the few exposed things on him—twitched and jerked, as if he was talking or gulping, but he wasn't making any noise.

"All right," he said, voice rough. He pushed his gun against my chest.

Jillian shot me a look. If her hands had been free—I saw that she was bound like I was— and if we weren't bagged and if ...

If if if. If I had been in charge of things, I'd just have rather not be captured at all. But since none of those ifs were true, we let him polarize our bags. When we got hustled out of the room, it was to the sound of the alarms shutting down, leaving only the distant sound of the city ... and underneath it, the occasional staccato burst of gunfire, which always seemed to coincide with a scream.

Then silence.

Chapter 14: Reporter

5/22/2068 (01:12)

Chinese-American Alliance, China, Xin-Shanghai

~~T-Minus L-Day: 88~~ REINITIALIZING

TANGOS: Unknown (Tracing netwar attack)

Response Time: 220 seconds

When we got the bags off our heads again, we were already on our knees. The zip-cuffs didn't come off, so the whole thing could have been a wee bit more comfortable.

I blinked.

Wee bit more comfortable?

That was what I was worrying about?

Well, yes and no. I was thinking of maybe fifteen thousand things every second, every heart beat bringing in a series of new ideas and concerns. The problem was all these new ideas and concerns were all half formed gasps of ideas which immediately floated away the instant I blinked. The only thing that remained stable, moment to moment, was the ache in my shoulders from my posture.

Well, I think their guns—

But they have net—
Drone had to be subverted—
The police will be soon—

I shook my head. The room Jillian and I had been debagged into was another office, but this place hadn't just been abandoned, it had been fought over. A series of bullet holes stitched through the wallpaper, leaving behind a series of weird holographic artifacts as the material tried to work around the lead that had punched through it. Blood flecked the wall and stained the floor, like someone had been dragged out. There was only one other prisoner in the room: an elf-thin, ethereally beautiful woman from Africa, I could tell, thanks to her pitch-black skin, the cut of her hair—short cornrows and dreadlocks—and the cut of her clothes, which was a futurist blend of African and Chinese styles.

"Jillian Zhang," Jillian spoke up.

The woman—who looked remarkably calm—nodded. "Affanii Wanaga."

"Drusilla Zhao."

Affanii Wanaga smiled, weakly. "You can call me AF. If you prefer."

Her English was better than most of the people I'd met in Shanghai—at least, if they were trying to make themselves understood beyond the local dialect. I smiled back at her.

"So, uh, did they leave any bugs?"

She shrugged, looking at Jillian. "They did destroy my equipment."

"Legal expert?" Jillian asked.

"Reporter."

"UAB?" I guessed. It was an easy guess, because there were only so many African broadcasting organization that sent reporters to other countries. As far as I knew, there could be anywhere from one to a billion other local African news channels and feeds, but only one of them actually got out to the rest of the world and that was United African Broadcasting.

She nodded.

"So ..." Jillian hung her head forward, sighing. "Sit here and wait it out or try to escape?"

She was asking me, but AF answered first. "The second."

I looked at her, startled.

AF saw my look and smiled. "If we simply let terrorists get away with everything, they win. I have been in two hostage situations before, and both times trying to escape almost killed me ... but staying almost killed others." She shrugged.

"Well, that's just wonderful. Got any sage wisdom?" I asked, looking left, then right, then up and down. There was nothing in the room that leaped out to me as being a possible escape help. The terrorists, for some ungodly reason, hadn't left us with cutting tools or guns or anything useful like that.

"I do have a sense for sieges ..." She frowned. "I'd wager they are not here for a siege."

"What gave it away?" Jillian asked, her voice oddly pinched and groaning. I blinked, looking at her. She had rolled onto her back and was contorting her body, eyes closed, teeth straining as she tugged her shoulders almost out of their sockets to get her ankles between her hands. She rolled back around, gasping in pain ... but her hands were in front of her. The zip-cuffs started to flash and blink.

"*Tā māde!*" she swore, looking around. "Dru, throw yourself flat at the door!"

I nodded, and then used my thighs and knees to throw myself, belly flat, right in front of the door. Jillian stood and AF—bless her soul—rolled back so that she was hiding behind the legs of the desk.

The door opened. I buried my face against the ground, just in case.

A foot slammed into me, right at tit-height (ow) and then a body pitched over me, a pair of shins cracking into my shoulder blades and the curve of my back. Someone shouted—loudly—but then Jillian was on them.

"HANDS UP!"

I rolled onto my belly, drawing up a leg. I kicked at the man in the doorway—the one who had moved to cover their buddy. He turned at the last second, my heel thudding against his thigh instead of into his groin.

Jillian, though, had gotten her zip-cuffs to spread just enough to let her slide the connection cable that bound her wrists around the tripped man's throat, working it up under his gas mask.

She rolled around so that he was between her and the man with the gun. She shouted.

"Drop it or I garrote your friend!"

She used pure English, and I was worried that the guy wouldn't understand her. But he understood ... understood enough to swing his gun to bear. I kicked the barrel into the air as it went off, turning the ceiling into so much confetti. I braced a shoulder against the doorway, rolled myself up, cocked my leg back and kicked as hard as I could, aiming for his gut.

He had body armor, it took most of the force and left my ankle feeling numb and tingly. It still staggered him backwards. I scooted forward, ungainly, and took advantage of the fact that I had pretty good support down here, even if my arms were a dead-weight behind my back. I got my legs between his and he went down, shoulder hitting the ground. I got my foot against his throat and pushed him. He rolled, then I caught him.

I pushed. He kicked, struggled, but by then I'd managed to rear up, my core burning as I took advantage of every bit of my cardio and muscle building. The extra gravity helped as I went from foot to the full point of my knee, pressed against his throat. Just where Cao Cao had showed us to put it.

The dude's gas mask had gone askew, and I couldn't see his eyes.

It made it way easier.

His kicking stopped.

I kept on him for another few seconds. Then a few seconds more.

Then, Jillian snapped me out of my focus.

"Dru!"

I slid off the corpse, standing. Jillian managed to get her make-shift garrote off the man's throat. I winced. Blood was way messier in orbit, but that didn't make it the best thing to look at down here. The thin wire, driven with enough force, had almost cut down to his spine, only stopped because Jillian wasn't *that* strong. She knelt beside his corpse, feeling around with her hand at his belt.

"Are you two okay?" AF poked her head out from behind the desk.

Jillian stood, holding a smooth, egg-shaped object in her hand. She squeezed and a buzzing blade snapped out of the front. I turned my back to her, heart pounding. The zip cuffs sliced with a faint snapping noise. First thing I did was grab the gun on the ground —a modified hunting shotgun with a tube shaped magazine built into it by some backyard blacktech. It was heavy, like a club.

I crouched by the door, covering the left quadrant of the corridor with the barrel, keeping up trigger discipline.

"Yeah," Jillian said, before shoving the handle of her blade in her teeth. She bit down, then carefully worked her zip-cuffs against the edge of the knife. They came free and she grabbed the knife from her teeth.

"They ... really train you well ..." AF sounded a bit dazed as Jillian cut her free. I, meanwhile, had kept my eyes on the hallway, sparing only momentary glances back, so I caught everything in stuttering flashes, everything else filled in through inference and clues.

"Yeah, well, we're supposed to kill people for a living." Jillian pocketed the knife. "Anything out there, Corp?"

"Nada ..." I said, noticing the word with a faint twinge of irony. I shook my head. "Hearing a thumping, no alarms ..."

"I got an SMG, two magazines, another drum, rolling it."

I felt the drum-magazine for my shotgun roll against one of my feet. I grabbed it with one hand, not taking my eyes off the corridor.

"There's LCW harness on each of 'em and gas-masks, looks like full chemical/bio warfare defense kit, though there's nothing for contact, *tā māde* ... aha!" Jillian sounded pleased. "Three spare hypos with ... *tā māde*, you know what drexicolin does?"

I shook my head.

"I know!" AF said. "I did a story on it; it's a suppressor of Twitch, the riot gas that the Alliance uses."

"How long does it last?"

"I ... uh ..." AF trailed off.

"Then we'll inject if they gas us," Jillian announced. I didn't have much time to actually move my mouth, but that sounded about right.

Jillian moved around a bit more, then whacked my shoulder. I glanced at her and saw she was wearing the LCW harness—a combination of carbon fiber weave anti-projectile plates and a metric ton of pouches, pockets and hooks for all sorts of combat minutia—and holding the terrorist's SMG at her shoulder, covering the same corridor I had been covering.

I dragged the other terrorist into the room and started getting his harness off. It fit pretty good, though I had to adjust it for my taller, skinnier form. I got my own collection of hypos, then paused, my hand resting on the nozzle-nose of his gas mask. If I pulled it off, I'd be looking into the face of the man I'd ...

I took it off and looked aside, reaching out to where his eyes would be. I pushed one eyelid down with a finger, but the other finger rasped against something hard and lurchingly unfamiliar.

I jerked my hand away and looked back.

"Jesus, Gods and every lazy-ass Bodhisattva!" I whispered. "Jillian!"

Jillian glanced back, looked at the corridor. She seemed to think it would be clear a bit longer, because she stood and came back to me. She whistled.

The man was a transie—a transhuman. His left eye had been replaced by a tube of metal and glowing fiberoptics. I didn't know how long it would work off internal batteries or if that was from burning some still active biochemistry in a warm but dead body. There were other signs of implants, most of them around the back of his neck, on his bald scalp ...

"Shit. Shit shit shit shit shit shit shit shit." Jillian kicked his corpse. "We're in it. We're deep in it."

"Maybe, uh, maybe I will be staying here," AF said, weakly. I looked at her and she sobered as I realized she had been trying to make a joke.

"That's why they're shooting anyone they want ..." I said.

Jillian looked at me. Her eyes were unreadable. Her expression set. I felt defensive.

"Well, they're transies, so—"

"Uh, Dru, you don't have to be special to shoot prisoners in cold blood." Jillian looked down at the corpse. "This just means that we need to get moving now. AF, you stick between Dru and me and if bullets start flying, then—"

"I get down. I understand this. I've done this before."

"Good." Jillian looked back at the door.

I held up a hand, looking at Jillian. That hand gesture—we'd learned them in Basic, but hadn't gotten many chances to use them (and now, now I felt an obscure whiff of gratitude towards the bloody-minded tradition that had gotten us to go through all the ground-marine shit that didn't make a damn lick of sense in space)—indicated that everyone should shut up and listen.

Thump. Thump. Thump.

"*Tā made*, move," I said, realizing what it was. "Jillian, let's head further in the building."

She didn't ask questions—she was still a good Marine—but AF did blurt it out. "In? Not to the exits?"

"They have command and control on the drones," I said, moving out and covering the corridor in the direction of the thumps.

And, just as I expected, the dog-like riot drone waddled in. Jillian slid her gas mask on and dragged AF along. I took aim and tugged back on the trigger, bracing myself for a kick.

I wasn't ready. The shotgun had a kick like a genetically engineered mule—something Sarah had demonstrated on a plank of wood before she let me near one. The spray of pellets or whatever the thing fired hit the side of the drone, making a flurry of discolored marks across the drone's armor, but otherwise doing absolutely nothing. I worked the pump and swore, backing up as the drone got out into the corridor. Its left shoulder turret turned and chuffed, sending out a gas grenade on a light, "underhanded" trajectory that sent it clattering past my feet. I grabbed my gas mask and shoved it on, gasping as I felt twitches start to work through my arms and legs.

I almost grabbed for a hypo.

Reconsidered.

Instead, I leaped forward and hit the floor, skidding belly first around the corner as the first streamer of anti-personal bullets ripped through where I had stood. I forced a hypo onto my shoulder and shouted—muffled—to Jillian.

"Go! Go! Go!"

Jillian, though, grabbed my arm and hauled me to my feet. "It can hound us through the whole base!"

"Yeah, I know," I said. "I have a plan, come on!"

We went forward, Jillian pushing a hypo—one of her spares —against AF's neck. AF stopped twitching and went with us, looking around nervously as we got out of the haze of Twitch gas.

"So, the plan is?"

I breathed through the mask. The muffling made it hard to really see beyond the curved hemisphere of the goggles, but that was nothing next to the difficulties of drawing in enough air to bring oxygen to my burning muscles. But, then again, it was a hell of a lot better than twitching out on the floor.

"We find a place where it'll have to come out into a blind spot, then we fill it full of holes at very close range," I said.

Jillian nodded. I could practically hear what she'd normally say, what she *would* have said if we were in space and not on the Earth: *Not as much fun as making an improved explosive out of bat shit and bailing wire, but hey, better than nothing.* Or something like that.

But as we were on the Earth, we didn't say much after that. Instead, we fell back on old tactics, old training: I'd move forward, cover, then she'd move up, check the corners, tap my shoulder, move out. We never let anything get uncovered by our gun barrels and we always made sure that AF stayed between us and near a piece of cover if we could.

We made it to a cubicle farm.

I caught Jillian's eyes, nodded, the pointed out a corner for her, turning to AF, whispering. "Find a cubicle, far from us, and stay there. Got it?"

"Got it."

She turned and ran off, staying low. I ducked into a cubicle that wasn't directly across from Jillian—which sounded like a great way to get shot repeatedly shot by my BFF—but instead, a bit to the side. I got behind the cubicle wall, intensely aware of how little protection it would give from bullets. But ... I hoped that the drone didn't have really good thermographics.

Or that it was still programmed for riot duty and that even the hack-job that the transies had pulled didn't override some basic protocols. As far as I knew, any drone with lethal weapons had to have a certain series of parameters filled for it to be a 'clean shoot', and even that sometimes lead to headline-grabbing, net-consuming debates and even trials over drone riggers who hadn't stopped the drone from blowing away a perp who *might* have not been a clean shoot.

Well, the public's paranoia, our reward, eh?

The drone thumped down the corridor, slow and plodding and unstoppable feeling. My spine tingled and I breathed in and out, in and out. Each time, I felt the gas mask press against my face and felt an intense itching *need* to rip the gods-damned thing off and just-

Chuff! Chuff! Chuff!

The drone didn't immediately waddle into the room. Instead, it landed three grenades in a wide arc, one landing into the cube next to mine. There was a loud hissssss as the gas started to spray out, but the mask and the injection kept anything too bad from happening. The drone thudded forward.

I knew, right now, it'd have a great firing lock. A quick burst, and the bullets would rip me to bits like a...

I knew too well what it'd look like.

I closed my eyes.

Thump. Thump.

The delay only made my shake harder.

It wasn't going to shoot, not without a 'clean shoot'. That gave us just enough time. And then, I noticed something.

The magazine in my shotgun had two colors. Red and green. Green for frangible—that is, pellets that would stick into someone rather than going through and beyond. Red for …

Better than nothing. I twisted the magazine, pumped the shotgun. That was the only noise that Jillian needed. She snapped up and opened fire on the drone, using short, controlled bursts. I heard a faint whirr.

I snapped out of concealment and fired.

The drone was stuck between two targets of opportunity, two clean shoots. The underslung gun had half turned to face Jillian, and now it froze. But the shell I'd landed in the thing's face—well, optical covering—had blown part of the armor open. It was some heavy, armor piercing slug. I worked the pump, aimed, fired. The drone's left leg twisted and it shifted its weight, staying up on a second leg. Jillian focused her fire and managed to start ripping into the side.

The damn thing still managed to fire a gas grenade into Jillian's chest. She made an ooof noise and fell, backwards.

I fired again. This time, I took out the forward optics. I fired again, then again, then again, aiming for the hole Jillian had started. The slugs ripped into the drone, the first few stopping inside, but then the fourth or fifth going out the other side, ripping open a serious exit wound. The drone twitched, smoke hissing from it.

Down.

"Jillian?"

"Fine!" She coughed. "Just … ow … gonna have a huge bruise there."

I nodded. "AF?"

I stood to peek around, and spotted AF, waving at us, though she had covered her face and mouth with her shirt to keep from inhaling any of the Twitch.

We left the drone in the dust.

Chapter 15: Safe-Zone

5/22/2068 (01:24)

Chinese-American Alliance, China, Xin-Shanghai

TACNET COMPLETE

TANGOS: 14 (Possible transhuman affiliation, running background sweep)

Subverted Assets: (4 TX-33 Riot Drones, 12 TIC-412 Gun-Drones, 35 TIC-111 Eye-Drones)

Response: Arrived

XSPD, Special Response Unit (Cmdr. Wong on scene)

I had expected a bigger attempt to stamp us out. I mean, two trained Marines with guns and kit, plus a hostage free. We'd taken down one of the drones ... so ... I'd thought more would be coming.

Nope.

We found a room with a thick door—a kitchen area, one of the half a dozen that served the normal swarm of people that worked the building—and settled down to collect ourselves. AF, despite her brave words, had started shaking, and I felt thirsty enough to drink a whole comet.

After it had been purified, of course.

Jillian tossed me a recyclable bottle of water and I threw my head back, drinking it down.

"So, think that there's a police response yet?"

AF clenched her hands. "Yeah. Without a doubt. This is one of the largest cities in the entire Alliance."

I nodded. "So, special response units and drones, assuming that these assholes can't just hack those."

"They'd better not, or someone's going to need a new contractor." Jillian rubbed her face. "All right, they haven't brought a hammer down on us yet."

"Maybe they can't find us?" AF said.

"No, if I were them, I'd get into the optics of the whole building," Jillian said. As she spoke, she started to move along the wall, her borrowed vibro-knife cutting along the seam of the wall. As she walked, the wallpaper slumped down, revealing the wall it was stuck to and ...

There. Jillian paused in her cutting and I walked over. "We're not important," I said.

Jillian frowned as we worked together to cut through the connection cable that filtered into the wallpaper and fed into the wall. "Who is more important than us?"

"The judges? Lau?" I paused. "The servers? I don't know."

"Servers?"

I realized that Jillian might have had more things to do with her time while waiting around than reading the specifications on the building—I'd gotten really bored and Sarah wasn't always around to start chatting with me over I.M. I got distracted from responding, though, because our knives had worked their way through the cable and, with a spark and a flash, the whole wallpaper turned off, leaving the room a dull gray. In the silence, AF spoke up.

"This building is one of the major server farms for this region. I had to come here to register my cloud."

I whistled. It was a bit of a risk, cloud-computing. I could see why someone like AF would want one, as it would let her continually transmit and update her vid streams without having to worry about a local calamity claiming all of her hard earned data. But, personally, I didn't like the idea of continually broadcasting both my location and what I was doing.

AF shrugged. "You'd be surprised how many people think that if they can de-mag your hard-drives, you'll be helpless to blow the whistle on them."

I nodded. "Well, they have the netwar capacity to take these servers on ... which means they'll be focused at the center of the building, where the farms are."

"Howdoyouknowthatthefarmsarethecenterofthebuilding?"

"I don't, I just figure that those would be a good place for 'em," I said, shrugging off my shirt. It took a few seconds of fiddling with the annoying interface to start broadcasting more than just colors out of the back. Once I got that up, I crossed my arms over my chest and waited for the visiting information map to show up on the back of the shirt. The image was low resolution, but very very bright. I winced, glancing at Jillian and AF.

"So, I'm guessing that the server farms would be somewhere here," Jillian said, pointing to the middle of my shirt. I really wished we had a better I/O device, but right now, the idea of using any plugged-in equipment—and thus, shooting up a big electronic flare to any hacker that was tapped into the local data loop—really seemed like a bad idea. The middle of my shirt was dominated by a large, vaguely defined blob that the fuzzy characters claimed was 'classified, top secret.'

"That's most of the building, Jillian."

"I have a question ..." AF looked up from the shirt to the two of us. "Why does it matter? Shouldn't we, instead, be trying to head to the exit as fast as we can?"

I clicked my tongue. To be honest, that idea hadn't quite crossed my mind. I was thinking of this as a military operation—regulations said, in this kind of situation (well, okay, not THIS kind of situation, but in a situation where you were detached from command structures and surrounded by enemy elements) you were supposed to gain information, engage the enemy in any means your local CO thought possible, then fall back and regroup.

"Falling back means going through the XSPD," Jillian pointed out.

"Uh, AF, do you know how bad that would be? I've never had to deal with a major metropolitan police force."

AF looked nervous. "They're not exactly shy about fully automatic weapons fire. That is, about using it at anything that twitches wrong."

I nodded. "So, I figure, we're stuck between a vacuum and a solar flare, so we need to pick which one is more likely to kill us..."

"I'd still bet on the XSPD," AF said, her voice quiet. "They have numbers on their side."

I sighed. She was right, but something in me bucked at that idea. It was that something that had been slammed into me in Basic, by months of fighting, by something I really didn't want to admit, but I ...

"We're Marines," I said.

It felt like betraying everything that I'd worked for while on the Cayer farm. Every agonized night spent dreading the war, dreading being called up, away from Sarah. And here I was, away from Sarah, in the middle of a war, my heart racing, knowing that if I made the wrong move, I'd die. Jillian would die.

But what was I doing?

Was I trying to find a way out, a way to escape?

No. I was trying to find a way to stick my dick into the meat grinder. And I didn't even have a dick. A queasy image of the sausage that Sarah's mom had tugged out of the carni-culture vat rang in my head. I shook my head again.

"The XSPD are going to be walking into a trap. They can't know that we're facing transhumans, right? So the transhumans could have any number of nasty surprises. But if we can at least weaken and distract them, the police force has a better chance."

AF didn't look convinced.

"So, stay here and wait for the police to come sweep you up," I said, putting my hand on her.

She frowned, shaking her head slightly. "There's a better thing I can do with my time ... if they're going to be focused on you and the police, then I will be safe if I access the computer systems here. I'm not a transhuman, but I have some moderate talent with accessing security systems for reasons I hope are fairly obvious."

Jillian smirked at her. "AF, that sounds fine, but we've got a little problem: If you stick by a console, we don't have a radio."

AF sighed, brushing her hands through her hair. "So, I just stay here and—"

"Yes," I cut her off. "You stay here, and you stay safe."

AF looked at the ground. I didn't know her as well as Sarah or Jillian, but it wasn't that hard to tell when someone looked mutinous. But she distinguished herself from most people I knew by closing her eyes, breathing in, breathing out, then nodding.

"Okay."

I patted her shoulder.

Of course, AF was also ten years older than most of the people I knew, save for Mrs. Cayer. And Mrs. Cayer wouldn't just have gotten mad and argued. She'd have shot me dead right here.

"So, this all sounds good, but we've got almost no intel and they've got drone support," Jillian pointed out.

I grinned. "We've got one thing."

Jillian waited for me as I looked around the room, just to check and make sure that I wasn't completely insane. There, I saw it, in the upper right hand corner of the room, revealed by the slumped wallpaper.

A ventilation tube.

I looked at Jillian, my grin not entirely happy.

"We're not claustrophobic."

Chapter 16: Claustrophobia

5/22/2068 (01:32)

Chinese-American Alliance, China, Xin-Shanghai

TANGOS: 14 (ID as New Dawn transnational terror organization)

Subverted Assets:(4 TX-33 Riot Drones, 12 TIC-412 Gun-Drones, 35 TIC-111 Eye-Drones)

Response: Prepping entrance, shots fired–officer down

XSPD, Special Response Unit (Lt.Cmdr. Abdul on scene)

This turned out to be both the best and worst idea I had ever had. And, once, I thought it had been a good idea to begin a forum debate about communism. Once, I had thought that someone could be noble and heroic in war and not get totally screwed over for it—that thought had lasted right up to David's spine snapping in half. And once, I had thought that ventilation systems in a secure military base would be the best way to sneak around.

On the one hand, that was true. The shafts were—by code— large enough to be accessed by drones and humans for when the drones broke down. That didn't mean they were large enough for our combat gear, or large enough to move all that quickly, even with our skinclothes set to the tightest fit. I really hoped that Jillian didn't mind at least a half hour of my ass in her face, because that was what it looked like it would take to get anywhere appreciable. I pushed a bit further and then checked my wrist. The map screen didn't show our position, so I had to make judgments based off what I could see and the indications in the tube itself, which I could only see thanks to the lamp feature on my collar, which was chewing through my clothes' supercaps with a worrying speed.

I pushed myself forward a bit more, and Jillian followed. She moved even slower than I did, and that paid off. I didn't even hear the thing she was dragging: a makeshift sled that held our longarms, such as they were, and the combat kit.

Right now, our main advantage was stealth. A bad noise, at the wrong time, and I was uncomfortably aware of just how deadly guns could be through what looked like comfortingly thick metal and wood. At the end of the day, unless it was carbon weave and pretty thick carbon weave at that, most bullets these days could chew through it. Fast.

We got to another intersection of tubes. My collar light—dimming perceptibly now—shone on the wall and I saw the indications of which way headed to the server farms. A quickly painted stream of characters along that indication also told me something else.

"Think that they left the vent security on?" I asked, looking over my shoulder, craning around to see Jillian—her face was pressed against the vent ground, her way of resting for just a bit.

"Hope not."

I sighed. "Pass up the shotgun, just in case."

The shotgun rasped forward and the lights went dim.

Darkness.

I'd been telling the truth, that we weren't claustrophobic. If anything, this was more comforting than some times out in the big, wide forest. But the darkness and the sheer silence we had to use in our movement, combined with the omnipresent press of gravity made me clench my jaw tighter and tighter with every movement forward.

But I kept moving.

Sounds filtered through the vent—distant gunfire. I hoped that was the police mopping up, and that we'd emerge to find the situation completely under control.

I doubted it.

After an eternity and a half—or at least a half hour by the chron I could barely get to flicker onto my clothes—my face bumped against a blank wall. I put my hand against it, shotgun left resting on the floor of the vent.

The blankness, when I put my hands against it, resolved into a very, very fine meshwork. The servers here were pretty sensitive, so they'd want to keep as much dust and other bugs out of the room as possible.

"Knife." My voice was so low that Jillian didn't hear me. I looked back and hissed, louder, "Knife!"

The pod shape of the vibro-knife rasped on the floor to my hand. I winced at the noise the buzzing little blade made, but it slipped into the mesh easily enough. And, because the Gods are kind sometimes, the alarms didn't go off a second time. The mesh opened, first one corner hanging open—I grabbed that— and then the rest came free. I pulled it in, not wanting it to drop and give us away.

The room beyond was a CQC nightmare—or wet dream, if you liked a highly challenging tactical environment. And, see, the only people who liked highly challenging tactical environments were rear echelon *wángbādàn*. The walls were a pale gray, with ventilation shafts clear and exposed—no wallpaper here—and a single door that led out. The door itself had been opened part way, the hydraulics had been cut, but I couldn't see anyone outside proper. The inside of the room was full of a crisscrossing grid of supercomputers, their heating elements exposed and circulating through the room, giving it a bake-oven temperature. The computers themselves were a monolithic black, each one almost two meters tall and five meters long.

They were almost threatening in their silence.

Two terrorists—both women—had the guts of half the computers open, revealing a haze of complex machinery within—wires and quantum blue-boxes mostly—and were attaching devices that looked so ancient that they had stepped out of the paleolithic era or 1999, take your pick. They actually had to plug the gadgets into USB converters to upgun them to be able to even talk to the machinery inside the supercomputers. But the end result looked like it wasn't just feeding information into another computer ... because the devices had a second layer of connections, connections that slipped into a nerve-shunt mounted at the back of one of the woman's head.

Decking.

I held up a hand to Jillian—she could see my silhouette, I hoped—and flashed the hand sign for two tangos and covering fire.

There was no way to do this quietly.

I put the shotgun out first, then used it to drag myself forward. I ended up tumbling out and not *quite* rolling properly. I ended up flat on my back, a computer between me and the transies.

They reacted fast. Bullets sparked and flashed around the vent I had rolled out of, footsteps—but no shouting—telling me they were moving. *Tā made.* Jillian started opening up, her SMG's silencer keeping her from going deaf in the enclosed space and keeping the flash down. I got onto my knees and then my feet, staying low, trying to keep my situational awareness up. I went to the corner of the computer I was ducked behind and peeked. Clear. I looked back at the vent, to see if Jillian could get the combat webbing down—she'd actually draped one of the vests across the ventway, giving her an even better cover situation. The other vest was on the ground, waiting for me.

"Tango down!" Jillian called after her second shot. "Moving to the left."

I grabbed the vest, pressing it against my chest and letting the semi-adhesive back stick it. It wasn't as good as getting the whole thing on, but it was better than nothing. Then, with shotgun at the ready, I went right.

That turned out to not work as well as I'd hoped. My plan—sweep around and flank—shattered with my vest as a bullet punched into my chest. I staggered backwards and tumbled back around the corner I'd just cleared.

Jillian fired a short burst, swearing. I gasped, feeling an intense pain right above my right breast, but at least I wasn't coughing up blood and thrashing around. I stayed still for a moment, waiting for some hint of where I should jump to next.

Jillian shouted, "Dru!"

I turned. A ... a blurring shape moved from the top of the computer to right beside me. It wasn't invisible, it wasn't even close to invisible, but when it moved, it made it hard to tell if I was actually seeing something or just imagining it. It was like the scenery was shifting and warping, bubbles and changes in perspective making it look as if the air itself had turned into warped glass.

It was just weird enough to give me pause, even with Jillian's shout.

A knife appeared in my chest. It had been not there ... and now it was. I stepped back, ever so slightly, blinking. The knife had gone straight through the bullet resistant vest and into my ... chest ...

I blinked again.

Then ...

Then it actually started to hurt.

And my legs didn't work.

I landed on my back, gritting my teeth, the shotgun—I could barely even remember what a shotgun WAS through the pain—slipping from my hands. The blur over me shifted and it was gone, falling back, going out of my red lined vision. I grabbed at the knife, but then—moments before I wrenched it out—military discipline slammed back into me with both feet ... and Jillian.

"Don't you dare die on me, Dru! *Nǐ gǎn sǐ, chǔndàn!*" Jillian shouted.

I gritted my teeth and —with every iota of will I had—I let go off the knife. Ripping it out felt like it should be the only thing I could, the only thing I *should* do, but ...

Right now ...

Discipline held.

Remove the knife ... and you start to ...

Oh gods ...

I was starting to really, really get this. I closed my eyes, not wanting to see it, but every tiny breath I made, every motion—voluntary or not—made it ...

It ...

Jiggle.

I could FEEL it GRINDING against me.

"Shit shit shit shit shit shit shit shit ..." Jillian whispered, again and again.

If she was so *māde* concerned, why didn't she *MĀDE* HELP ME?!

My hand closed around the shotgun and I whimpered. It was not a noise I ever wanted to make again.

"God damn it!" Jillian pushed her cover out of the way and pulled herself, carefully, out of the vent, dragging the makeshift sled with the supplies out, catching it. I had lifted up my head, lifted it up to see her land. Lifted it up to see the blur behind her.

Real nasty trick.

Hurt someone.

Kill the medic.

Nasty.

I lifted up the shotgun, remembering position 4—Supine—from Basic. I'd hit targets at almost fifty kilometers, simulated. I hadn't used it since Basic. I'd thought it was easily the stupidest position of the five we had to learn—crouched, prone, standing, sitting and supine.

Supine.

Laying on your *back*.

Even with a knife, I took it.

The shotgun almost broke my wrist—it didn't like being used as a pistol and I couldn't bring my other arm around without pushing the knife deeper into me.

But blood fountained out of the back of the blur, the blur itself rippling, crackling, sparking like a badly attuned wallpaper. The cloak—that's what it was—slid off the body as it fell, the two landing next to each other.

I'd gotten the transie bitch in the chest.

I grinned, laying my head back.

Now I could whimper and feel marginally less guilty.

Chapter 17: Puncture

5/22/2068 (01:37)

Chinese-American Alliance, China, Xin-Shanghai

TANGOS: 11 (I.D as New Dawn transnational terror organization)

Subverted Assets:(3 TX-33 Riot Drones, 4 TIC-412 Gun-Drones, 25 TIC-111 Eye-Drones)

Response: Breeching clear, shots fired.

XSPD, Special Response Unit (Lt.Cmd. Abdul on scene)

The antiseptic had painkillers. That was the main reason why I loved them, but the fact I wouldn't be getting gangrene or any number of other blood infections were some of the other reasons. The knife that Jillian had yanked out of my chest wasn't serrated—thank the god of battlefield medicine—but it still looked odd to my eyes. For one thing, it didn't have a single drop of my blood on it once Jillian set it down next to my head, her hands pressing the battlefield dressing against the wound.

The edge shone.

Monomolecular. Of course. I closed my eyes and clenched my jaw as the battlefield dressing dug in, starting to sew the wound shut with a soft, whirring noise.

"These *zázhǒng* have better tech than we did …" Jillian grumbled.

Now, I tried to think of a quip or something to say, but nothing came to mind. Instead, I gritted my teeth a bit more as the dressing finished its job of cleaning and sealing up the wound.

"Here." Jillian handed me the rippling cloak she had torn off the dead transie. My shotgun blast had ripped into the side, so the visual scattering effect wasn't quite as nearly perfect as it had been before, but Jillian and I both knew the value of even half-good camouflage. Not that we'd ever had a chance to use that knowledge, not in space. But everything down here was so hot and noisy and fast and close, camouflage and stealth could actually work.

I sat up, wincing. Now that I wasn't in total agony, I could feel my legs again. Moving felt off, stiff, the dressing trying its best to keep my range of motion from triggering any pains or reopening my stitches. I ignored it as best as I could, taking advantage of my painkillers. I threw the cloak over my shoulders and Jillian nodded.

"Looks halfway decent."

I sighed. My breath blew back against me and I felt a vivid memory shoot through my brain like a solar flare. My skin tingled, as if hoping to feel the familiar restriction and mass of a Government Issue Space Survival Suit. The memory faded as Jillian moved to take point.

I overtook her, tapping her shoulder, hissing. "Let the invisible girl go first."

"That's—" She cut herself off as we got to the doorway, the one that had been partially sliced open by the terrorists. I peeked around the corner and jerked back.

"Three drones," I whispered. "Little disks with guns."

Jillian sighed. She didn't need to say it. Each drone was a small, fast moving target, with enough bullets to turn us into hamburger. The only chance we had would be if we could get them by surprise before they started zipping around at fifty KPH.

"We know you're in there."

Well, *wǒkào*, I suppose.

The voice had a harsh, raspy sound to it. Like someone whose throat had been scraped and cut up by a knife being swallowed the wrong way. Like someone who carried around more than their share of hate. I closed my eyes, reminding myself to not throw stones ...

I hated too. Sometimes.

More than sometimes ...

"Okay," I called back. "And, unless I miss my guess, you can't do much about it. Not with the XSPD on your ass."

"They're not an issue."

I took a risk of peeking again. This time, the gun drones either were more on the ball or had some programming switched around, because one of the guns made that louder-than-expected silenced bang of a suppressed weapon. A bullet zipped past my ear and I jerked back, heart hammering.

Movies got silenced weapons wrong. Every single time. But I had definitely seen blurs this time. Anywhere between one to five other transies, all in cloak mode. Goodie.

"Don't try and come out without surrendering your weapons. We won't kill you, not at first."

"That's really ... r-really comforting." I closed my eyes. These guys had been shooting people at the drop of a hat. Did they expect me to *buy* that? Jillian squeezed my hand. She found it without even trying, through the invisibility robe's bloody, jagged hole. I squeezed back.

"You have fifteen seconds before we send the drones in and the gas. You don't have to be intact to be alive."

I frowned. They wanted us alive?

Jillian sighed, releasing my hand.

I looked at her. She was ready to go. I watched her, feeling the ache of my stab wound. Jillian looked ready to go down fighting. She was checking her SMG's ammo. I swung my gaze down. Closed my eyes. And in that moment, everything felt like it was going slower and slower and slower. I could feel the ache of my heart beat, grinding against my ribs, like my chest had been replaced with a shoddy knockoff.

Making the same mistakes again, huh, Dru?

Making the same bad calls.

Do something because it *felt* right. Fighting the good fight.

I didn't have a platoon to get killed this time.

I didn't have *anyone* left, but Sarah ...

I looked at Jillian.

"Five ..." the terrorist's voice echoed down the corridor.

They're going to try and take us alive, I thought. We're wearing gas masks, and have contact drugs. They're going to gas us, and it won't work, and then they're going to use guns. There will be drones and lots of them and they won't be ambushed. They'll know where we are and they'll flank us out and slaughter us.

"It's been fun, Dru," Jillian said.

She knew how this was going to end too. We've been here before. Done this before.

"Two!"

I held out the shotgun, pushing it out underneath my cloak. I let it drop to the ground with a clatter. Then, I stepped out, tugging the cloak off my face.

Not. Again.

I could see Jillian's stricken expression and it was niǎoshì to me.

The drones whirred forward, their frames blurred by their ionic thrusters. They were so *fast*. The guns remained trained on Jillian and me. I put my hands behind my neck.

Jillian stood, looking like she was carved in stone. Then she threw her SMG to the ground and put her hands behind her neck as well.

"I don't suppose you'll be gloating at us ..." I said. The figure that stepped away from the wall and let his cloak drop was lean, clothed in what looked like leather but probably wasn't, with a rifle in his hands. His ... face ...

His face had been replaced. I could see the seam of scar tissue along where the jaw should have been, raised and jagged, like he'd been burnt. But above the jawline was blank metal, crudely welded together into a collection of boxes and rectangles that resolved into a skull shape. The forehead bulged with optics. The back of the head had a series of raised cooling fins, which radiated intense heat, glowing brightly. His arms had been hacked off and replaced by more home grown augmentations.

He approached Jillian and me. The barrel to his assault rifle looked bigger and bigger as he got closer and closer. I couldn't move. I couldn't even think, I could just look at those whirring optics, those arms and legs, that chest, that head. That inhuman head. What kind of person would *do* that to themselves? What kind of monster were we looking at?

"You've been a major thorn in our ..."

He stopped. He looked at me, then at Jillian. Jillian glared daggers at him. He performed a pitch perfect double take, a kind of humanizing gesture that snapped me out of the spell that his appearance had cast over me.

"Well, we try—" I started.

"Who the hell are you two!?" he asked, looking from Jillian to me to Jillian. Jillian glanced at me. I glanced at her, my hands still behind my head. I looked back at the transhuman leader, then shrugged.

"You're not—" the transie started.

A blur moved behind him.

I looked at it, eyes widening.

He noticed my glance and that saved his life. Considering everything, I shouldn't have let on.

He spun around, rifle snapping up. Bullets whipped past my ear before I realized the rifle had been pushed out of the way, sent spinning down the corridor. The ripple-blur shivered and flowed away like water, revealing a man who barely came up to the transhuman leader's chest. He wore a skintight black outfit which had a shoulder patch. That was all I saw before he blurred into motion, moving faster than I properly could see. His arms thrust forward and the transhuman leader leaped backwards, a knife appearing in one of his whirring, clicking hands. The knife flashed, sparking-

Sparking off the blades that had burst from the other man's forearms.

Jillian started dragging me backwards, shouting something in my ear. I didn't tear my eyes away from what I was seeing. It was inhuman, unreal: The two transhumans danced, and each time they touched, it let out a cracking *thump* that sounded like it should have been the impact sound used by a wire-fu movie. But in real life, humans didn't *make* that sound when they parried a punch or kicked the other in the chest.

The transhuman leader swung his knife in an arc, the Alliance soldier—that's who he had to be—parried with his forearm blade, then returned with a haymaker punch that the transhumanist ducked under. The Alliance soldier—the Alliance supersoldier—put his fist through a hunk of wall, sending out a haze of shattered plastic and wood. He jerked his hand out and knocked aside a blow that looked just as strong.

"We need to leave!" Jillian shouted.

I shook my head, breaking the spell. Jillian started dragging me, clearly thinking that I was telling her no. But I turned, going to run with her.

"This is getting too *niǎobī*—" she started.

We ran around the corner and into three of the other terrorists. These guys weren't nearly as augmented as their leader, but they had guns. We didn't.

Jillian kept running straight forward. She had banked on even an augmented mind being susceptible to a shock. She was right. The three paused and that gave Jillian time to tackle one to the ground. When she rolled off of him, she held the shimmering, monomolecular knife that had, only a short while ago, been sticking out of my chest. The man she'd tackled was missing his heart.

Given a choice, I might have tried to surrender again.

Maybe that was why Jillian forced the issue.

I slammed, shoulder first, into the woman to the right, but I kept my stance while she staggered, her gun practically falling into my hands (after I wrenched it out of her grasp, at least) as I felt my field dressing strain to hold my own chest wound shut. The gun, though, was angled wrong for me to use it immediately. So, instead of trying to shoot the third guy, I swung the gun around.

He met it with his forearm and the gun was the one that shattered.

"*Sǐ pì yǎn!*" I snarled.

He started to swing, but his punch held no weight behind it as he twisted to the side. For a second, I didn't understand it, but then I saw the hilt of the knife sticking out of his neck. Any armor plating he had hidden under his flesh, it didn't stop that knife.

He fell, limp. Boneless.

And the girl I shoulder-checked threw her arm around my neck. She got her forearm against my throat and her hand against the base of my spine. I growled, but then she tightened her grip.

"Drop it or I snap her neck."

Her voice was harsh, flat, an accent born out of the North American Midwest. It wasn't exactly a common accent, at least not in the culture I was used to.

I didn't like it.

Jillian, who had picked up one of the discarded guns, didn't drop it. But she didn't swing it to aim at me or the terrorist who was using me as her human shield. Guilt gnawed at my gut.

The girl tightened her grip on me. "I said drop it, *shăbī!*"

My head bubbled with a million thoughts. I could see the same swirl of possibilities on Jillian's face. I didn't know if I wanted her to try and take the shot, or if I wanted to blubber and beg to just see Sarah one more time before I died.

And, lo, salvation came around the corner in the form of the leader.

He was holding a severed head in one hand. The Alliance supersoldier. Blood dripped from his neck and his eyes were closed, a grimace of pain on his face.

The leader looked at the girl, looking through me—for all I knew, he had X-ray vision or could emit T-rays or something like that—and I had the distinct impression that a conversation happened in complete silence.

If they didn't have implanted radios, I'd stick my hand into my own chest.

Which I could do, right now.

I didn't know what they discussed. But I knew that they had to have needed us for *something,* because the girl pushed me away from her, then slapped another pair of those zip-cuffs on my wrists. They didn't have, or didn't bother to use, the smart-bags, so I got a full look of Jillian's face as she got cuffed as well. She looked mad, but resigned. Like: *Hey, at least we tried.*

"Hostages, huh?" she asked, looking at the metal freak that walked past the girl, still holding a dripping head.

The transhuman turned his head a slow, eerie one hundred and eighty degrees, some magic of his augmentation making the motion possible. I had read about—and seen documentaries—about owls and other extinct creatures like that. Seeing it in person was way, way creepier.

"Yes," he said.

Then, his head snapped back to the front and he continued walking.

Jillian and I didn't have any questions after that.

Chapter 18: Rod

5/22/2068 (01:40)

Chinese-American Alliance, China, Xin-Shanghai

TANGOS: 5 (I.D as New Dawn transnational terror organization)

Subverted Assets:(1 TX-33 Riot Drones, 5 TIC-111 Eye-Drones)

Response: Preliminary hostages secured, building check (55%)

XSPD, Special Response Unit (Lt.Cmd. Abdul on scene)

The roof winds whipped against my face, bringing tears to my eyes as I gritted my teeth and glanced aside, trying to protect myself from the vicious cold and the burning sting of shunted pollutants. I was fairly sure that no one without face masks was supposed to be on the roof of the administration facility, because the roof sat slap bang in the middle of a section of Xin-Shanghai that had either enclosed buildings (like the surrounding arcologies) or uninhabited architectural artifacts. That was the best term that I could think of for the vanes and flutes and curved, plastic half-tunnels that were built into the side of the arcologies and skyscrapers around me, all designed to help channel the wind that blew through the city.

Channel it right into my face, that's how it felt to me.

I blinked away the tears and tried to look at the rest of the roof. It looked like a load of heating elements and other things you put onto roofs. But, nestled amongst the boxy structures that bled off waste heat and sent out radio transmissions and what not, was a sleek and very stolen-looking Alliance VTOL. The frame didn't have the same quantum dot wallpapering that the last one I'd ridden in had, but instead sported bulkier, thicker engines and equally thick and powerful-looking armor.

There weren't any drones supporting the terrorists, but I only saw two other bipedal terrorists ('cause I didn't really want to call them *human* until I knew how much cybernetics they had) join the leader and the girl who kept reins on me and Jillian. Those two hit a middle point between their inhuman leader and the girl who had a gun pressed against my spine: one was taller and spindlier than a human should be, but as I watched, he ... folded in on himself, metallic skin clenching shut to cover up with false flesh that looked like one of the technicians that I had seen yesterday, complete with his swarthy cast and slightly out of place ethnic features.

The other looked normal, save for the fact that their right arm had been replaced by a pivoting gun, further supported by backbone bracings and leg clamps that looked like they'd let them settle down in a single place and put out the din of gunfire that I normally associated with heavy battle tanks.

They continued the eerie—and downright frustrating—habit of not talking out loud, but instead just looking at one another as they spat lines of code through the EM spectrum. I wondered why they had used verbal language earlier, but it didn't seem that important now.

Jillian, her head kept down to keep herself from being blinded by the cold, stinging air that shot past us, hissed, "Do you hear that?"

I looked at her.

"Hear with your feet."

That was something I hadn't done—and, frankly, hadn't needed to do—in a while. Up here, sound went through the air to my ears. But in space, you learned to hear through a lot of weird places. Hearing through your feet was a good way to feel any major changes in a space station, as feet were always aimed at the outer edge of the station—at least, it was if you had any kind of gravity. I closed my eyes (a relief) and let my thin shoes press against the roof.

I could hear faint bangs and thumping noises, down there.

Then the girl snarled at us. "On the VTOL. Now."

Jillian and I started to move, Jillian muttering very uncomplimentary Mandarin under her breath. The girl didn't hear, didn't understand, or didn't care.

The inside of the VTOL had crash-webbing, but no vid feeds for the exterior. The seats had also gone from eighteen to only twelve, maybe fourteen if you counted people standing in the middle of the central corridor. The girl shoved Jillian and me into the first seats near the entrance, which opened up and out of the yawning back of the VTOL. She webbed herself in, the others doing the same. The leader, though, he stepped onto the ramp of the VTOL, then looked back. He watched the roof as the engines whirred and groaned to life.

"Gonna strap in?" Jillian asked.

"Yeah, don't you know, buckling your seatbelt saves lives," I added.

Hey, if Jillian was going to try and verbally spit into the eye of Death, I couldn't very well let her do it without jumping in too.

The leader ignored us.

"He's not going to make it," he said, out loud. "Damn it."

The VTOL lifted off, the engines screaming so loudly that I didn't hear Jillian's question, though when I glanced at her, I did see her lips move.

Inside, though, I felt a moment of disquiet. My imagination leaped to hurried life, trying to fill in and construct a plausible story to frame around those words. Clearly, we hadn't knocked off all the terrorists—or even most of them. Someone was down there, in the building. Was he trapped, pinned down by the XSPD? Was he remaining behind to open up a chance for the others to escape?

That sounded ...

Uncomfortably heroic.

The face of Jorge Friedman, the teenage kid who I had turned into so much hamburger meat on the Forge—which I still couldn't eat if I watched it being cooked—floated into my mind. I shook my head.

The VTOL banked away from the building and I could see it. I could also see the armored XSPD response vehicles, most of them on the ground level, their red and blue lights flashing. I saw a sleek, one-man VTOL with underslung weapons move over to fly behind us. It was painted with the same colors as the police, blue and white. Before I could do anything, though, the transhuman grabbed me by the shirt and dragged me out of the webbing, which automatically disengaged. Traitor webbing.

He thrust me out, dangling me over the edge of the still open ramp.

"You son of a bitch!" I screamed, feeling the intense vertigo that normally only hit me when I was in orbit. I could see all the way down to where Sarah would work, my heart hammering as the ground rushed up to meet me. But no, the hand still held me. Wind blew through my hair and I looked up at the VTOL, trying to not ... not ...

The VTOL pilot. I could see her, though half her face was covered by a helmet. I couldn't see her eyes, but I saw her mouth. It was moving, shaping words in Mandarin. Without the tones, I couldn't imagine what she was saying. But I did see that her voice cut off hallway through a sentence and then she shaped a very pungent, very English and very satisfying word. A word that I was throwing at the transie with the wild abandon of the terrified hostage.

"Cào! Wo cào nǐ mā de! Cào, cào, cào!" I kicked my feet, eyes unwilling to close because my eyes were bastards.

The police VTOL backed off. Its engines whirred and tilted backwards, sending it flying away. The transie dragged me back into the VTOL, letting me go. My ass slammed into the floor plates and I growled at him. I don't even remember what bravado I had been about to throw at him. I just remember the first word.

"You're—"

What happened next ...

What happened next took me a while to figure out. It took me minutes to understand. No, wait, that's a lie. It took me a nanosecond to understand. I saw it, after all. But it took me minutes, no, hours ... no, days to *comprehend.* There's a vast gulf between that. I understood the Slump, I knew the reasons and the effects and what happened. But I didn't comprehend it like Sarah's mom did. I didn't feel the same gut-instinct that pushed me to hoard food, to hoard ammo, to build my house into a fortress that could withstand the armies of homeless and dispossessed that wandered the countryside in those grim, grim days.

I understood what happened next.

It had to have begun at least a half hour ago, on a time-table that Jillian and I, in all our ... stupid, ignorant, naïve ways, imagined that we could somehow alter. But we couldn't. It was just math.

It began with an orbiting satellite, one either captured or retrofitted or even built and launched by the Loonies, taking advantage of their still crushing orbital supremacy. That satellite ... the hell of it all was that it wasn't even a very complex satellite. It didn't even need more than a few computerized systems, and just one radio. All it needed was a way to determine its own position and orientation and two long rails. Coilguns were more re-usable, but railguns were cheaper and easier to build. Either way, the effect was the same. A magnetic field, created by electromagnets powered by anything from solar to micro-fusion to rad-batteries, shoved a rod of tungsten down the rails and towards the end of the satellite.

The math was all fairly simple. The orientation, the angle was all calculated who knows how long ago in advance.

And, in the fierce, tight, bloody fighting that I had thought was so damn important, that magnetically launched rod of tungsten shot towards the Earth. It didn't need a heat shield, it had no complex parts that could fail or melt or be fused together. It didn't need deceleration rockets, because it wasn't going to land or coast to a stop or even adjust its trajectory. It didn't need to be aerodynamic or graceful or elegant. It didn't even need to be hewn properly.

It didn't even need explosives.

All it needed, all it had, all it used was its mass and its velocity—nearly all of it imparted by the coilgun.

The stolen VTOL was almost out from underneath the top of Xin-Shanghai, almost out in clear water. The laser defense systems didn't shoot us down, the ship had hostages.

I had my eyes on the terrorist, but his ugly, misshapen, inhuman, impossible head was framed by the metal sky, the iron sky of Xin-Shanghai.

That was why I saw it. A roaring streak of pure white flames, created by the sheer speed of the rod as it ripped through the atmosphere like a bullet the size of a freight train.

Within less than a second, the rod punched through the hydroponic gardens and the support structures and the hidden tunnels. As it punched through, it shed some of its mass and some of its speed in a kinetic shockwave that moved along the metal superstructure like the ripple in a pond.

Xin-Shanghai was built to withstand wind shear and even major explosions.

Not this.

The superstructure bucked and metal hunks already started to rain down, smashing through buildings. But my eyes, half blinded by the heated, white hot streak of the tungsten rod, still saw the administration complex first.

The rod impacted the armored side and the armor parted like plastic under a heated scalpel. The rod, though, still received enough of a 'stop' for it to end its long fall and release most of the kinetic energy that it had carried, mile by mile, kilometer by kilometer.

The VTOL bucked and a sound like the end of the world— that was the end of the world—slapped against my ears. I bounced and almost went flying out as the VTOL went into a hard spin. I grabbed onto the still extended ramp, holding on tight as my shoes were ripped off my feet. The city and horizon spun.

A metal hand grabbed my wrist and hauled me in. The VTOL righted itself, coming out of the spin with a scream I felt through the deck plating, not through my ears. My ears rang. I looked up and saw Jillian, hanging against the webbing. Vomit dripped down her lips and tears streaked her face. The trans-human looked down at me. I didn't know what he was thinking.

I sat up and looked back out the ramp.

I couldn't hear anything.

The VTOL was over the sea now.

The spires of Xin-Shanghai remained standing, the arcologies.

But the sky had fallen.

And, rising from the now open air above the city, expanding with an inner illumination born of half a million fires and the searing glow where the tungsten rod had cut the air itself … was a cloud.

A mushroom cloud.

I slowly lay back on the floor of the VTOL … and started to cry with Jillian.

I spoke a name, and I could not hear it.

Chapter 19: Last Words

ERROR: ERROR: ERROR: ERROR: ERROR: ERROR: ERROR: ERROR: ER-ROR: ERROR: ERROR: ERROR: ERROR: ERROR: ERROR: ERROR: ERROR: ERROR: ERROR: ERROR: ERROR: ERROR: ERROR: ERROR: end of line

My hearing hadn't come back. I didn't know how long it was, but it was long enough for us to be over the Pacific for a while. We hadn't gone towards Japan, though even they wouldn't have waited to shoot us down, even with hostages. I didn't know how the rest of the world was doing. I didn't know how Jillian was doing.

I could only imagine. And, somehow, I smiled.

Even if I got out of this alive ...

Mrs. Cayer would kill me.

It wasn't funny. It wasn't even *mā de bī* close to funny.

The VTOL started to go down. I felt it rather than saw it, I couldn't bear to look out the ramp for more than a few seconds at a time, as the mushroom cloud was still visible on the horizon.

Then, quite suddenly, the horizon wasn't. A thick wall of concrete or something close to it rose up and blocked everything save a tiny line of washed out sunlight that came over the lip. I started to stand, but one of the transhumans dragged me to my feet.

We were on what looked like a recycling platform, one built out by the huge plastic flows created by the early 21st century's excesses, dumping trash into the oceans. They were primarily automatic, but I did see a few corpses here and there, most of them shot with looks of surprise on their faces. The whole structure was made to take out plastics, and I could feel/hear the noises of the machinery below the deck, chugging and humming away against the soles of my shoes. If the transhuman pushing me along had anything to say, I didn't hear it. Jillian's lips moved when I looked at her, but I couldn't tell what she was saying ...

And ...

Frankly. I didn't give a damn. I plodded along. We went through a doorway, down a corridor, and then into a large chamber. We stood on a balcony, a catwalk, that lined around the upper part of the chamber. The floor was completely invisible, though, covered with layers of biomatter—seaweed and decaying fish—and layers of meshwork and other bits of machinery. The whole thing was fed into and fed out of by a series of tubes, which sucked away and sprayed in water in a continual streamer. It had something to do with the recycling, but I couldn't for the life of me figure it out.

The transhuman turned us around. Jillian and I stood shoulder to shoulder. The transhuman was the one who had folded back down into a more compact, more human-looking body. His lips moved. Jillian jerked her chin, saying something.

The transhuman shrugged, tugging out a curved piece of plastic and metal. He stepped forward and jammed it into my ear. There was a sharp, stabbing pain, then a squeal as I gasped, feeling sound come back in a dizzying rush. It was a static filled, crummy quality, but I could still hear.

"Any last requests?" the transie asked, again, stepping back.

"Yeah, you let us go ..." Jillian said, her voice muffled—the earbud was on my right side and she stood to my left. "And we get to go home."

"No can do."

Jillian sighed.

I glanced at her. She glanced at me. Our eyes met.

"No requests. Unless you feel like telling us your nefarious plans, you know ... just to satisfy our curiosity," I said, looking at the man. He shook his head, but he could have told us whatever he wanted. I didn't have a plan. I didn't have a goal. I didn't have anything. I just felt *tired*. And to think. I had sacrificed our dignified last stand to survive long enough to get here. Looking down the barrel of a gun.

The transhuman had pulled out a pistol. It was a sleek model, built almost entirely around one hunk of molded and shaped carbon composite.

Jillian stood up straighter. "If you ever get interviewed, my last words are officially ..." She spat on the ground. "Up yours. Die."

The transhuman shot her in the head.

Jillian's body pitched backwards and fell over the side, into the recycling pit.

The transhuman tilted the gun around.

He shot me in the chest.

Chapter 20: Armor Piercing

5/22/2068 (02:22)

Unknown, Unknown

Tracking: Drusilla Zhao Jillian Zhang TOP PRIORITY

I opened one eye. My head ached. I shifted around on a spongy, bouncy mat of flesh and seaweed. My chest ached, my head ached, my wrists ached, my soul ached. But ... I was ... alive. I closed my eyes, unsure if I was going into shock or if this was a really crappy version of the afterlife. I sat up and felt so dizzy I almost passed out again. Everything had a grayish tinge to it, and sounds came muted and distant.

I closed my eyes. I opened them again, breathing.

My field dressing didn't have a hole in it. It had a scar, where its materials had drawn taught again, still powered despite almost an hour and then some of trying to keep me together.

Wow.

They ...

Really did have good tech. I looked around again, automatically, doing things without trying to think beyond the moment. I saw that I was laying on top of a load of seaweed and fish, the mound being just slightly above the water line. I saw a body floating face down in the water. Jillian!

I shifted forward on my ass, using my legs to push against her. She actually thrashed. She rolled onto her back …

One of her eyes was half open. The other was closed. When she thrashed, she twitched with a kind of boneless randomness. Her brain had had a hole punched through it by an armor piercing bullet. She wasn't …

She …

I looked away, eyes closed. I had to have an exit wound on my back, and it had to be bleeding. Right?

I didn't know. I could still move. I managed to get my feet under me and looked around for something, anything I could use. I saw that the wall had some spinning gears, which were used to translate motive power into a pair of machines that looked like they acted as an automatic shaker for large pans that shifted out the smaller particulates of the sea water. I walked backwards towards it, looking to the ceiling.

My metal fingers got jammed into the machinery. They held up, just long enough, for me to twist around and get the zip-cuffs' chain there instead. The machinery groaned … and with a crunch, I was free. I rubbed my wrists with my hands, panting.

Well.

I was dying. I'd either bleed to death or freeze to death—the water level was getting higher, and the thick, wet stuff around my thighs felt colder than space.

There was one thing, though, one thing that the cold and the pain didn't drown out.

Rage.

I … I was beginning to realize how I had been *sǐ dìng* from the day I had been born, hadn't I? Here I was, knee deep in the rot, with my best friend's blood still smeared on my hands, because of things I had been born dealing with. Loonies and separatists and the grinding mass of the Alliance, all of it just …

Just …

Taking. And taking. And *taking*. They took my parents. They took my *life*. They took my friends. They took…Sarah…I closed my eyes and felt the rage boiling and sparking and *roaring* through me like a fusion sun. They'd even taken my *gestures*. My surrender to save Jillian?

Nothing.

Nothing.

Lián diǎosī bù suàn de nothing. But I had one thing left that I could do. One. Last. Thing.

I grinned a slow, sick little grin.

Getting out of the pit was easier than I thought. There was a ladder nestled against the corner, a ladder I took carefully, not wanting to slip and fall. By the time I got to the top, I was panting. The transhuman was gone, and my hearing aid partially slipped out of my ear. I forced it back in, wincing at the pain that it sent through my head. I got onto the catwalk and, my feet bare thanks to me losing my shoes, I padded to the door.

Weirdly, my brain started to make some …

Jumps.

Connections.

These guys were technical. They were expert hackers, duh, they hacked the drones. They were very, very radical transhumanists. Their remaining ethnic features said Latino. Texan, maybe.

The Loonies had the orbit, but they couldn't stand up to the Alliance once it finally got on its war footing on and started launching.

Alliance.

Loonies could drop supplies, supplies that let them augment themselves as much as they could in their forest and mountain hidey-holes, wherever it was they'd gotten to. I pushed my back against the wall and closed my eyes. My hands clenched and unclenched, trying to get them to feel again now that I was out of the cold water. It worked, slowly. I wished that they would go from not feeling to feeling, without the horrible part in-between them: the part where my skin felt like huge, jagged shards of glass were stabbing into my muscles.

Loonies would want something in return. Something in exchange for orbital support.

Netwar. A good netwar attack could cripple me. Could cripple...

Memory, the gun I had been using on Mrs. Cayer's roof, jamming up. The drones, subverted. Painful memories, but they painted a pretty damn clear picture.

"The computers ..." I whispered.

That meant ... they couldn't send a signal to the Loonies, they couldn't beam the information they'd stolen, they couldn't mail off their viruses and Trojans and other nasty electronic surprises, without-

I opened the doorway into the corridor. The corridor beyond wasn't patrolled. I crept forward, my ear-aid straining to try and hear, my feet ready to sense any vibrations I could. One of my hands was on the wall, to keep my balance. I had to balance. Had to move. Couldn't think of names, faces, friends. Think of *now*. Right now. Think of wars.

Where had the moon been? I hadn't seen it. If it wasn't in the sky, they wouldn't have line of sight to beam their intelligence to the Loonies.

I heard voices.

I froze.

"They're both dead?"

A voice I didn't recognize. The footsteps were heading perpendicular to where I was. I saw an intersection ahead. I hurried forward, then peeked around to see two men heading down the left, away from me.

The transhuman nodded.

"Godsdamn it, I hate this ..."

They kept walking.

That voice. That man.

No. No. No.

No.

That was impossible. I closed my eyes and jerked myself back behind cover, breathing in, becoming aware of just how much I hurt, just how numb I was starting to feel. This was a different kind of numb, something inside me felt broken. Something emotional, something physical.

The transhumans needed an in. Most hacking was just an in. A backdoor. An opened door.

A traitor.

Daniel Lau was walking down the corridor with the transhuman.

I trembled. Still rage. If you were curious.

First, he abandoned me and my troopers. Then he tried to use banned weapons. And now he was conspiring with terrorists. The rage I felt crystallized into something white hot, like a sun going from proto-star to star, burning bright. I clenched my teeth hard, hard enough to break some. That's how it felt.

I moved around the corner, trembling.

Lau and the transie headed out through a door by the time I got to the corner they'd went around. The door opened to the courtyard, where I saw the VTOL and a laser transmitter being set up by the two other transhumans. I didn't have a gun. I didn't have ... anything ...

Think. What did these places do?

Recycled. Plastics. Plastics broke down into petrochemicals.

Petrochemicals, some of them at least ... were explosive.

I looked at the wall, really looked at it. The signs said that I had come from biomatter reclamation. Another line pointed towards chemical recycling. I padded down the corridor. I fell once or twice, my body becoming dizzy, my fingers numb, then my hands. I dropped to my knee every time, and every time, I thought of what would get me up, what would get me moving.

Sarah.

Jillian.

Everyone.

Not seeing Sarah again. I'd never see her again. I'd never see either of them again. That? That never seeing them again? It was my new motivation, fed into my body, giving me the energy to keep going, with a few holes through me and nothing but adrenaline and grit pushing me forward. I wanted to *hurt* these sons of bitches. I wanted to hit them, stab them, blow them into bits of hamburger. I wanted to space them, gas them, meme-bomb them. I wanted to nuke them until they glowed, then shoot them in the dark.

I got to the chemical recycling facility. There were no self-destruct buttons, but the console near the corner of the large, intricate room, did have a few buttons enclosed by glass to keep people from accidentally pressing them. One of them, in fact, had a few characters.

Emergency Gas Evacuation.

I smirked.

Pushing the button made the entire place rumble and shake. I started moving, my feet slapping against the ground. I headed to the back corner of the chemical facility, where stairs headed up with signs declaring that they were emergency exits. I ran up the stairs, staggering, thumping against the wall, dragging myself.

The door at the top opened.

I saw a gray sky, but I also saw a great gout of gas shooting up, up into the air. I didn't know why the facility would have to evacuate gas, but it was clear there were reasons. Maybe in case of fire? I didn't know.

What I did know was that I had just sent up a two, maybe even three-hundred-meter-tall plume. That, plus no one responding to hails ...

That had to count for something.

I fell to my knees, then landed on my face.

I closed my eyes.

Breathed in.

Breathed out.

I had to apologize to Mrs. Cayer. That was my other big goal, the big dream, almost as impossible as getting to Earth had been back when I was in space. I understood now. I got why she didn't want Sarah to move away ...

To the dangerous places.

I didn't know how long it was before a foot got under one shoulder and rolled me onto my back.

The sky was dark. But the head wasn't augmented, female, or swarthy.

Lau.

I hadn't talked to him since I'd told him to go screw himself, after the battle of the Forge. I felt the same then as now. Wrung out. Spread over too little. He held a gun in one hand, and his voice was tinny, scratchy and distant. It was like he was talking to me from the past, when radios were new and humanity had only dreamed of the stars.

"You never know when to quit."

I guess that was a compliment.

I grinned at him, then.

"*Cào nǐ kūwěi de júhuā.* Sir."

He moved his gun. He aimed it at my head. Then ... his hand shook. "I ... I can't ..."

He looked to the side. Something exploded, out of the corner of my eyes. I could see it, a coiling bloom of fire and smoke that caused Lau to stagger and a vibration to run through my spine. I laughed, rolling my head to the side. Two Alliance VTOLs, drawn here by the smoke, were opening fire. A transhuman—the one with the arm-cannon—was firing back. Twin streams of high caliber bullets took him to pieces.

I looked back at Lau, who was gaping in shock. I closed my eyes and figured ... hell ...

I could do one last thing.

I kicked Lau in the knee. I had the leverage and the position, and he wasn't even looking at me. And, his knees were—unlike most knees I'd been kicking—Spacer knees. He, like me, worked on them, but that would never make up for the lack of gravity and constant pressure that Earthers got.

His leg bent, unnaturally, and he fell, his scream overloading my earpiece in the same way that whump-silent explosion had. His gun fell and I grabbed it before he even took his hands away from his knee. I pushed myself away from him, sitting up. I almost blacked out, my head hanging forward.

The earpiece squealed and began to work again.

"Drusilla, please ..." Lau was saying, around clenched teeth. "I didn't have a choice! You don't—"

I shot him in the head. The gun bucked in my hand and his brains splattered the floor. Then, I shot him again. Then a third time, and a fourth and a fifth. Then, with a grunt, I hurled the empty pistol at his corpse, which twitched and jerked. I leaned my head back, resting it against whatever it was that I had pushed myself against, a wall of some kind or other.

I closed my eyes.

And I died with a smile on my lips.

Epilogue

5/31/2068

Chinese-American Alliance, China, Neo-Hong Kong

T-Minus L-Day: 79

When I woke up, I could hear things. I could hear the faint bleep bleep bleep of biomonitoring equipment. I could hear a distant rumbling noise, like I was in a city. And I could hear a tap tap tap tap tap.

A foot. On the ground.

I opened my eyes.

I was in a hospital bedroom. My body felt like it had been wrapped in bandages, but I knew that couldn't be true because I lifted my arm to my forehead and saw that my hand wasn't wrapped. My wrist had a bracelet, and the bracelet had at least fifteen billion (or, you know, three) wires that went into something looming over me. When I tried to turn my head, my neck didn't want to move all the way.

Then, as if my brain suddenly remembered how to gauge relative importance, I remembered the tapping. I craned my head around and saw a woman in the corner of my room. She was slender, knife thin even, with a black bodysuit that clung to her like a skinsuit, though a bit thicker around the joints. She had a badge on her shoulder, a similar badge to the ...

To the supersoldier, the one whose severed head had been carried off by the transie for reasons that totally escaped me.

This time, I could really see what it was, but I didn't care, not for a few long seconds.

The woman was bald.

And I recognized her.

Major Mary Singh. The woman who had read my brain scans. The woman who wanted to see if my fingers, my gleaming, metal, cybernetic fingers were a fluke or not.

"You ..." I croaked.

She stopped tapping her foot. Her arms had been crossed over her chest. She smiled, slightly.

"You have a good memory."

I decided to not mention K.

"You are memorable. Where am I? Where is Sarah?"

Singh held up a hand. "You are in Neo-Hong Kong, in one of the best hospitals in the entire Alliance. Your friend, Sarah—"

"She's more than that," I said, my voice rasping out. Sandpaper.

She lowered her hand. "I don't know. Shanghai was, for all intents and purposes, nuked. The only upside is that there's no radioactivity and no firestorms, but it will still take longer than you've been out to sift through the rubble."

I closed my eyes, tight.

"However, from reports about damage and what I know about where she worked, it's unlikely she survived."

Singh spoke softly, not ... without emotion. I could actually hear the regret and sadness in her voice.

That didn't help. It wasn't the rending sadness I felt, it was a clinical sadness. A kind of 'oh I *should* feel bad' sadness. I clenched my fists and closed my eyes. I tried to breathe. I couldn't. I tried to reach out and grab that hope ... that dream I'd had, that dream that Sarah made, that dream that kept me alive in space.

It wasn't there.

It was like trying to take a step up a flight of stairs in the dark and then finding that the next step had been erased, vanished away, leaving you tumbling, falling ...

I managed to breathe in, then breathed out.

"She'll be okay." My voice was ragged. "S ... She'll be okay ..."

Singh didn't respond to that. For the best. When she spoke up, she asked me some questions. She asked me about what I saw and what I did. She asked me about Jillian and the transhumanists and the drones. She asked me about AF and she asked me about Daniel Lau. And, together, we laid out what we thought happened.

As I connected Lau's desire to avoid prison to him letting the terrorists into the Alliance network systems, Singh nodded. She launched into her own expositional spiel. She elaborated on just who the New Dawn were and what they stood for and how they had been created and all of that floated past my head and didn't actually connect to my brain. Instead, I looked at the patch on her shoulder.

It looked like a snake, coiled around to bite down on its own tail, surrounding the interlocked hoops of a biohazard warning sign. Underneath it was a series of characters: S3TA. Above, curving with the snake's body, were letters that were English ... spelling out words that definitely were not.

Per meliorationem, ad astra

The only Latin I knew was sewn to my jacket, and it wasn't that.

But Singh saw my look.

"Through Augmentation, the Stars," she said, sliding her finger along the words. "The motto of the Space Special Service ..." She paused, just a moment. "Transhuman Arm."

The supersoldier.

The first responders at the Forge. They'd been the same, though I hadn't seen their abilities then.

I grinned, slightly. "I wish ..." I shook my head, trailing off.

Singh smiled. "You wish you could do what we can do?"

I nodded, looking to the side. The hope was gone. But the anger, the raw burning hatred that burned and burned and didn't stop. That remained, that stuck with me. That, I could grab and squeeze with both hands.

"Yes."

Singh smirked. "I was reading your brain scan, when we first met. I know that might sound odd, but there is a reason why we're not widely publicized."

Well, yeah, I thought, remembering the Singularity Scare and the horrors of the early days of the Slump, when transhuman soldiers had gone amok. I remembered my grandfather, with his dead eyes and permanently crippled body.

"And, there is a reason we exist at all," she said. "Cyber-affinity."

I nodded, remembering K.

"Some people have it. The technical definition is long and complicated and involves words like psychosomatic and body dysmorphia. The practical upshot, though, is that people who have cyber-affinity have the ability to accept it when their arms are removed and replaced with better ones. People without go psychopathic and try to do all sorts of horrible things. When you exhibited the ability to use your fingers, and your adroit ability to use virtual reality, I began to monitor your progress. I'm quite impressed."

She opened her mouth, but I held up my hand. "Permission to speak freely, ma'am."

She nodded.

"Are you sure you want someone … like me?" I asked. "I'm only a corporal."

Singh chuckled. "Corporal Zhao, the S3TA isn't about experience. It's about psychosomatic capacities and neural plasticity. The best kind of recruit has the ability to learn how to control the augmentations that make us so effective. That is all that is required, not age and not decorations, though your combat actions have some promise."

I nodded, slowly.

I closed my eyes.

I had spent so long, months, trying to get out of the war. To try and stay home.

It took me maybe five, six seconds to decide.

"I'm in. What do I do?"

"In a week, you'll be taken to one of our training facilities. Two or three months later, L-Day comes. Launch day. Invasion day. We take the Moon back. We *end* this," Singh said. She stepped back. "Officially, though, it doesn't exist." She smiled, then. Her smile had a ghostly quality to it. Then, with a jolt I realized she was actually fading from my sight, the edges of her body blurring and shimmering and becoming like the wall and window behind her.

"I was never here."

She was gone.

I lay back in my bed.

The window that sat across from me showed the blazing city lights of Neo-Hong Kong, which spread out where Shanghai built … had built up. But what drew my eye wasn't the lights or the millions of people …

It was the sky.

I could see the blazing lights of thousands of satellites. I could see the refracted glow of the debris field, still glittering up there. I could see, or thought I saw the occasional flash and searing line of high-powered space combat. I could see the fuzzy, purple shroud of still descending climate control particulates, spewed out by the now mostly defunct terraforming effort.

And beyond it all, I could see Luna. It looked half gone, darkness shrouding it. But on the darkness, cracks made of light expanded, as if the moon was about to … break apart.

I lay there, alone, in the hospital bed, dreaming of blood and steel.

Underneath a shattered sky.

LUNAR CYCLE BOOK 3
LUNA'S LAMENT

6/25/2068

Republic of Deseret, NAU

T-Minus L-Day: 43

"Today, we are going to teach you eighteen silent ways to kill a man."

Of the many things that I could call Selection out on, I could (at the very least) say this one single positive thing: They don't *fahn leong jian* about what they're teaching you. I sat up and paid attention—not that I really had a choice, not in the VR sessions, where you weren't just required to attend, your brain was hooked in and pumped with military grade neurotropic drugs. And let me tell you: The fact you can't *not* think about the instruction helped.

It helped a *lot*.

Our instructor for this little tween chop seminar was a gray-skinned transie that looked like he had come right out of a Bol-lywood slasher film: Machined lines ran along his joints and his arms were made of matte-black carbon composites, molded into the crude shapes of muscle and joints. He summoned a virtual bad guy and tapped him twice on the shoulder.

The bad guy—dressed in Loonie yellow and black—half-turned to see who was bothering him before our instructor smashed his face in with the mother of all sucker punches. It was fairly silent—nothing more than a soft crunch—and the man fell, his face dutifully simulated with a crumpled jaw and scattered teeth.

It seemed silly, but that was the Selection motto: Simplicity breeds success. Why bother with kidney strikes or eye gouging or fancy kung-fu when you have a 1000 PSI harder-than-steel piston for an arm? Of course, that was just one of eighteen "silent ways" that our instructor had to show us. By the time he was done, I was feeling a little green around my virtual gills, drugs or no drugs. The Class Two Cyberlimb wasn't just strong and tough, it was also flexible. Joints could bend in ways they never could with a human arm, as demonstrated when the instructor grabbed a virtual bad guy by the head and spun him three hundred and sixty degrees with his articulated wrist. That kind of thing upped your lethality from scary-good to suit-soiling terrifying because most of the process of winning a fight was based on an intense understanding of how people moved and how to move them right.

Well, move them wrong.

From the point of view of their bones, internal organs, nerves, blood vessels and so on.

Once the show was over, we all got dumped straight out of the VR. Total time, subjective, three hours. Total time, actual—that is, recorded by clocks in the real world, not by brains hopped up on neuros—was something close to three *minutes*. That's why they called them "tween chop" seminars: you could hit them up between your meal and your physical training and not even miss a beat.

Theoretically, at least.

Each time we had one of the tween chop lessons, I was reminded of an earlier training run I had gone through—and that kind of reminder made me wonder what the hells I was doing here. I'd gone through this mill once before—and now, here I was, going through it again. And why?

Because in the S3TA—the Space Special Service, Transhuman Arm—I'd get to kill Loonies. Loonies had kicked off the first war in space by flying a shuttle into the unfinished space elevator—the elevator that my parents had worked on for their whole adult lives. Their ashes were mixed in with the ashes of a few million other people in Kenya, where the elevator deorbited and smashed into the ground like a city-smasher nuke.

And yet, if that had been it, I might still ...

I shook my head. Trying to focus on the lessons that had been seared into my thoughts—trying to keep everything *straight* in the swirling rush of coming down from neurotropics. Focusing ... focusing ... focusing on how to kill Loonies. It made everything feel slightly less raw when the neuros finished draining—though less raw wasn't saying much. I still felt like I had a hole punched through my chest.

So I tried to force my brain to settle into the present, tilting my head up and down, back and forth, all to overload any feeling of pain with visual stimulation. I was in a gray, plastic tube and felt hot, the VR shunts blazing against my skin. I still lurked in the tube for just long enough to be considered slacking, at least by the vicious standards of Selection.

Why?

Well, because outside of this *feh feh pi goh* tube was ...

The world. And the world was a terrible, terrible place. That thought wasn't helped by the raw fury and terror of Deseret winter, which could flay a man to ice shards faster than a vacuum. It also didn't help that we were outsiders in this place, staying only because the Chinese American Alliance had the military wherewithal to make the Mormons do whatever they wanted and because the CAA had been plastered from orbit since the beginning of last month, when the war had taken the last shred of my future from me. That was the real reason the world was a terrible place.

In the tube, I felt too hot, too cramped, and there was not enough air.

But at least the gray plastic hid the ghosts.

And so ... I waited. I waited until the nanosecond after slacking.

I opened the tube from the inside, shaking and quaking from the VR dumpshock and my own nerves. Selection didn't ease you out, like commercial VR systems always did. Dumping you out produced a load of pleasant neurological symptoms, such as muscle tremors, low blood pressure, dizziness, fainting spells. That kind of thing. But if you couldn't hack dumpshock, then you couldn't hack Selection.

My bare feet hit compacted dirt and I rubbed my shoulders, catching some glances from Alvarez, his face and barrel chest showing he was from the southernmost parts of the North American Union under the Alliance's jurisdiction. His forehead furrowed, pulling his scars into new constellations of ugly as he sent me a look that combined irritation and psychopathic rage. Or maybe it was lust, I couldn't tell when it came from him and, more importantly, I didn't care.

"L-l-look somewhere else, Lightfoot," I muttered, rubbing my shoulders to try and get the post VR-dump shivers out of my system. Being the youngest girl in Selection was its own special kind of hell, made all the worse by being stuck in this freezing cold, dirty, low-tech, backward hellhole full of religious nutcases. "Or I might practice on you."

Technically impossible, as none of us had been augmented beyond what we had come in with. Alvarez had stepped on a land mine during a police action in Brazil or something, so his left leg was all chrome and metal. He, like me, was one of the one-in-a-million combinations of decorated combat soldier who also had a *jing tian dwohn di* immunity to Cybernetic Psychosomatic Rejection Syndrome and its many delightful side effects, starting with dissociative personality disorder and going on through intense body dysmorphia, schizophrenia, megalomania, and psychosis.

At least, we hoped we were immune.

Alvarez smirked. "Hey, I don't see you sometimes, PR." He whacked my shoulder and padded off toward the stairs that led from the basement with the rigs to the mess hall. You wouldn't think a man with a foot made of synthetic parts could be so quiet. Other candidates walked past, some of them talking, most of them not. They were all cut from different cloth. Selection plucked from across two continents and most of the orbital arena, so they had all kinds. Bulky guys, skinny guys, girls with more scars than I have hair, and so on. There weren't any other Spacers though, not naturally born ones like me. And none of them had a nickname like mine.

See, the DIs here, unlike the DIs I had to deal with up in Space, loved their sardonic nicknames. Alvarez steps on a mine, they call him Lightfoot.

I do *one* high profile stunt, mostly by dumb luck and my even dumber decision-making process, and the entire Chinese-American Alliance press (and what passed for Deseret press, for that matter) glommed onto my story and started shouting it from the rooftops. So, I got to be called PR. Well, hey, it could have been worse. They could have called me Media-Whore.

The mess hall sat in a building designed to look remarkably like a Mormon hut. Packed earth, no electricity, no running water, no nothing. Now, see, the Salt Lake Arcology held all the normal citizens of Deseret, insofar as such a thing could exist. When they peacefully seceded from the Chinese-American Alliance, they'd also splintered their own selves. Some, more used to modern amenities than others, went to the arcology. Others ...

Others built their own towns, following their own interpretation of their holy book. And our selection training facility had been built right into one, subtly, over the course of a few weeks. These are the kinds of things you had to do when the enemy has orbital superiority on you and is willing to throw rocks at anything that looks military. That thought caused a flash of pain in my mind.

I put it out of my head and stepped through the door and headed inside, which looked just as impoverished as the outside, with metal tables and chairs and a guy ladling out food from a big old pot in the corner, heated by a fire. A wood-burning fire.

And I had thought that Sarah's cabin was primitive. My heart ached at that thought, and I kept my face dead, totally dead.

Our commander watched us get in and I watched her out of the corner of my eye as I got in line. Major Mary Singh had been a bit odd when I had first met her on a VTOL from Quebec to Shanghai. I knew enough now to know just what she might have under her skin. That was enough to know how very afraid of her I should be. I forced myself to not wonder about her career. Her past. How she'd ended up in S3TA, with a body mostly made out of killing machines. Instead, I tried to focus on what was important right now.

I got my chop, shoving my hand through a scanner held out by the cook. The scanner looked totally out of place in this hut, but since we weren't in line of sight from orbit, it didn't matter. The tracking chip they'd slipped into me at the start of Selection was scanned, and the scanner dinged and the spoon ladled out a hunk of slop, perfectly balanced for my projected nutrient output. We'd had some washouts from that, people who were too used to eating slightly too much. I didn't have trouble with it. Standard procedure for space.

I took a table besides Chin and Lee. There were like a million Lees in the CAA, and exactly three had ended up in Selection. The one sitting beside me was younger than Alvarez, but still a few years older than me. He looked up at me and got right to the point. "Got any smokes?"

"No," I didn't pause in my eating.

"Shit."

"Got any infosec?" I asked, glancing at him sidelong.

He snorted. "Oh, so, you expect some computer time for free? Do I look like a Maoist?"

"No, but I can get you some smokes." I grinned. It, like many of my expressions, was halfhearted. "I know a guy."

"She's talking about me." Gloria said over her shoulder.

"I said I know a guy," I glanced over my shoulder at Gloria. She smirked. She had her hair at the longest allowed length, tied into a tight bun that drew her face taut. The blond was an injection, her skin was space black. And that was the blackest black I knew words for. It was also exquisite in a way that made me feel a sharp, knife twist of utterly illogical guilt.

"Exactly." She said. "I'll give you smokes if you spot me for this night's watch."

I side-eyed her. Gloria ...

Gloria and I ...

My heart didn't know whether to speed up, slow down, or stab my lungs and commit suicide like a Japanese Samurai. But still, taking watch for her meant both infosec and making things easier for her. That cinched it.

"Deal." I pursed my lips. Gloria grinned and slipped me a battered box of crappy smokes, thoughtfully smuggled into camp by some gentiles that visited the town to trade with the locals. The

Selection's stance on smokes, infosec and trading watches was pretty strict: If we got caught, we'd be sent through CAPE. And not the wimpy kind of CAPE that I'd gone through in the Marines, no, but the Selection's idea of CAPE. The kind that could actually kill you. Not that it was likely to kill you if you were inhumanly attentive to detail, brutally strong, and lucky. Easy.

But they also expected us to do it—be sneaky, that is. Slipping stuff past them was a sign of "clever" minds, and the S3TA wanted the sneakiest killing machines they could make. So they left holes in their security. Except for when they didn't.

Lee pushed a pebble of gray plastic along the packed earth of the floor. I slipped it into my shoe with one of my toes, eating as fast as I could. I managed to get it out of my shoe before we hit the night run, thank the Gods, and it settled into my pocket as we ran, following our training instructor, whose legs whirred and clicked as he jogged backwards, his torso held perfectly level.

"Get the lead in!" He shouted. "Come on, come on, come on, show me you mean business, you flats."

I gritted my teeth and thought of what infosec could buy. And I tried to feel both eager and not eager and guilty and not guilty, logic be damned.

We got back when we were bone tired and half frozen. As hot as Deseret could get in the day, it got so much colder at night, and winter made it worse. We stood beside our beds for inspection. Our training instructor walked along the row, examining our feet and hands and everything. You'd think they would not care so much, as our limbs were all going to be gone when Selection was done. But the way it was explained to me was thus: We went through physical hell less to build muscle and more to train our nerves, so they could adapt to our cyberlimbs once we had them.

And, more than that, it washed people out. People quit when they could not hack it, or they got kicked out by being stupid or unlucky or both. Two people—Singer and Hung—had fallen off a training platform and broken their spines. They were in Beijing, getting their nerves knit back together, all expenses paid. I wasn't sure if I envied them.

Once we were inspected, the lights slammed out and I slipped into my coveralls. I picked up my flashlight and started to patrol on night watch. Gloria stayed in bed. Thankfully, the gray skies that had been threatening cleared, giving us a crystal-clear view of the night sky and the full moon. I sighed slowly, my head surrounded by an illusory and temporary atmosphere as my breath condensed. The fog cleared and I remained staring up, at the Moon.

The Moon.

You'd never think it'd be so ugly. I hadn't thought the Moon was ugly until almost a year ago, but maybe it was because I was transferring some of my anger from the people who lived there. But if there had never been the Moon ... then, well, the Earth would have sunk into a new dark age in 2034. No moon, no lunar regolith. No Helium-3. No fusion reactors. No way to support a planet-sprawling civilization, not one hooked on fossil fuels for so long.

I shook my head and went back to patrolling. I was technically supposed to report any people shacking up—against the rules down here, a nasty change from my time in the Marines. I just tapped their bed when I noticed, so they'd know to be quieter, and went on walking, going from the inside to the outside to the inside.

Eventually—finally—the night watch ended. I crashed and didn't dream. That was a kindness.

>+<

Three days later, I got to spend my infosec. I slipped the pebble into the secure lock on one of the armory closet doors. The armory didn't hold anything more lethal than practice rifles and a few stunner-guns the instructors could use. Right now, we were at chop, but some things were more important than chop.

Gloria slipped in after me, and before I could say anything I was against the wall and her lips were on mine. I grabbed her hands and she pushed her hips against me. I trembled and my knees felt weak.

I ... was so godsdamned horny that I was going cross-eyed. Gloria's mouth drew back. She had a fierce bite to her kiss, more ...

I desperately tried to not think of Sarah. It didn't work. I started to cry. Gloria slid her arms around me, comforting. "I'm sorry, I'm sorry..." I whispered.

She whispered soft nothings in my ear. My hands tightened on her. And then I kissed her again, through the tears, desperate to feel something that wasn't deadness and nothingness and sorrow.

The infosec, which had shut down the security systems of the armory, gave us time to burn away the world in physical training that didn't hurt. Oh, no ...

It didn't hurt at all.

Until it was over.

I sprawled on my back, one arm over my head, feeling the weight of Gloria's head on my stomach. The hurt came with the closeness. My eyes closed.

"So, PR," Gloria murmured into my skin, her voice soft and her breath warm. "What are you brooding about now?"

"Life," I said.

"Heh." Gloria didn't really laugh. She just said the word "heh." Like a verbal punctuation. Her lips glided along the lines of my belly muscle. She nuzzled me slowly, then brought out: "Ever tried lightening up?"

"Yeah," I said. "Then everyone I loved died."

Gloria was silent for a bit. "Changing the subject. What are the odds you think that someone's got a bug in this room and they let us slip through the firewall as a test."

I was silent for a moment. "Depressingly likely."

Gloria pushed herself up, her hair falling around her face. She tossed it back with a flip, then smacked my belly. "Come on, PR. Lets get dressed before they stop testing us and start drumming us out."

Watching her dress made the hurt different. It didn't make it go away.

I should be here with Sarah, not with a near-stranger. What did I know about Gloria? Beyond her warmth, and the corded muscle of her arm, and the feeling of her lips on mine. But...the only thing worse than watching her dress and aching for what wasn't there was not watching her dress and ache twice over. For Sarah and for a loss of contact.

I'd gone celibate for, like, a distressingly long time for a Spacer.

Then I got a shot, and now I was alone and, holy shit, I was thinking about getting laid when Sarah was dead. I put my head in my hands and my shoulders started to shake. Embarrassment warred with self-horror and I tried to stop the sobs, to choke them off. But Gloria just sat down and slipped her arm around my shoulders. She squeezed me against her and I kept on crying and crying and crying.

>+<

The next day, we kept our distance.

That was why I took a roundabout route to the sim-units, weaving my way around the back of a building that I'd normally pass in front. I was crunching through shin-high sooty snow that had brushed up against the back of the primitive house when I realized that going this way was just as obvious as if I had walked arm in arm with Gloria. But it was too late.

Far too late.

I stopped. I had a clear view from the back of the house to the headquarters building, which looked like every other hovel.

Outside of that, underneath a copse of scrawny, shitty trees, was Mary Singh. She was leaning against a tree, and chatting with a woman in black. The woman in black had no rank insignia, no clear indication of service, and the kind of face that'd vanish the instant you took your eyes off it. A small, circular drone hovered next to her.

It was armed. My skin prickled as I remembered the buzzing police drones from the courthouse shootout. This one looked about two decades more advanced. The tiny nubs along the forward disk shape had been beaten into my head during the tween chop seminars. Seeker darts. Each one was a tiny rocket with enough Delta-V to zip across half a kilometer and hit you where their laser targeting sensors said you were weak. Their payloads were small micro-charges tipped to drills.

The idea was they'd hit, and that'd hurt. Then the drills dug in, and that hurt. Then the micro-charges went off under your skin and turned your organs into jelly.

I froze, though I knew it was pointless.

The two women saw me. Mary smiled. She shimmered and vanished with a faint ripple – like an optical illusion. I blinked stupidly, shocked that she had done it despite having seen the exact same freaking thing in Shanghai.

The other woman, the one in black, smiled.

She lifted her hand—and, for a terrifying moment, I thought she was going to plant a targeting laser on my forehead. Instead, her hand formed an "O" with the pointer and thumb finger, her other fingers fanning out. She tapped the middle finger to her forehead, then swept her hand towards me in a mocking salute.

ABOUT DAVID COLBY

A fan of old school sci-fi and tabletop roleplaying games, David Colby started writing almost fifteen years ago. It went poorly. But despite these early setbacks, David continued to work and write and send out submissions until someone was mad enough to accept him. Currently living in Sunnyvale, California, David's day job involves leaping in front of cars for fun and profit (he's a crossing guard.)

Website: ThinkingInkPress.com/LunarCycle
Blog: http://QuantumSpinPlates.blogspot.com
Facebook: Facebook.com/David.Colby2
Twitter: @TheRealZoombie
Email: DavidColbyAuthor22@gmail.com

ACKNOWLEDGMENTS

Thanks go out to my parents, Paul Colby and Marion Barker, and to my siblings, Brian Colby and Kathleen Lloyd. Thanks, too, to my friends: Scott Ballatore; George Richbourg; Daniel Lofgren; Meghan Collins; Steven Cline; Morrigan Rose; Robert Donahue; Elesha Chidley; Nathan Ravenwood; Jason Cayer, whose name I cheerfully stole; Alex Rasgon; Alex Aldenbrook; and Jay Durant.

Thanks, also, to my editors Anthony Francis, Keiko O'Leary, Betsy Miller, and Gayle Schultz; and last, but far, far, far from least, my teachers: Greta Vollmer, in whose class on young adult literature I hope to one day star, and Robert Coleman-Senghor, may he rest in peace.